THE Peasant Queen

THE Peasant Queen

Discover your magic!

CHERI CHESLEY

Cheri L. Chesley

Bonneville Books
Springville, Utah

This is a work of fiction. The characters, names, incidents, places, and dialogue are products of the author's imagination, and are not to be construed as real.

ISBN 13: 978-1-59955-416-7

Published by Bonneville Books, an imprint of Cedar Fort, Inc., 2373 W. 700 S., Springville, UT 84663
Distributed by Cedar Fort, Inc., www.cedarfort.com

LIBRARY OF CONGRESS CATALOGING-IN-PUBLICATION DATA
Chesley, Cheri, 1975-
  The peasant queen / Cheri Chesley.
    p. cm.
  ISBN 978-1-59955-416-7 (acid-free paper)
  1. Women peasants--Fiction. 2. Abduction--Fiction. 3. Kings and
rulers--Succession--Fiction. 4. Queens--Fiction. I. Title.

  PS3603.H485P43 2010
  813'.6--dc22

  2010013579

Cover design by Danie Romrell
Cover design © 2010 by Lyle Mortimer
Edited and typeset by Megan E. Welton

Printed in the United States of America

10 9 8 7 6 5 4 3 2 1

Printed on acid-free paper

This novel is dedicated to all those who supported this journey—you know who you are—but in particular to the one person in my life now who was part of it then . . .
Stephan, thank you.

Acknowledgments

I HAVE BEEN EXTRAORDINARILY blessed in my life to have the constant, unfailing support of my husband, Bryan, and my five children. I also have the support of my extended family and friends, who have waited for this book with almost as much impatience and excitement as I have. A huge thank you to my friend Jen Healey, for nudging me back onto my true path. I'd be remiss if I did not acknowledge the talented Richard Paul Evans, Rober G. Allen and their WriteWise group, and Karen Christofferson in particular for their mentoring and support. Thank you, CFI, for giving me this chance. It would be impossible to list the names of all the talented authors who acted as mentors by helping me through the process, but to all of you—thank you. And, of course, I must thank my loving and generous Heavenly Father for His faith in me and for the talents and gifts I have been given in my life.

Chapter I

"THERE WILL BE NO MORE DISCUSSION!" Andrew slammed his fist on the desk for emphasis. "You've done nothing but argue about this for a week now. You will marry Curtis Belvey."

Krystal stood motionless. "I will not."

"Don't try my patience," he said. "I'm head of this family. You will do what you're told."

"Don't make me laugh!" Krystal folded her arms across her chest. "You're only head of this family by default. You've turned this room into your personal study so you can sit behind that desk like the lord of the manor. Do you honestly think this is what Father had planned for me?"

"Do you really think Father wanted you to spend your life looking after Mother?"

His words stung, and she drew back. Krystal felt hot tears prick the corners of her eyes, and she knew she had to get away. "You know this isn't right."

Her eldest brother threw up his hands. "Arranged marriages happen all over Brynne, but for you it's wrong? You're being childish."

Krystal didn't wait to be dismissed. She fled from her brother and the house to the barn. She raced up the ladder to the hayloft and collapsed in the straw, crying tears of frustration.

"I thought I'd find you here."

She looked up and saw Douglas, her middle brother, through an opening in the floor of the loft. Krystal shifted away from him, not sure if she wanted company. She felt him sit down next to her. "Did Andrew send you?"

Douglas didn't offer a direct answer. "He's in some kind of mood."

"He should be," she said. "He's accepted an offer for my hand in marriage."

Douglas nodded. "I wondered about that."

"An *offer*." Krystal threw a piece of straw. "It makes me sound like I'm a horse or something. Is that all the value I have?"

"Don't be dramatic. You *are* sixteen, after all. You had to be expecting this."

She sighed. "Did all of my brothers conspire in this? Are you so eager to get rid of me too?"

"If it's any comfort, I voted to keep you," he said. "You're the only one who can cook anything decent."

"I'm in no mood to be teased."

He sighed. "So he didn't tell you this is the third offer for your hand?"

Krystal drew up sharply. "What? That's ridiculous."

"You're right," he said, the sarcasm evident in his tone. "The parade of young men marching past our farm every afternoon must be a coincidence."

She glared at him. "What does that have to do with anything?"

He laughed. "You're smarter than that, little sister. You can't tell me you think Justin Broun takes a *shortcut* to his place across our field. His family's fields are nowhere near our property."

Krystal huffed impatiently. "What are you talking about, Douglas?"

"Those boys come by here to see *you*," he said. "They *like* you."

She threw straw at him. "They do not!"

He flicked the end of her nose. "Don't beg for compliments. It's not my job to give them to you."

She smiled, though not happily. "With a blind mother and a dead father, whose job is it?"

He frowned. "I hadn't thought of that. But it's awkward for a brother to tell his sister she's one of the prettiest girls in the region."

She looked at him. "I guess I'll have to settle for that."

"Your friends should compliment you," he said, as though that just occurred to him. "Don't girls flatter one another?"

"How should I know?"

"You have friends."

"I have Damen."

"I meant friends who are people. Your pet doesn't count."

"I'll be sure to mention that next time I see him."

"I hope not," said Douglas. "I'd hate to have Damen eat me."

She smiled. "He wouldn't eat you. You aren't his type."

"I'll choose to be flattered by that." He sighed. "Are you ready to come make dinner?"

"I see your plan," she said. "You're trying to cheer me up so you can get fed tonight."

"I'd leap to my feet in offense if I wouldn't bang my head on the beams."

She poked his muscular arm. "You never get offended."

Douglas bumped her with his shoulder. "Maybe if I did, I'd get more respect around here."

Krystal fixed him with a dark look. "Like Kayne does?"

"He'd probably annoy you less if you didn't needle him so much. I don't know why you seem to spark his temper so easily."

"He's made it his duty to see that I know my place." She twisted a piece of straw around her finger. "And that happens to be under his boot."

"You're being dramatic again," said Douglas. "If it's any comfort, I talked to him about how he treats you while we hunted today. I doubt he listened to me, but I tried."

"Kayne doesn't listen to anyone." Krystal sighed and dusted her hands on her apron. "All right, I'm ready. Let's go."

"Don't worry, little sister," Douglas said. "It will all work out."

She moved to the ladder and smiled up at her brother. "I'll make certain of it."

As she went down the ladder, she heard him say, "I was afraid of that."

ॐ

Krystal scrambled from her bed at the first sign of dawn the next morning, dressed in her nicest skirt and blouse, and tied her hair back in a braid. She made a simple breakfast for her family, took some up to her mother, and then rushed back to her room to finish getting ready. Will pounded on her door a few minutes later.

"We're going. Come on."

Krystal sighed. Her brother: a man of few words. While Andrew had educated himself enough to run the farm, learning to balance the accounts and read the ledgers and Krystal had learned to read at her mother's knee, her other three brothers hadn't concerned themselves with much education. They knew their farm responsibilities inside out, but neither Kayne nor Will read well. Will knew a smattering of the financial responsibilities Andrew normally took care of but only enough to manage the farm on the rare occasion Andrew had to leave it. Many local nobles, and possibly those throughout Brynne, discouraged the education of peasants.

Krystal brushed the last of the flour from the sleeves of her blouse, took off her apron, and headed downstairs to the wagon. At dinner the night before, Andrew had agreed to let Krystal come to town to meet her new fiancé while her brothers got supplies. Will and Douglas were already in the back. Andrew climbed up to the seat and reached down to her. He paused to take in her appearance and gave her a smile, which Krystal returned. It warmed her to think she'd pleased him. While they didn't always agree, Andrew remained the closest thing Krystal had to a father.

They passed the short trip into town in silence. Krystal hid her hands in the folds of her skirt in an effort to conceal her nervousness. She told herself to stop being silly. Krystal didn't know Curtis Belvey well. It hadn't been fair to reject the young man out of hand. Maybe Andrew was right. Even a farmer's daughter from a more prosperous farm couldn't expect much more from life than marriage into a solid, respected family. But the thought of tending a home and caring for her children the rest of her life made Krystal shiver.

Andrew stopped the wagon by the blacksmith's shop, where they parted ways. Will and Krystal started down the street. Many of the local men knew Will and greeted him as they passed, but Krystal walked beside him in silence until they reached the Belvey store.

Curtis and his mother, Darva, both stood at the counter.

"Give me the list," Will said. "Stay at the counter where I can see you."

Krystal nodded. Her throat tightened and she could not speak. She walked woodenly to the counter where her future waited. Tall with broad shoulders and a wide chest, Curtis had arms like tree trunks. His hands, Krystal noticed, could easily span her waist. Curtis gave enormous new definition. Why had she not noticed this before?

Darva Belvey stood beside him, a tall, thin woman with sharp eyes. She wore her dark hair in a severe bun. "Hello, Krystal," Darva said. "Curtis, say hello to Krystal."

"Hello."

Krystal nodded to the mother and looked into the face of the son. Instant despair gripped her. She saw wide brown eyes and a slack jaw. He looked at her with the interest a wolf would gaze at a lone lamb.

She forced herself to speak. "Hello, Curtis."

Curtis did not seem acquainted with subtlety. "You look pretty."

"Thank you."

A heavy silence followed. Darva watched Krystal intently, so she felt compelled to continue the conversation.

"I confess, I don't know much about you," she said awkwardly. "My brothers hunt. Do enjoy hunting?"

"Yeah."

"Do you fish?"

"Yeah."

"What other things do you like?"

"Pretty girls."

His mother coughed suddenly. "Curtis, tell her about your birds."

"I keep birds."

Krystal waited expectantly for a moment before she realized he'd finished telling her about his birds. "That's nice," she said. "I like to read. Do you read?"

"Of course not!" Darva interrupted. "My son has better things to do than waste his time with something so frivolous. Curtis has never opened a book in his life."

At that moment, the last glimmer of hope Krystal held for a good life extinguished. She could not be the wife of a man who didn't read, could hardly carry on a conversation, and whose mother seemed to control his thoughts. Every instinct she possessed screamed at her to run. Her pride, however, foolishly kept her rooted to the spot.

"My mother taught me to read, Mistress Belvey," she said. "I do not find it frivolous."

"You will find, young lady, that there will be no time for reading as the wife of my son," the woman said in a brisk manner. "You had better put such childish pastimes behind you." At that she whipped her head to the left. "There is Adelaide. Excuse me."

Krystal watched her future mother-in-law move away to assist a woman buying cloth. Reluctantly, she looked back at her betrothed. Curtis had been staring at her, and now a small drop of drool crept down his chin. She shuddered.

"You're pretty," he said again.

Krystal took a step backward. "Curtis, why do you want to marry me?"

His silence lasted so long Krystal thought perhaps he hadn't heard her. Just as she got up the nerve to repeat herself, he said, "My father told me to get married. He liked the look of you and went to your brother. I'm glad you're pretty. I don't want to marry an ugly girl."

She just stared at him. "But you don't know me. Surely if you plan to spend the rest of your life with someone, you'd want to get to know them."

"You'll be my wife. You'll do what I say. Mama says you have to."

Krystal backed away again, this time in fear. Did he not have a thought of his own?

Curtis took a step toward her and grasped her arm. Krystal tried to free herself, but he held her fast. His thumb dug into her arm painfully as he pulled her closer. Horrified, she realized he intended to kiss her.

"No, Curtis, please."

He ignored her and bent his head to hers.

Krystal lashed out with her booted foot and kicked him in the shin. Surprised, he let go. She whirled around and charged out the front door. She passed several shops before she looked back. No one followed her.

She saw the wagon up ahead and headed for it. Krystal's heart sank and her steps slowed as she thought that her future husband was the man Andrew, her own brother, had chosen for her. Abruptly, she turned to the road that led out of town to her home. She couldn't bear facing her brothers only to have them ask about her meeting with Curtis. Andrew would be furious with her for leaving town without them, but right then, she couldn't bring herself to care.

Fury warred with despair. She'd been right all along. She couldn't marry Curtis Belvey. Now she just had to figure out how to get out of it.

Krystal approached the house and was relieved when she didn't see Kayne. She went up to her room to change into her regular clothes and put on her apron.

❧

A few hours later, Krystal heard the wagon pull up while she scrubbed the hall floor. Andrew threw open the front door and bellowed her name.

"Krystal!"

He spotted her before she could respond. She jumped to her feet as he approached, ready, she hoped, for the explosion.

"Do you have any idea how you worried us?" He halted a foot away from her. "We looked everywhere! If Douglas hadn't suggested we try looking at home, we'd still be searching all over town for you! You know better than to run off like that! What possessed you?"

Anger erupted inside her. "I met my future husband, the man to whom you would banish me in a terrible marriage!" she said in a yell to match his. "Tell me, Andrew, how much time did you say you spent talking with him? It couldn't have been more than a moment, or you'd have done anything to end the torture!"

"What are you talking about?" He shook his head. "It doesn't matter. You never, *ever* run off without telling one of us where you went. Anything could have happened!"

Krystal took a step closer. "He tried to kiss me! After he drooled all over himself, that is. I won't marry that man!"

Andrew took a deep breath. "Go to your room," he said in a voice deadly quiet. "We will discuss this later."

"There is nothing to discuss," she said, tossing her scrub brush into the bucket at her feet. "I will not marry that man, Andrew. Not in the spring, not ever."

"*Go!*"

Krystal ran for it. She bolted the door of her room and threw herself onto the bed. All her fury poured out of her in the form of tears as she wept into her pillow.

She didn't wallow long in self-pity. Maybe, if nothing else, she could convince the Belveys that she'd make a terrible bride for their son. As a last resort, she could always run away; although with no money or connections, it would just doom her to a hard life.

The unknown did not frighten her. She was sure she could earn her keep, if need be. She could cook and clean and perform basic chores on the farm. Her chief concern would be getting far enough away that her brothers could not find her.

❧

The next morning, Krystal tried to talk to Andrew at breakfast. He cut her off, stubbornly refusing to discuss the engagement. She tried again a few days later with the same result. Despair and helplessness gnawed at her. Frustration welled up and threatened to suffocate her. She feared if Andrew denied her again, she was in danger of losing that increasingly fragile control over her temper.

As she climbed the stairs to her mother's room one afternoon, Krystal knew she had to get away, if only for a little while, but helplessness ate at her and she hated it.

She fought for calm before she opened the door. "Hello, Mother."

"Hello, my dear." Elyce sat in a rocker near the small window with Krystal's stool next to the chair. Aside from the bed and trunk for Elyce's clothes along the opposite wall, the room remained essentially empty. Krystal's mother usually made her own way around her room, and more furniture would only make things more difficult for her.

"I've brought lunch," said Krystal as she placed the tray on the stool.

"Thank you, dear," said her mother.

"Did you need anything before I go?" It suddenly struck Krystal how ominous those words sounded, even though she said them every day.

"I have everything I need," said Elyce. "Are you all right? Your voice sounds strained."

Krystal should have known she couldn't fool her mother. "I'm fine," she said. "Don't worry about me."

"Have your brothers been teasing you? I could have Andrew talk to them."

"They don't tease me so much anymore, Mother. They have more important things to do."

"All right," Elyce said. "But I don't want you thinking your mother is useless."

"Of course not," said Krystal. "I don't think that. Good-bye, Mother."

"Good-bye, dear."

Krystal shut the door as she left and sighed. She put a hand on the wood and thought of all the things she longed to say. *I'm not ready to marry, Mother. I can't stand Curtis Belvey.* The words jumbled in her mind, but Krystal knew she'd never dare say them. How she envied other girls whose mothers helped them work through their worries. What sort of a miracle would it be to have a mother in whom she could confide all her fears?

Krystal stole away to her own room and dug in her trunk for the old clothes she'd taken from Kayne. Andrew hated seeing her in her brother's trousers, but they were better for running than her skirts. Besides, he hadn't started objecting until a year or so ago, when the local farmers' sons had started passing by the farm.

Krystal changed quickly, slipped her dagger into her boot, and then crept down the stairs and into the kitchen. The pot of stew simmered happily. She added another log to the fire. With any luck, it would be ready by dinnertime, and she'd have an hour of peace. She opened the front door, scanned the yard for any sign of her brothers, and raced to the forest.

Chapter 2

KRYSTAL LOVED THE SECLUSION of the woods near her home. A mere ten steps into the trees, and she could imagine she was in another world. At least, she had felt that way in her childhood. Even now, more so than the hayloft or her bedroom, the forest remained a haven for her—a place she could be alone.

The feeling didn't last. She heard a branch snap and froze, alert to any sound coming from every direction, feeling eyes upon her. She turned her head slightly and watched for movement.

Suddenly, a huge black form leapt from the trees and knocked her down. They rolled for several feet before the creature pinned Krystal with large paws. She looked up at her captor and laughed. A large black dog, nearly the size of a man, held her to the ground. She brought her hands up and stroked the animal's side.

"All right, Damen, you win. Now let me up." She shoved him aside.

He sat back while Krystal got to her feet and then started circling his mistress.

"You must have been watching for me," she said. "I didn't expect you so quickly."

Damen growled from the back of his throat.

Krystal scratched his neck. "Some of us weren't born hunters. Besides, I haven't got your ears." She patted her leg, and he fell into step beside her.

They walked deeper into the forest to one of her favorite clearings, where she sat and reclined against a tree. Damen lay down next to her in the grass, and Krystal idly stroked his broad black back as she thought.

"He isn't going to give in, is he?" She didn't really expect an answer. Damen dropped his head in her lap. "Andrew, I mean. He won't let me convince him this marriage is wrong."

Krystal sighed. "Do you think if I act crazy enough I could get the Belveys to break the contract? I could mash dirt in my hair and run screaming around their house at all hours of the night. That might do it."

Damen yawned and shifted onto his side. Krystal shook her head. "I didn't think it would work anyway. But what's left?"

Damen scratched behind his ear with his hind paw, and Krystal brought her knees up to her chest. She sighed again and dropped her head onto her knees. Damen stood and nudged her head with his nose.

Krystal looked at him, eyes wet. "I can't marry Curtis, and I can't get out of the contract. I think the only way out of this marriage is if I am not here for the ceremony." She put her arms around Damen's neck and buried her face in his soft fur.

After a time, she sat up and sniffled, wiping her eyes on her sleeve. "Mother will miss me, and my brothers will try to find me. If I go, my family will be disgraced. What a choice to make."

Realizing it was time to get back to the house, Krystal got to her feet and looked down at her dog. "Come on," she said with a sigh. "You can walk back with me to the edge of the woods. No farther, though. I don't want to risk Kayne catching sight of you."

Andrew claimed that Damen disturbed the livestock and ate too much, and Kayne had been threatening to put an arrow in her pet the next time he saw him on the property.

Krystal took her time. She knew it would be the last few precious moments of peace she'd be able to enjoy in awhile. That cheery thought did not make her want to hurry.

In a rather quiet section of woods, Damen stopped suddenly, and his hackles went up. Krystal looked at him quizzically as he let out a low growl. She looked around but saw nothing unusual.

Damen had his eyes on the trees to her left.

Krystal trusted her dog. He had an uncanny awareness of danger, even for an animal. She peered more closely into the trees and found a pair of eyes gazing back at her.

"I believe your pet is troubled by my presence." A stranger stepped out of the woods. He wore the uniform of a guardsman but not from Brynne.

Krystal stepped back. She thought first to be civil, but Damen's initial reaction to the man concerned her. "Why are you in these woods? Are you lost?"

"We aren't lost," the man said.

In answer to her unasked question, more men in the same uniform emerged from the forest. They had surrounded her—two men behind her, one on either side, and two in the trees above her. The men on the ground all carried swords while the two in the trees had crossbows.

"Who are you?"

"Introductions can come later," he said. "Right now you need to come with us."

"I'm not going anywhere with you," Krystal said. Her eyes moved to the sword at his belt, and her mind flew from one scenario to the next. She could try to run past him. After all, she knew the forest well and might get away. She hadn't finally determined to take control of her own destiny simply to fall captive at the hands of strangers.

Before she could move, Damen dove for the man nearest her. Man and dog tumbled to the ground. His sword flew from his hand, and Krystal dove for it. She grasped the hilt and came to her feet to face the group's presumed leader. She heard the dying man's last sounds as Damen delivered a final, deadly blow. The dog leapt off the fallen man's body and moved to protect her back.

Krystal's opponent had drawn his sword. He tapped her blade with his. "Now, what do you think you're going to do with that?"

She tapped back. "That depends on you. Let me go."

He smiled. "I can't do that." He lunged, and Krystal blocked him deftly.

"You can," she said.

He raised his eyebrows. "So you know something about the blade."

She smiled without humor. "I had an indulgent father."

He attacked more earnestly, but she blocked again.

"You really need to stop this," he said, "before you get hurt." He swung the sword at her again, this time with more force.

Krystal bit her lip and blocked his swing. Her arm stung from the force of his blows. As she stepped back, she felt Damen at the back of her legs.

Her opponent smiled again. "If not for yourself, then surrender for your pet. My archers have him in their sights. Are you ready to watch him die?"

Krystal's blood ran cold. "You wouldn't," she challenged, knowing the truth.

"In a heartbeat," he said.

She glared at him. "Damen's a big boy. He can take care of himself."

"Then why have you tried to maneuver yourself between him and my archers? You can't fool me, little one. You're trying to protect him."

Krystal dared a glance at her pet. He snarled menacingly at the men behind her. Though she knew he was her only hope of escape, she could not knowingly put him in such danger. He would have to go.

"Damen!" she said. "Go now."

The dog halted. He turned and growled his protest, clearly itching for another target.

"Get away from here! Now!"

Slowly, ever so slowly, he turned his black body and melted into the forest. Krystal wanted to sigh with relief, but could not do so with the odds still stacked against her.

The evil man gloated. "I knew you'd see it my way."

"You haven't won yet," she said.

He flicked his sword at her, which she easily blocked. "Come now. You aren't really going to go through with this are you?"

"I won't surrender."

"You can't fight us all," he said with a smile.

"You can't all attack at once," said Krystal. "That would violate the rules of fair play."

"In the real world, fair play has no place. We fight to win. Losing often means death."

Krystal whirled as the others approached. She tapped the tip of each sword as she turned, trying to keep them all in sight. She actually bloodied one man before being disarmed. Two men sheathed their swords and came at her. They grabbed her arms, holding her fast.

Krystal twisted against their hold. "What will you do with me?"

Their leader leaned down and pulled her dagger out of her boot. He examined it for a moment before he spoke. "My master would like the pleasure of your company for a time."

"Who is your master?"

"Too many questions."

"Why me, then? Why not snatch a girl from some other forest?"

"He wants you. His instructions were quite specific."

Even outnumbered and unarmed, Krystal still tried to fight her captors. The archers dropped from the trees to lend assistance. Working together, the men bound and gagged her, and the leader slung her over his shoulder. "Let's get out of here before someone comes looking for her," he said. Then, looking at the black dog's fallen victim, he said, "Bring the body. The master said we must leave no trace."

With each step her captor took, Krystal felt his shoulder slam painfully into her belly. They moved through the trees to where their horses had been tethered, and there he handed her to another man while he mounted his steed. When she was securely seated on the saddle in front of him, with her bound legs off to one side, he leaned forward. "Try to escape, and you will find things much worse for you," he whispered in her ear. "I am not a patient man. I am not a kind man. You might be surprised at what indignities I can inflict along the way."

She responded with a withering glare. He laughed in her face.

They rode through the trees as quickly as the low branches would allow. Once clear of the forest, the leader set a faster pace. Krystal had no choice but to grip the pommel of the saddle with both bound hands and hope she wouldn't fall or be sick against her gag. She closed her eyes and prayed the ordeal would end soon.

Night fell before they stopped to make camp. The men had found a dense collection of trees and brush off the road that would shield them from any travelers. Two of the men rode off with the body of the man Damen had killed and returned later without it. Two other men took Krystal to a tree, where they left her to tend to their horses. As they settled in for the night, each man withdrew dry rations from their packs. They had no fire.

The leader approached. "Are you hungry?"

She ignored the question.

He laughed and came closer to her. "I said, are you hungry? I will feed you if you can keep a civil tongue and do not try to escape." He loosened the gag around her mouth.

"Why shouldn't I try?" she shot back. "Why should I make things any easier on you?"

He opened his palm, displaying a small vial of dark liquid. "If you continue to resist us, I am authorized by my master to give you this."

Krystal looked at it. "What is that?"

"A sleeping draught, or so I'm told. You will sleep the remainder of our journey."

"Where are you taking me?" she said. "And why?"

He sighed. "Again, you ask too many questions." He leaned forward. "Are you hungry?"

Fiery sapphires glared at him. "Yes."

"Good." He reached for her feet, his voice and actions deliberate. "I'm going to untie you. If you run, I will order my men to shoot you down."

Krystal didn't doubt his sincerity. She rubbed feeling back into her limbs. One of the other men brought over a portion of fruit and dried meats.

"There is a clear stream nearby. When you have eaten, you may go there and drink some water. Also, I will give you a few moments alone to see to your personal needs."

Krystal only nodded. Even in her anger, the vial he held made her wary.

She ate only enough to settle her rolling stomach. When she moved into the trees, a dark shape approached her. Krystal bit her lip to keep from crying out. Recognizing him immediately, she scratched Damen behind the ears. She knew he could not risk getting any closer to the camp.

When Krystal returned to the camp, a man gave her a blanket to sleep on and then tied her up again. Two guards were posted to keep watch. The other men positioned themselves around her and slept. She couldn't move without bumping into one of them.

The next day the company headed east. Krystal could only guess that had been their direction all along. Her geographical knowledge—most of which she had been taught by her brothers—began and ended with the borders of Brynne and the western-most edge of Bettania.

They made camp that evening in another secluded area. This time one of the men tied Krystal's bound hands to a tree so she could not get away. She watched the men gather around the leader as he pulled an object from the pouch at his waist.

"It has nearly been seven days," he said. "Tomorrow the artifact should be fully charged."

Krystal strained to hear more.

One of the men spoke up. "Captain Bennett, will there be any difference without Lewis?"

"I don't see why there should be," Bennett said. "With the girl, we are the same number returning as we were when we left. Even so, he said nothing about there being a difference when he gave me my instructions."

"I still don't like it," someone else said. "It doesn't seem natural. Give me a horse and a long ride over this method of travel any day."

"The master said time was of the essence," said Bennett. "I think it would be unwise to challenge him. You know how he hates alterations to his plans."

The others nodded or grunted their agreement. Krystal glared at the leader, now identified as Captain Bennett. Knowing his name didn't help her like him. Nor did his loyalty to his master sway her.

"Get some rest," Bennett said to his men. "We leave at dawn."

"What of the horses, sir?"

"Release them," he said. "We won't need them any longer."

This confused Krystal. How could they leave at dawn with no horses?

Bennett brought her some food. "You should sleep right after eating. We leave at first light."

"How?" she asked. "You turned the horses loose."

He smiled. "We have another way."

Krystal ate a little and then settled down to sleep. The men set up a perimeter around her but did not untie her from the tree. Two guards took positions at either end of the camp. She leaned back against the tree and searched the darkness for any sign of Damen. He had to be close—if she could just get her hands free of the ropes, she could melt into the darkness and join him.

Krystal managed to loosen the knot that tied her to the tree before she decided to get some rest. She awoke as the first hint of pink showed in the eastern sky. Tense, she listened for any sound of movement. She did not dare turn around to view the men.

Soundlessly, she untied herself from the tree and scanned the brush but could not see any sign of her pet. Knowing she was taking a risk, she slowly crouched under her blanket. Her muscles protested the movement, but she ignored them.

She had yet heard no sound from the men. Gathering her courage, Krystal let the blanket fall away and dashed into the brush. One of the posted guards called out the alarm, but she ignored him.

The men would pursue her, certainly, but the lack of horses might lessen their advantage. She tucked her bound hands to her chest and let her legs do the work. She had two options: find a place to hide until they gave up or outrun them. Her nerves screamed to run.

Krystal was surprised that she hadn't found Damen yet, but she resisted calling out to him. He would turn up soon.

Krystal noticed the trees and bushes starting to thin, much to her dismay. Across open ground she'd be easy to spot. She turned to her left and kept running along the edge of the trees. She thought she heard a sound, but even if it was Damen she couldn't stop.

Suddenly she felt something large crash into her from behind. Krystal fell forward and hit the ground as a man's knee dug painfully into her back to keep her pinned.

"Captain Bennett!" he shouted. "I've got her!"

Chapter 3

STUGGLING AGAINST HER CAPTOR as hard as she could, Krystal only succeeded in having her face pushed roughly into the ground.

"Don't move," he said.

Krystal lifted her head and spit grass from her mouth.

In a moment, two more men crashed through the bushes. The man on top of her let up his hold and pulled her to her feet. Another man grabbed her other arm, and together they marched her back to the campsite and tossed her to the ground at Bennett's feet.

He knelt down next to her. "You are becoming troublesome."

"Then I'm doing something right."

He stood up and addressed his men. "Who found her?"

"Saunders did, sir," said one of the men.

"Good work, Saunders," said Bennett. "This will be remembered."

Saunders nodded. "Thank you, sir."

"Now then," Bennett said. "Let's get going."

To Krystal's surprise he knelt down again and withdrew a scroll and a small, rough-cut medallion from his belt pouch. As he placed these on the ground in front of him, each man in turn knelt around them. Two still held Krystal's arms.

"What are you doing?" she asked.

"Silence," said Bennett. "I must concentrate." He put his hand on the medallion and began reading in an unfamiliar language from the scroll. As he spoke, Krystal caught sight of a movement near the trees and she turned to see Damen emerge. She dared a look around. Each man had closed his eyes except Captain Bennett, and he seemed absorbed in reading the scroll.

Hope surged within her. If Damen could sneak up on the men, she might have another chance at escape. But before he got close enough to attack, a shimmering silver shield formed between Damen and the group. The dog hesitated before circling the barrier.

Krystal couldn't believe her eyes. The shield seemed to hum with its own energy, and it grew more solid as Bennett's voice grew stronger.

She opened her mouth to speak, but a horrible dizziness struck her. As she felt the bile rise in her throat. Damen barked urgently; she saw him fade from view.

"Damen!"

Krystal's entire body tingled. She shivered violently, and her ears started ringing. She saw Damen make a flying leap for her just before she fell forward onto soft earth.

Her stomach rebelled and Krystal heaved. Since she hadn't eaten she had nothing to lose, though that didn't make her feel any better. Her head felt like it would explode. The ringing in her ears started to subside, and she heard voices.

"Look out!"

"Move! It's coming this way!"

The snarling reached her. She tried to raise her head but couldn't make her body obey. She heard a man scream and tried to open her eyes. She felt Damen's cold nose on her cheek.

"Get your bows! Kill the creature!"

"Damen," she croaked. "Go. Get out of here."

He whimpered at her.

"I can't come with you. Just go, now!"

She heard the men around her and heard Damen move away.

"Don't miss!" Krystal recognized Bennett's voice now.

"Sir, the beast got Saunders!"

"So kill it!"

"He's almost out of range!"

Krystal forced herself to look up. Her eyes, slow to focus, finally caught sight of Damen as he disappeared over a hill. She closed her eyes again and collapsed onto the ground. She rolled to her side and tried to stop her head from spinning.

After a moment she felt hands on her arms as someone pulled her to a sitting position. "You look green," Bennett said to her.

Krystal opened her eyes. Her words came out in gasps. "What did you do to me?"

"Teleportation is hard on the body," he said. "My men and I were affected nearly as badly as you were our first time. This time wasn't as bad, though your pet recovered first. The blasted beast tore out the throat of another of my men before we could chase him off."

Krystal squinted at his face. "Teleportation?"

"Yes," he said. "It's the act of moving from one place to another by magic. Look around—you'll see we aren't where we used to be."

It took a great deal of effort, but Krystal did as he suggested. Instead of the tree where she'd been bound the night before and the bushes and forest beyond, she saw fields of grass with low hills all around them. Nothing resembled the place they had been just moments before.

Bennett leaned close to her ear. "Welcome to Fayterra," he said.

She pulled back from him. "Where did you say?"

"This is the kingdom of Fayterra," he said. "You are a long way from home, little one."

"Impossible," Krystal said.

"Can you stand yet? We need to get going." Bennett motioned with his hand, and two men pulled Krystal to her feet. They held her there while she steadied herself. Her head felt like fire and her stomach protested, but she managed to keep her feet.

"Where are we going?" she asked him.

Bennett had picked up the medallion and scroll and now placed them into his belt pouch. "Teleportation is not exact," he said. "We will have to walk to where we left our horses. We arrived some distance away from them."

Though she could understand his words, they held no meaning to her. She kept her silence and instead concentrated on putting one foot ahead of the other. The men holding each of her arms had started walking, so she could either walk or be dragged.

She noticed some distinct differences as her clarity returned.

Once she could walk on her own, the men released her arms but kept close. They also did not worry about keeping out of sight, nor did they worry about hiding the body of the other man Damen had killed. Bennett simply said they had no time to bury him and they went on their way.

Her captors didn't leave her time to ponder her pet's plight. As they approached a town, the men tightened the circle around her with Bennet taking the lead. Any people they met stayed clear of the men; Krystal noticed they eyed the guards uneasily, almost fearfully.

"I'm hungry," she said to the man next to her. "Can't we stop and eat?"

Bennett answered her. "No. We're moving on. Now be quiet."

Krystal bit back a rude retort. She glared at the back of his head for a moment. "I don't see why we can't stop for a few minutes and buy some fruit or something," she said.

Bennett spun on his heel to face her and raised a single finger. "You are becoming quite a nuisance," he told her through clenched teeth. "If you had a brain in that pretty little head you'd keep your mouth shut."

She stuck her tongue out at him.

Bennett's hands came up, and he clenched them into fists. Krystal thought he might be imagining her neck in his grasp. His eyes spoke promises of bodily harm. Finally he sighed and turned around. They walked on in silence.

They stopped at a stable near the other end of town. Bennett directed his men to go in and retrieve their steeds while he waited with Krystal, and when they came out he went in to do the same. He exited the building with two mounts.

"Our numbers have been nearly halved thanks to that mutt of yours," he said. "You will take this horse. Your hands will be tied and I will hold the reins, but we can make better time."

"I'm surprised you let me have my own horse," she said.

"I considered having you ride with me," he said. "But I think this will be safer."

She didn't ask him what he meant. Something about the hostile look in his eyes warned her off.

"I shouldn't have to remind you to behave," he said. "But I will anyway. Your horse will be tied securely to mine, so any attempt to escape would be useless."

"Where would I go?" Krystal asked him. "I don't even know where I am."

He smiled. "Good point," he said. "But if you fight me, it will be the worse for you."

"I don't think so," she said, meeting his eyes.

He narrowed his eyes at her. "And why is that?"

"I'm not stupid. You've threatened me plenty of times, but you have yet to follow through with any of them." Krystal smiled at him. "I've been paying attention. I suppose your master has given you some sort of order that no harm should come to me."

Bennett smiled at her. "You're a clever girl, but there is one thing you should consider. My master, the man who ordered your abduction, strikes fear in the hearts of these seasoned soldiers you see around you. I'd be willing to bet my life that everyone you encounter from here to the Capitol fears him. *You* may not be afraid of what I can do to you, but you should wonder what *he* may do to you if you continue to defy his will."

Krystal's chin came up. "I will not fear your master until he gives me reason to fear him."

"Don't worry, little one," Bennett said. "I'm sure he'll do that soon enough."

"He must be a man of some power," she said. "Perhaps he is a baron or some kind of lord. Tell me, who is he?"

"I've told you enough as it is," he said with a shake of his head. "Be patient. In time you will learn all you need to know."

Krystal sighed with frustration. She gained the horse's back and settled herself in the saddle. Bennett mounted his steed, tied Krystal's reins to his saddle, and motioned the group onward.

Once outside the town, Krystal spotted Damen keeping pace with them. The men saw him too. They spread out, and the men nearest to him raised their bows.

"Don't bother," Bennett said. "He keeps just out of range, curse him. We will make camp at sunset. I don't dare ride through the dark with that beast on the loose."

Sanford spoke up. "Sir, won't that make us late?"

"There is nothing I can do about that," said Bennett. "We can only hope he will understand the reason for our delay."

Krystal watched the men exchange skeptical looks.

They stopped for the night in a sparse wood near the next town. The men surrounded Krystal as before, and the assigned guards took their places. They slept with no fire.

Krystal woke in the dead of night. As she had done before, she carefully worked at the rope binding her hands to the tree. She loosened the knot and moved to a crouching position, waiting for her eyes to adjust enough to make out the shapes of the men around her. She had no desire to step on one of them and ruin her escape.

She froze when she heard a fierce whisper next to her. "Don't even consider it."

Krystal sighed. "Bennett," she hissed.

"You don't give me any credit," he said. "Give me your hands."

Krystal thrust her hands into the darkness between them. She could not see his face but felt him grope for her and then tie the rope more securely around her wrists.

"Why should I listen to you?" she demanded. "You are my kidnapper. It's my duty to try to escape from you." She relaxed again on her blanket. "What gave me away?"

"When I mentioned your possible escape, you pointed out you had no idea where you would go," he said. "A resourceful girl such as you wouldn't give up so easily."

Krystal sighed again. "I thought I'd go back to the last village and ask around," she said.

"What makes you think anyone would help you?"

"I'm one of them," she said.

She heard Bennett sigh. "You have the absurd confidence of youth," he said. "And you have become more than a little inconvenient. If we weren't so close to our destination I would force feed you that sleeping potion."

"I'd only spit it back in your face."

"Go to sleep," he said. "You'll need your rest for tomorrow."

"Why?"

"I should think you'd want your wits about you when you meet the man who ordered your abduction."

Chapter 4

KRYSTAL AND HER CAPTORS rode into the capital city of Fayterra and directly through the castle gates. Bennett pulled her off the horse and used his knife to slit the rope binding her hands. Worry settled in Krystal's stomach when Bennett and two of his men led her into the castle and through the stone corridors. Bennett stopped at a doorway and motioned for her to wait. He stepped in alone.

Krystal heard a deep, compelling voice. "Bennett. I expected you yesterday."

"Yes, sire," said Bennett. "We encountered unavoidable delays."

The voices faded. Krystal stepped toward the doorway, but her guards stopped her. She glared at them.

Soon Bennett stepped out and took her arm. "Behave," he said.

They could have entered Andrew's study, Krystal thought, if her brother had expensive tastes and more gold than sense. Near the fireplace sat two high-backed, cushioned chairs, and across the room from the door stood an ornately carved desk. Behind the desk she saw the figure of a man, standing with his back to them.

Bennett stopped and pulled her down as he knelt. "Kneel," he whispered.

Krystal had no choice but to comply. "Why?"

But the man turned around before Bennett could answer, and Krystal lost her train of thought. Handsome did not do him justice, though his age had to be beyond thirty. He stood taller than Bennett by several inches, his shoulder-length ebony hair given to curl at the ends. Bright green eyes studied her intently, almost hungrily. Krystal shivered, feeling exposed and vulnerable under his gaze.

The man nodded to Bennett, who rose, pulling Krystal along with him. "May I present King Gregory Gildresleve of Demarde and Fayterra?"

Krystal looked to Bennett, caught his mischievous smile, and knew he delighted in her surprise. She glared at him, knowing he'd gotten the better of her.

"She isn't a puppet, Bennett. Release her." The king's voice cut across the room.

Krystal jumped. She dared a look back at King Gregory and noticed he still stared at her with that same hungry expression. Never before had she or, to her knowledge, any member of her family been in the presence of royalty. She wouldn't have guessed it could be anything like this.

King Gregory motioned to a chair. "Come, my dear, you must be tired. Do sit down."

She moved automatically to the chair, though she hesitated to sit. The chair had to be the finest thing she'd ever seen, and she knew her clothes carried at least three days' worth of dirt.

The king didn't seem to notice her hesitation. "You may go, Bennett. Send Miraya in here. She should be waiting in the next room."

Bennett bowed. "As you will, sire." He turned on his heel and left the room.

King Gregory sat at the desk, across from Krystal. "I trust your journey here was as comfortable as could be expected."

Krystal found her voice. "I survived it."

"No doubt you have questions."

She nodded. "Sire, why am I here?"

King Gregory opened his mouth to speak, but then she saw his eyes flicker from her to the doorway. Krystal peeked around her chair to see who had come. A maid with long black hair and wide brown eyes stood there. She curtsied to the king.

"You sent for me, sire?"

"Yes, Miraya," King Gregory said. "Have a bath sent to the chamber I had you prepare yesterday. Our new guest will want to freshen up, I'm sure."

"New guest?" The maid's eyes went from her king to the chair where Krystal sat.

Krystal watched her eyes widen. She stared at Krystal as though she recognized her. She didn't take her eyes off Krystal until King Gregory cleared his throat.

"You are dismissed," he said.

Miraya curtsied again and left the room. Krystal stared after her.

King Gregory cleared his throat again. "I'm sure all of this must seem strange to you."

Krystal turned to look at him. "I am at a loss to explain how strange."

"You asked me why you are here," he said. "I ordered you to be brought to Fayterra."

"But why? How could you even know of my existence?"

"The kingdom of Fayterra has an ancient bond with magic," said King Gregory.

"I've encountered it," she said. "Two days ago I was in Brynne, and now I'm here. Your man Bennett called it teleportation."

"He used an artifact I own to get you here as quickly as possible."

"Please, sire, tell me why you have brought me here."

King Gregory smiled at her. "You have a certain importance to my enemy," he said. "I brought you here so you can help me further punish him."

"I could only be important to my family," she said.

"I have no quarrel with your family," he said. "Prince Jareth is my enemy and, unfortunately, my nephew."

"This prince has been to my home then?"

"To my knowledge, he has never left Fayterra."

Krystal sighed. "Then how does he know of me?"

"We're going in circles, aren't we?" King Gregory stood. "Allow me to show you." He motioned to a low wooden table behind him. "My sister, Jareth's mother, once gave her son a gift." Gregory lifted the cloth to reveal a round, clear ball. "This crystal sphere allowed my nephew to see other places, other lands. Through it he found you. I'm afraid you became quite important to the young man. I would even dare to say he thinks he's in love with you."

Krystal rose to her feet. "I don't even know him."

King Gregory lifted the sphere in his hand. "Young men often feel more than they think. I took this sphere from him and learned of you, and I must say I can understand his fascination."

Krystal could feel herself blush, though she trembled with anger. "That doesn't explain why you had me kidnapped and brought here."

"Jareth feels he should rule Fayterra," he said. "He is impulsive and completely unworthy to take the throne, but he refuses to listen to me. When I am crowned King of Fayterra at the end of the year, I want you to be there to show him the futility of his ridiculous dreams."

"You can't expect me to remain here all that time. I have to go home."

King Gregory looked at her through furrowed brows. "I would ask that you remember your place, my dear," he said. "I have no patience for disrespect."

Krystal took a deep breath and let it out. She fought desperately to keep her temper under control. "You said he could see me through this sphere? How is that done?"

He approached her. "Hold out your hands and I'll show you."

Krystal accepted the sphere. He cupped her hands and looked into her eyes.

"Look into the sphere and think of what you want to see," he said.

Krystal thought of her family first. They had to be frantic looking for her. To her amazement, she saw a fleeting picture of the farm inside the sphere. The vision jolted her, and she lost it. Krystal peered harder into the center to try and find it again.

"What did you see?" King Gregory released her hands to move behind her.

"I saw my home, I think," she said. "I can't find it now."

"Think harder."

Another picture suddenly formed inside the sphere. Krystal saw a person, a figure in some kind of prison cell. As she watched, he raised his head, and she gasped. He had to be the most handsome young man she had ever seen. Under the layer of prison dirt, she could see his striking face and long blond hair. He turned his head and it seemed as though he saw her watching him.

Krystal gasped again, and the sphere fell from her hands. King Gregory made a frantic grab for it but missed. The orb shattered on the stone floor.

She stepped back, away from the mess. "I'm sorry."

"No matter," said the king. "The sphere has been so well used it had begun to lose its power. I'll have someone clean that up. What did you see that so startled you?"

Krystal saw in his eyes he had seen it too. "I saw a young man. He sat in a prison."

He smiled. "The sphere's magic has become unpredictable. Put it out of your mind."

"Sire, I don't understand your plans for me," she said. "With respect, I ask you again to send me home. Surely your goals can be accomplished without a mere peasant girl."

King Gregory stepped closer and lifted a strand of her hair in his hand. "I don't want you to ask me that again. And as for being a mere peasant girl, you are that no longer."

"What do you mean?"

"I own a tiny bit of land called Avolonya," he said as he moved back to his desk. "It is in my authority to name a princess of Avolonya and I have. You are now that princess."

She looked at him in disbelief. He acted as though he expected her to fall at his feet in gratitude. Instead, she shook her head. "No, thank you. I have no wish to become your princess."

King Gregory frowned. "You cannot refuse."

"I believe I just did."

"The title carries no responsibilities," he said. "There is no point to your refusal."

Krystal felt her hands clench. "I just want to go home, sire."

"You are not leaving Fayterra."

"And *you* are not my king," she said. "You have no power over me."

He laughed. "Your king doesn't even know you're alive. Who do you think would rescue you? Can your brothers track you through teleportation? They don't even know what it is."

"You have no right to keep me here!"

King Gregory pinned her with an emerald glare. "You will not raise your voice to me. Your future—your life—now rests in my hands."

She glowered at him. "You have stolen me from my home. You have ruined the plans I made for myself. But know this, King Gregory, you will never control me."

He took a step toward her but then stopped. "Guard!" A guard appeared in the doorway. "Take her to the prince's old chamber. And stand at the door. She is not to leave that room."

Krystal jerked away from the guard, who moved to take her arm. "I can walk by myself."

He led her to a room where the maid she had seen before had just finished filling a tub of water. Krystal hardly noticed the guard close the door. The maid hurried out before Krystal could utter a word. Alone, she stripped off her filthy clothing and bathed quickly. Another maid entered just after she'd wrapped herself in a robe she found on the bed. This new maid had curly blonde hair, green eyes, and a ready smile. She gathered up Krystal's dirty clothing and left the room, only to return a few moments later and take a gown from the closet.

"You should be comfortable in this, my lady," said the maid.

Krystal touched the dress. "It's the finest thing I've ever seen, but I can't wear it. Don't you have something more like what you're wearing? I could wait until my clothes are cleaned."

The maid looked confused. "The king ordered your clothes to be destroyed, Princess."

Krystal fought the urge to roll her eyes. She sighed instead. "I'm no princess."

Once Krystal was dressed, the girl insisted on doing Krystal's hair. As she sat before the mirror while the maid brushed her hair, she asked, "What happens to me now?"

"I'll fetch your lunch tray," said the maid. "What would you like to eat?"

"Whatever you have," Krystal said. "I'm not picky."

The maid patted Krystal's hair. "I'll be right back with your lunch."

Krystal watched her leave and then turned back to the stranger in the mirror. She almost didn't recognize herself. She lacked only a crown to complete the image of a princess.

Krystal had no luck with the window in her room. It had either rusted or been sealed shut. Nor could she find anything in the room that could be used as a weapon. If she wanted out of this chamber, she'd have to rely on her wits.

Her lovely gown quickly became a hindrance as did the infrequent arrival of castle servants. The blonde maid returned with a tray of fine food that Krystal found she could not stomach. The blonde left again and returned awhile later with fresh water to drink and a full pitcher for her basin. Finally Krystal moved to the bed to wait for things to settle down.

The day must have caught up with her, for the next thing she knew, someone was shaking her awake. "Princess Krystal," said the voice. "The king requests your presence in his study."

For a brief moment, Krystal thought she must be dreaming. It sounded so strange. She sat up and looked into the eyes of the dark haired maid. "What does he want?"

"It is not my place to question," the maid said. "I have been sent to bring you to him."

Krystal looked at the candle the maid held. "How late is it?"

She moved to light the room. "It's just after sunset. I am to have you in his study by the time he finishes dinner."

She sat up. "Can't you just tell him I'm not up for another round of shouting?"

The maid stared at her in astonishment. "You truly raised your voice to him?"

Krystal shrugged, trying to seem unconcerned. The maid's reaction embarrassed her. "I lost my temper. I don't think it's any secret to your king that I don't care for his company."

"He is not my king." The maid put her hand over her mouth, looking horrified. "I did not mean to say that. Please forgive me."

"I didn't hear anything," said Krystal, and the maid rewarded her with a smile.

"Thank you."

"What is your name?"

"I am Miraya, Highness."

Krystal rolled her eyes. "Please don't call me that. I don't know what King Gregory hopes to accomplish by naming me a princess."

"It's difficult to know what scheme is in his head," agreed Miraya. "Though one thing is certain. It is clear that he has a specific plan in mind for you."

"That's hardly reassuring."

Miraya brought Krystal her dinner tray. "Please eat. It will help you feel better."

"I don't see how food can help," said Krystal.

The maid smiled thinly. "I wish I could do more, but in this kingdom, King Gregory's word is law. Most Fayterrans support him. They prefer a seasoned warrior to an untried boy."

"What do you mean?"

"I thought you knew," Miraya said. "Prince Jareth is the rightful heir to the throne of Fayterra. King Gregory stole it from him."

"Isn't Jareth his nephew? Why would he do such a thing?"

"His reasons are his own. Please, Princess, I must ask you to eat. He will be expecting you soon." Miraya moved about the room, straightening as she went.

Krystal ate and watched her. "Why do you stay here? Why not leave?"

"I wish I could," she said. "The king prefers to keep me here. He's made sure I'll stay."

"How?"

"I wish I could tell you, but even talking about it brings risk." She put down the pillow she'd been fluffing. "I can tell you this. It entertains King Gregory to cause suffering. He enjoyed tormenting Prince Jareth, and now I am his target."

Krystal put down her roll. "And now perhaps I am as well." She stood up. "Let's get this over with. The anticipation is driving me mad."

Chapter 5

THE KING SAT AT HIS DESK when they entered the room. Miraya curtsied and nudged Krystal, who copied her. Gregory came to his feet. Krystal couldn't help but notice how his eyes traveled the length of her more than once. Miraya left quietly.

"You are breathtaking." Gregory took Krystal's hand. "That color suits you."

She responded automatically. "Thank you."

"I'm glad to see you are in a better mood," he said. "I'd hoped to enjoy our time together."

"How can we do that? I am your captive."

The king frowned. "I would prefer you not refer to yourself as a captive."

"I see no other way to define it," said Krystal. "Your men brought me here against my will, and you will not let me leave. I am a captive and you, sire, are my kidnapper."

Clearly King Gregory did not like being referred to as a criminal. He straightened to his full height. "Are you always this flippant to your betters? For a peasant, you speak too freely."

"You claim to have made me a princess. You can't have it both ways, King Gregory."

He sighed. "I brought you here to have a civil conversation, but I see that is impossible. Sit down and listen to what I tell you."

"I prefer to stand."

"Sit!" The command had a fair bite to it.

Krystal sat.

"I intended to tell you that you could have freedom to roam the castle and the grounds," the king said. "However, since you seem determined to be regarded as a captive, I can treat you as such. I can leave a guard posted at your door day and night and only allow maids in to bring your meals. I see no need for us to be enemies, Krystal. That choice would be yours."

"And if I choose to cooperate with your rules?"

"You will have your freedom," he said. "Within reason. You may spend your days in the gardens or within the castle. You will dine with me in the dining hall along with the rest of my nobles." King Gregory leaned forward. "But any attempt at escape will be punished. There are enough isolated rooms and dungeons to teach you the true meaning of captivity."

Krystal crossed her arms. "You win, sire. I will abide by your rules."

He smiled at her. "I knew you could be reasonable."

Until I escape, she thought. Krystal rose to her feet. "If you are through with me, sire, I would prefer to return to my room. It has been a long day."

He stopped her at the door. "You must wait to be dismissed from the king's presence. This is not your home, Krystal. You may not come and go as you please."

She turned to him and gave him a surprisingly graceful curtsy. "May I be excused, sire?"

King Gregory frowned at her. She thought he might have caught the derision in her tone. Then he waved a hand and a guard appeared at her side. "You may go. Wilson will escort you."

"Thank you, sire." Krystal led the way back to her room and shut the door in the guard's face. She turned and found the blonde maid by her bed.

"I can help you ready for bed," she said.

"I can dress myself."

"The hooks for that dress are in the back," the maid said. "Allow me to assist you."

Krystal sighed and offered the girl her back. Once dressed in the soft cotton nightgown, she watched as the maid gathered the clothes they had just removed.

"I will see to it these are cleaned and returned to you," said the maid.

"That's fine. If you don't mind, I'd prefer to be alone now."

The girl curtsied. "Of course, Princess. Good night."

Krystal watched her leave. Being a princess would take getting used to.

The maid had pulled back the covers and Krystal climbed into bed, her mind still heavily weighted with her troubles. Sleep would not come, no matter how much she tossed and turned. How simple her life a few days ago seemed, with only an unwanted betrothal to worry about and the world open to her. When she finally slept, tears moistened her eyelashes and the pillow.

&

Krystal disappeared from her room just after breakfast. She didn't wait to see if someone would stop her but slipped down the corridor when the maid returned to take the tray. She followed the hall toward the king's study because it led to the main entrance, careful to avoid the study doorway in case anyone happened to be watching.

She stopped when the main entrance to the castle came into view. Krystal clearly remembered the large wooden doors she had been led through the day before. Guards were posted on either side. Escape would not be possible through the front doors, but a castle this size surely had more than one way out.

Once she found a means of escape, where would she go? Krystal had no idea how to find her way back home. She would need to find a map.

Krystal continued to watch the great doors as she considered her problem. She knew Andrew kept all the maps in his study. Perhaps King Gregory did the same thing. If she could sneak into the king's study without his knowledge, maybe she could find a map to help her get home.

As she watched, the great doors swung open. The guards snapped to attention as a woman entered the castle. She had cropped blonde hair and wore a uniform similar to the ones the guards wore, along with a sword and a scowl. Another man stepped inside and closed the door. Krystal backed down the corridor in search of a different area of the castle to explore.

Following her nose, she made her way toward the kitchen, hoping to find another way out of the castle. She found the dining hall before the kitchen, but figured she had to be heading in the right direction. The kitchen had to be close to a table large enough to seat thirty people. She found a hallway to the left of the dining hall and followed it. About halfway down the hall, Krystal heard the first clanging of pots and pans.

The hallway opened up to the largest kitchen Krystal could have imagined. Dozens of cooks and servants hurried from place to place in a rush of cooking and cleaning. As she watched, a woman pulled six loaves of bread out of an oven and put them on the counter. Her hopes of passing through unseen, however, were dashed in a moment.

A short girl with her curly hair tucked in a scarf stopped and curtsied to her. "Can I help you, Princess?" Several heads turned in their direction at her words.

Krystal looked at her. How had she known to call her Princess? "No, thank you."

Another woman stepped up. "Are you lost?"

"No," she said. "I thought I would explore the castle."

The curly haired girl giggled. "Well, you've found the kitchen."

The woman hushed her. "Maggie, that's enough. Get back to work."

Maggie's mouth turned downward but she didn't argue. She trotted away.

The woman looked up at Krystal. "You may wish to take a maid along, Princess, the next time you explore," she said. "You wouldn't want to get lost."

"No, of course not," said Krystal. "I'm sorry to bother you. Good day."

Krystal retraced her steps through the hallway and out of the dining hall. As she continued down the castle corridor, she paid closer attention to the people who passed her. All of them bowed or nodded to her in passing, each one seeming to recognize the rank King Gregory had given her. It made no sense. She wore no crown or emblem; how could they tell?

Without thinking, she started to climb stairs. She didn't know where they led, but Krystal suddenly felt the need to feel the sun on her face. She had seen men on the upper walls of the castle when she arrived with Captain Bennett. There had to be a way up there.

She soon found herself shielding her eyes from the morning sun. Krystal moved to a wall to take in the view. The beauty of the countryside entranced her. She could see the distant forests to the north and mountains to the south.

A shadow fell across her. Krystal turned around only to find herself face to chest with the largest and darkest man she had ever seen. He wore the uniform of a guardsman and looked more than a little imposing with his arms folded across his massive chest.

"May I help you, Princess?" His deep voice shook the stone, she was sure of it.

Real fear washed over her. "I was just looking around."

"It's dangerous up here," he said. "You shouldn't be here alone."

Krystal thought he sounded amused, but she couldn't see a smile through his thick beard. The sun behind him shadowed his face. She edged around him, but he turned to continue to face her. Krystal looked up into his brown eyes and lost some of her fear.

They definitely twinkled. He may not be as ferocious as he looked. "What is your name?"

"I am Voltimande, Highness."

"Voltimande, really?"

"Yes," he said. "My mother is the palace healer."

Krystal folded her arms in front of her. "And you are one of King Gregory's guardsmen?"

He inhaled and rose to his full height. She didn't think he could get any taller. "I am a guard of the kingdom of Fayterra. I serve the kingdom's best interests."

Something in his tone confused Krystal. "It isn't the same thing?"

"Sometimes serving the king is not the same as serving the kingdom."

She understood. "You are not loyal to King Gregory."

"It would mean my life if King Gregory did not believe me loyal."

"Why are you telling me this? What if I tell him?"

"I have it on good authority you won't," he said. "Besides, what could you say? I have served him for years. You have known him one day."

Krystal began to walk, and Voltimande walked with her. "It's dangerous for you to tell strangers you may or may not be loyal to the king. Someone might betray you."

"If I never spoke to anyone, how would I make new friends?" He looked at her. "No one should be alone. It's important for a person to have someone to confide in if they need it."

She looked at him sharply. It crossed her mind he may be trying to trick her. Perhaps King Gregory sent him to befriend her. Would it be possible to trust anyone?

Krystal moved on to a less hazardous topic. "The view is extraordinary."

"Fayterra is a wondrous kingdom," he said. "Some believe it has magic woven into every aspect of the land."

"I know nothing of magic," she said. "All I see is beauty."

"You will learn of magic if you stay here," said Voltimande. "You cannot escape it."

Krystal quickened her pace. "I think I will go back downstairs. The sun is quite warm."

He bowed at the waist. "Good day to you, Princess."

On her way through the interior of the castle, Krystal took several wrong turns and nearly got lost. She eventually found herself near her bedroom and more familiar surroundings. She wondered if the king would be in his study at this time of day. She'd spent a great deal of time wandering around the castle, so it had to be near lunch. Where did King Gregory eat?

She slowed her steps the closer she got to the study door. If he was inside, she had no desire to talk to him. She stopped. Voices came from within the room, and Krystal's heart sank. She turned to go to her room but then heard her name and stopped.

She moved closer to listen.

"What did she do then?" King Gregory asked.

"After my men caught her and brought her back, we teleported." She recognized Bennett's voice. "Thankfully she did not struggle much, but that monstrous dog of hers managed to get through the portal also. It's here now, in Fayterra. The beast got another one of my men while we recovered from the transition."

"How did Krystal react to teleporting?"

"It made her ill," Bennett said, and Krystal thought she heard a smile in his voice. "She recovered quickly and resumed her defiance."

"You've mentioned this defiance of hers several times now," said the king, an edge to his voice. "If I didn't know better, I would think you admire the girl."

"I think I might, in a way," Bennett said. "She never lost her spirit or will to fight, even when facing all of my men. Though it made my job more difficult, I admire that. A lesser person would not have struggled so to accept what she could not change."

Krystal heard anger in the king's voice. "That will do, Bennett."

"Well, well," a voice said beside her. "What have we here?"

Krystal turned in surprise and came face-to-face with the uniformed woman she had seen at the castle entrance. Her eyes burned with anger. The woman grabbed Krystal's arm.

"My king," she said as she dragged Krystal into the study. "I caught this girl spying outside your door."

Krystal looked at King Gregory. He looked even more handsome than before in a black shirt and pants with an emerald tunic. She watched him take her in with his eyes.

"Release her," he said to the woman.

She obeyed. "What would you have me do with her, sire?"

"Nothing," said the king. "Krystal, what were you doing outside my door?"

She could feel the eyes of the woman burning holes into her. Krystal searched her mind for a logical excuse. She lifted her chin and looked at Gregory. "I was not spying. I wanted to talk to you, but when I approached I heard someone with you and didn't want to interrupt." She dared a glance at the woman and found hostility. This strange woman stared at her with unmasked hatred.

"You see, Caprice?" he said to the woman. She looked at him. "I suspected Princess Krystal would have an explanation."

"I'm certain she was eavesdropping, sire," Caprice said. "She didn't even hear my approach."

"Come now, Lady Fordyce," said Bennett. "We all know you can move like a cat when you wish to. Perhaps you didn't make any noise."

She gave him a look that suggested she might disembowel him and then calmly looked back at the king. "I'm certain she would have heard me had she not been listening to you."

King Gregory smiled at her. "You needn't worry, Caprice. Even if Krystal *had* heard our conversation, I doubt she would have learned anything." He looked over at Krystal and his smile widened. "Why don't you and Bennett leave now? I'd like to talk to the princess alone."

They bowed and left Krystal with the king. Gregory moved away from his desk and approached her, stopping only when she was within his reach. Krystal watched him warily. She'd heard him snap angrily at Bennett. Now he seemed amused, almost genial.

The atmosphere of the room changed as he looked at her. Krystal resisted the urge to rub her arms. The intensity of his gaze made her want to run, but she didn't understand why. She couldn't stop herself from taking a half step backward as she waited for him to speak.

Gregory reached out and took her hand, as if he couldn't resist touching her. "What was it you wanted to talk to me about?"

Krystal's mind went blank. "What?"

"You said you wanted to speak to me," he said. "Don't tell me you've forgotten already."

Her mind raced. She couldn't think of anything that sounded good. "Breakfast."

He looked at her questioningly. "Breakfast?"

"Yes." Krystal sighed and moved away, forcing him to release her. "I wondered if the maids could bring less food in the morning. I'm not that hungry, and I hate to see it wasted."

"You can have whatever you want," he said. "But you could have simply told the maids this. You did not have to trouble yourself with seeking me out."

She pretended ignorance. "I'm sorry to have bothered you then."

He smiled again. "Please don't think you bother me. I could never mind an interruption as pleasant as you." He stepped closer.

"Have you enjoyed exploring the castle?"

Krystal looked at him, surprised. "How did you know?"

"I am king," he said. "It is my duty to know what happens in my own castle."

"I suppose that's true," she said. "I did enjoy myself, though I admit the castle is large enough that I can get lost in it."

"You disappeared quite early this morning," said Gregory. "I had planned to assign a maid to go with you."

Krystal tried not to sound too eager. "What about Miraya? Could she accompany me?"

His eyes narrowed. "Why Miraya?"

"She's the only one whose name I know," Krystal said, thinking quickly. "She seems nice and doesn't seem like she would talk a lot and distract me."

He seemed content with her answer. "Unfortunately, Miraya has a great deal of other duties. Perhaps Catrina or Lysabith would be better companions for you."

"I don't know them."

"You don't know anyone," he said. "I'm sure you would be satisfied with either of them."

She tried not to look too disappointed. "I suppose so."

A maid entered with a covered tray and put it on the table near the fireplace. "Have you eaten lunch?" asked Gregory.

"Not yet," said Krystal.

"Why not eat with me?" He removed the cover and set it aside. "There's plenty to share."

Again she felt the urge to run. "I'm sure there's a tray waiting for me in my room."

He frowned. "You don't need to go."

"Thank you, but I should. Good afternoon, sire." She curtsied and turned to leave.

He stopped her with a word. "Krystal?"

She turned. "Yes?"

"I'll see you tonight at dinner."

Krystal nodded. "Of course."

She returned quickly to her room. Krystal had forgotten about eating with the king and his nobles in the dining hall. It meant less time she would have in the afternoon to explore the castle.

Two maids entered her room after she'd finished picking at her lunch tray; the blonde and a taller brunette with a long braid down her back.

The blonde spoke. "Lysabith will take your tray. I will show you around the castle."

Krystal's heart sank. "You are Catrina?"

"Yes, Princess," Catrina said. "Lyssa will also return to prepare your gown for dinner tonight, so I will be at your complete disposal."

Krystal nodded. She hadn't wanted a maid who King Gregory believed was so loyal.

She looked at Lysabith, who had immediately moved to take care of the tray and now had almost left the room with it. She couldn't know if the new maid would be an ally or not.

"Shall we go, Princess?" asked Catrina.

"Yes, of course," said Krystal. "I'm sure there's a great deal still to see."

Chapter 6

EXPLORING THE CASTLE with Catrina proved to be a disappointment, though Krystal was hardly surprised. The bubbly maid talked endlessly about the king's many fine qualities. By her estimation, Gregory had saved Fayterra by taking it over. Krystal soon ended the tour just to escape her.

Lysabith came to help her dress for dinner. She had selected a lavender gown for Krystal and helped her into it with practiced ease. Already Krystal preferred Lysabith's quiet ways to Catrina's brashness. She did have difficulty, though, drawing the maid into conversation. She asked her about bringing less food at breakfast and only received a nod.

"Have you been here long?" she asked as Lysabith brushed her hair.

"I've lived in the castle my whole life," said the maid.

After a long pause Krystal tried again. "How many people usually attend these dinners?"

"I've never served at dinner," said Lysabith.

"The king said we would dine with his nobles," Krystal said. "Do they live in the castle?"

Lysabith put down the brush. "Some do. Duke Milford and his wife, Lady Dannaie, are here more than at their home. And I heard the Elder Patriarch arrived this afternoon. He is only passing through, so I don't know if he intends to attend dinner."

"Who is the Elder Patriarch?"

The maid looked at her with undisguised surprise. "He is the head of the Church. He travels from kingdom to kingdom to offer spiritual guidance. You have never heard of him? His name is Leodegrance Severin."

"My family didn't follow a particular religion," said Krystal.

"I don't believe the king likes him," said Lysabith. "Brother Severin has never acknowledged his claim to the Fayterran throne."

"Why does the king let him stay here?"

"Perhaps it is because Brother Severin is so well loved. People everywhere put a great deal of importance on his opinions."

Krystal fell silent and gazed at her reflection while Lysabith arranged her hair. She liked the idea of dining with the king even less now. What would there be to look forward to at a dinner with strangers? Would Gregory be hostile to the Elder Patriarch?

The maid stepped back. "You look lovely, Princess. I'm sure the king will be pleased."

Krystal noticed Lysabith hadn't smiled when making that pronouncement. "I'm sure King Gregory will have other things to worry about than how I look in my dress." The maid curtsied and turned to go but Krystal stopped her. "Do I go to the dining hall by myself?"

"If you need help I could show you where it is," said Lysabith.

"No," said Krystal. "I know where it is. I just wasn't sure if I was supposed to wait."

"I don't believe so," the maid said.

Krystal let her go. She spent another minute in front of the mirror, still unused to seeing herself dressed so well. She straightened her shoulders and walked to the door.

King Gregory stood just outside her door, his hand poised to knock. "You look lovely. The gown suits you."

"Thank you," she said. "It's beautiful."

"It belonged to my sister. I had guessed you to be about her size, though you are taller. May I escort you to dinner?" He offered her his arm.

Krystal put a hand on his arm. "Yes, thank you." As they walked, she continued. "Is that where all these clothes came from? They were your sister's?"

He looked down at her. "I could hardly have a seamstress sew clothes for you without measurements. When the time comes for your winter wardrobe, you will be properly fitted."

Since Krystal had no intention of being there for the winter, she did not take exception. She also didn't want to say anything that might put him on guard. For all he knew she planned to stay exactly where he'd put her.

The diners had gathered around the table. They rose when Krystal entered with King Gregory, and it seemed as though all eyes set upon her. He led her to the head of the table and kissed her hand before releasing it so she could sit at his left. She fought the urge to run or scream. Here stood a *peasant*, yet they treated her as the princess Gregory had made her. How odd that, when she needed it, she couldn't call up a shred of calm reserve.

Her dining companion leaned in to introduce himself. "Good evening, Princess. I am Duke Milford of Weston, and this charming lady next to me is my wife, Dannaie."

Krystal thought they looked more like father and daughter with his snow white hair and wrinkles and her black hair and pale skin. She nodded to them. "Hello."

On Gregory's right sat Lady Caprice Fordyce, who still seemed to take pleasure in glaring at Krystal. Next to her sat Captain Bennett. Krystal hadn't even considered that he might attend dinner. She frowned at him, the memory of how he'd treated her or that he'd been the one to abduct her in the first place—even if it had only been at King Gregory's order—still fresh in her mind.

Bennett smiled at her and raised his goblet. Her hands fisted in her lap. Even now he taunted her. She turned her head to look down the table and pointedly ignore him.

Two men caught her eye. One, a brown haired, balding man tried to blend into his chair. He sat far away from the king and moved out of sight every time Gregory looked down the table.

The other man, young, handsome, and blonde, sat surrounded by women both young and old. Krystal glanced at King Gregory, who smiled at her, then looked down the table at the blonde man. She thought she might prefer sitting next to him rather than the king.

Gregory motioned for dinner to be served. Krystal almost gasped when a servant placed her plate before her. She had never seen such a beautiful meal. She didn't cook pretty food. It would have been a wasted effort the way her brothers attacked their dinners every night.

As though he had been waiting for her, the king caught her hand when she lifted it to pick up her fork. "I had them prepare this meal in honor of your first dinner with me."

She smiled when she pulled away and pointedly picked up her fork. "Thank you."

The first bite melted in her mouth, and Krystal sighed. This did not compare to picking at trays the maids brought her, though a part of her did prefer the solitude. She hadn't eaten a meal that she had not cooked in years.

Again Krystal felt the king's gaze and looked at him. His emerald eyes smoldered at her with an intensity she could not understand. He didn't look angry, but he didn't smile either. A blush crept across her cheeks and she turned back to her plate.

He kept watching her, only turning his head when Lady Caprice spoke to him. Krystal found she couldn't eat under his scrutiny. A terrible thrill of spasms assaulted her stomach. She felt like she'd swallowed live butterflies. She put down her fork and reached for her water goblet.

A voice called across the room. "Announcing the Elder Patriarch, Brother Severin."

Everyone, including King Gregory, rose after hearing this, although Gregory did so with his goblet in his hand. A tall, lean man wearing brilliant blue robes entered the dining hall flanked by two black robed assistants. He took the seat at the end of the table. His assistants stood by his chair.

Krystal turned her attention to the newcomer. She found his age impossible to determine—although his hair and beard were white as snow, he walked like a young man. He looked at everyone at the table in the eye, and Krystal noticed some couldn't hold his gaze. Then he settled on Gregory.

"Good evening, Brother Severin," the king said in a formal and regal manner. "We are honored to have you dine with us this evening."

"The honor is mine, King Gregory." Even the man's voice seemed ageless. He looked around the table. "Are you representing Fayterran royalty this evening?"

Krystal felt the air around Gregory change. He rose to his full height in the chair. "Need I remind you I am king, Brother Severin?"

"Of Demarde, I know," the Elder Patriarch said. "I wonder how your kingdom fares without your leadership. I do understand, however, the familial obligations that necessitate your continued presence here in Fayterra. Young Prince Jareth undoubtedly needs guidance. Where is the lad? I haven't seen him once since my arrival."

Krystal watched with fascination as the king tried to conceal his rage. "There is, unfortunately, some doubt as to whether the *lad* will be able to assume the throne," he said with icy civility. "At present, he is away from the palace. Boys will be boys, after all."

Leodegrance Severin's diamond eyes lit on Krystal. "Sire, who, may I ask, is that charming young woman at your side? I have never seen her before."

The king reached out for Krystal's hand. She could feel the rage from him as they touched. "Princess Krystal of Avolonya, may I present the Elder Patriarch, Brother Severin?"

"How do you do, my dear?"

"Very well, thank you," said Krystal. "I am pleased to meet you."

"I wish I had more time to become acquainted with you," said the Elder Patriarch with a sigh. "Perhaps, once my business in the north is concluded, I will be able to return."

"It would be our pleasure to have your company again so soon," said Gregory.

Krystal looked at him. She found it incredible that he had not choked on the obvious lie.

She looked down the table again at Brother Severin. He accepted his plate with a smile and took a bite. He either had not noticed Gregory's hostility, or he chose to ignore it.

The other diners had picked up on the king's mood. Conversation had all but stopped, and as it slowly resumed, it did not regain its previous pitch.

King Gregory, however, did not recover. Krystal noted how he lifted his goblet more than his fork, and how he utterly ignored Lady

Fordyce when she spoke. He stared at his plate more than Krystal, but his distraction did not soothe her.

She tried to put him out of her mind by drawing Duke Milford into conversation, but she saw he had fallen asleep. Surprised she looked at his wife, who shrugged.

"He always does this, the poor dear," Lady Dannaie said. Then she turned back to her friend.

Krystal pushed her plate away. She could not eat another bite. Her stomach still fluttered, and she felt a vague sense of anticipation. King Gregory had shifted his gaze to stare down the table at the Elder Patriarch. He also demanded a refill of his wine goblet.

As the servants doled out dessert, Brother Severin announced his need to retire. "You will forgive me, King Gregory, but I have a long journey ahead of me tomorrow, and I need my rest."

Gregory motioned him away with his goblet. Krystal noticed Bennett snicker and nudge Lady Caprice with his elbow. She brushed him away, her gaze intent on the king.

Krystal tried to enjoy her fruit dessert, but the air grew thicker once the Elder Patriarch left the hall. She wanted to seek the sanctuary of her room, but no one would leave before Gregory. He, however, didn't seem the least inclined to leave his seat, or his wine.

Bennett leaned close to Caprice, whispered something, and then laughed. His attempt at whispering the phrase, "But I am king," could be heard above the subdued diners. Silverware clanged to plates. An urgent hush swept across the table. All eyes went to Bennett and then to Gregory. The king slowly rose to his feet, his hot, seething eyes boring holes in his lieutenant.

"Stand." Menace bled into the word.

Bennett had enjoyed his wine also but not enough that he failed to see the danger. "Sire, my humblest apologies. It was a poor joke, truly. I am your servant, sire! Surely you must know that."

"Stand," Gregory repeated, "or I will kill you where you sit."

"Over a bit of humor?" Bennett tried to laugh. He rose to his feet as Gregory moved around the table. "Surely, my king, you remember my years of service."

Gregory advanced and Bennett backed away. Tension polluted the air. Some of the women clung to their husbands. No one could leave, since the two men had moved to block the only exit.

"My title may amuse you," Gregory spat, his voice rising to match his fury, "but it is no laughing matter to me. *I am the king!*" He pulled his sword free of its sheath.

"Yes, sire, you are the king!" said Bennett. "Please forgive my ill-chosen words."

King Gregory continued to advance. "It is my right to rule this kingdom!"

Bennett had become frantic. "Majesty, please!" He drew his sword.

Steel clanged against steel as Gregory slashed at Bennett. "Your foolishness is boundless!" he roared. "You drew your weapon against your own king! Now I will kill you."

At first Krystal thought the two were actually well matched swordsmen. But soon it became apparent that while Bennett fought for his life, Gregory merely toyed with his opponent. Bennett would die. The timing of his death only depended on how long the king wanted to exercise his sword arm.

Bennett's end came between a suit of polished armor and a tapestry of a summer picnic. Gregory's sword slashed across the other man's chest and then cut right into his middle. Bennett fell to the ground with a thud, his bloodless sword clanged on the stone. Gregory stood for a moment over the body of his faithful lieutenant, tossed his sword to the floor, and stalked away. His eyes fell on Krystal as he passed her, but it seemed like he didn't recognize her.

"Get out of here, all of you!" he shouted to the diners over his shoulder. "Get out!"

Chapter 7

KRYSTAL DIDN'T NEED TO BE TOLD TWICE. She fled at a run, hardly caring where her feet led her. She only wanted to be as far from Gregory as possible.

Eventually she stopped and sat on the landing to catch her breath. She fought her heaving stomach, in serious jeopardy of losing her dinner all over her lovely gown. Never before had she seen one man take another man's life. She looked around frantically for a means to settle her nerves.

Only then did Krystal realize she had gotten lost. She had gone up some stairs and down others so quickly that she couldn't determine whether she stood on the same floor as her bedchamber or the dining hall. Not knowing how long she had until Gregory regained his senses enough to wonder about her, she decided to retrace her steps and try to find a way back to her room.

She stumbled upon the portrait hall by accident. Huge portraits of the royal families of Fayterra surrounded her. Krystal followed the time line of portraits down to the last, a painting of what she guessed would be Jareth and his parents. But the portrait revealed one little detail no one had yet mentioned. The beautiful queen seated on the velvet bench held not one, but two blonde haired babies: a little boy—by all accounts the young prince Jareth—and a little girl. Krystal stared at the tiny twins in astonishment. Why had King Gregory not mentioned his niece?

She looked at the faces of the king and queen. Jareth's father had been intensely handsome. The artist had captured him while still in his youth. He had eyes of clear blue, his hair light brown. He stood tall, broad of shoulder and narrow of hip, but power radiated from his stance and expression. His hand rested on the slender shoulder of his queen.

Krystal stared long at the replica of Gregory's sister. She looked nothing like her brother. A mass of honey blonde hair shimmered down to her hip. Her blue eyes hinted of violet.

Krystal frowned at the loving family portrayed on the canvas. *They should be here now*, she thought, *ruling Fayterra instead of Gregory*. What happened? What went so wrong?

The sound of boot steps in the marble hall made her jump. She whirled around and, spotting King Gregory, backed up several paces. He had gotten close enough that she could see him frown at her retreat.

He stopped. "Come, my dear, there is nothing here to alarm you." He held his arms out at his sides. "As you can see I am harmless. I don't even have my sword."

She continued to stare at him, wordless. He seemed calmer, but she had seen for herself how quickly his temper could change. For a moment she wondered what troubled her more, that he had just killed a man or that he didn't seem the least bit bothered by it.

Gregory sighed but did not approach her. "I see you found our gallery and my favorite portrait. My sister was a great beauty, wasn't she?"

Krystal nodded. She stepped forward cautiously, determined that if he chose to act normally, she could too. "They seem almost as though they could speak to us."

"It is how I prefer to remember her," said the king. "She lived for her children."

"The little girl," Krystal said. "Is she your niece?"

"Falina named her Alana."

"They were such beautiful babies."

"Falina gave birth to them far too soon," he said. "They must have been about a year old when the sickness spread through the palace. Both became ill but only Jareth survived."

Krystal did not speak. King Gregory became more agitated as he looked at the painting.

He looked at her when she moved. "Please," he said. "I wouldn't hurt you for the world."

She looked at him. How could he not understand abducting her had been hurtful?

"I can't forget what I saw," she said.

"Bennett drew on me," said Gregory. "What could I do but defend myself?"

Krystal couldn't stop herself. "Did you have to kill him?"

King Gregory took a step toward her. "Do not question me." His eyes flashed.

Krystal had never considered herself suicidal. She shut her mouth.

"I hope you never again find yourself in a position to see that," he said in a calmer voice. "But if you do, you will then understand I did what had to be done. We will speak no more on the topic."

That suited her. Her mind searched frantically for a reason to leave. "I'm quite tired."

The king immediately turned solicitous. "You should have said something. I shall take you to your room. You should go straight to bed."

Krystal let him take her arm and lead her, inwardly marveling that he had accepted such a weak excuse. She had hoped that he would let her walk to her room alone, but since she would have probably wandered the castle for half the evening trying to find it, she let him escort her.

"Try to stay close to your room tomorrow," he said as they neared her door.

"Why?"

"I would like to take you out to my sister's gardens," said Gregory. "They are exquisite. I'm sure you are tired of being indoors."

"Why can't I go out myself? Or Catrina could take me."

"I would hate for you to go out and get lost," the king said. "Besides, I want to be there the first time you see the gardens. I want to see your face."

"What is so special about them?"

"Falina received enchanted soil for a wedding gift. She cultivated it carefully, and after a decade, she had developed a garden that blooms all year round. It's where I feel closest to her."

They stood in front of her bedroom door. Krystal looked up at him. "You must miss her."

"It is never easy to say good-bye to someone you love," said Gregory. "But you know that. I'm sure you miss your father."

It unsettled her to hear him speak so casually of her past. He knew more about her than she realized. Krystal pulled away. "Good night, sire."

"Good night, my princess."

☙

As it happened, King Gregory did not have a free moment to take Krystal to the gardens the next day or even the day after. He apologized each night when they met for dinner, but on the third day, Krystal gave up waiting around for him. With Catrina in tow, she continued her exploration. She would find another way out of the castle.

She had to be careful, though. Catrina had no interest in the entrances and exits of the castle. The last thing she needed would be for Catrina to tell the king Krystal had been searching for a way out, particularly after Krystal had promised him her obedience. So, along with exploring the main floor, she also took Catrina to the second and third levels.

By the end of the week, Krystal felt confident she could make her way around the palace on her own. She hadn't returned to the upper level where she had met that unusual guard, but she knew how to get there. She had also discovered the dungeons, though that had been quite by accident.

Catrina had blatantly refused to allow Krystal to go down the stairs to explore the dungeons, claiming to be too afraid to go with her. That evening at dinner, King Gregory kissed her hand in greeting as usual but then said, "I hear you are interested in our dungeons."

She waved her hand in dismissal. "Curious is not the same as interested. I've never seen a dungeon and wanted to know what it looked like."

He laughed. "Most people do whatever they can to stay out of a prison. You are the first person I've heard of who seeks one."

Lady Fordyce had evidently heard them. "Curiosity can be dangerous."

Gregory nodded. "That is true. I would prefer you keep out of the dungeons, my dear."

Krystal looked across the table at Caprice, who sneered at her. Krystal hated these dinners. She felt isolated at the end of the table with the disdainful Lady Fordyce, the sleeping Duke Milford, and the overly attentive King Gregory.

So, Krystal sat quietly and picked at her food while she waited for the meal to be over. When King Gregory felt talkative, she had no choice but to pretend interest in what he said. Her options were few, but Krystal tried to get through dinner without screaming.

Gregory spoke to her again. "Tomorrow morning I will take you to the gardens. I made a point of keeping my morning clear of appointments."

Krystal's spirits rose. She did miss being outdoors. "I will make sure to be ready."

He smiled. "Excellent. I look forward to it."

Catrina waited for Krystal just outside her bedroom. "I wanted to ask you, my lady, if you would like a bath tonight."

"I suppose so. Why?"

The maid looked worried. "I was afraid of that. You see, the men are still busy sealing off a passage, and there's no one available to bring the tub. The maids and I simply can't lift it."

Krystal frowned. "The men are doing what?"

"Sealing the passage," said Catrina.

"What passage?"

"The secret one," Catrina explained. "Though I guess it can hardly be called a secret."

"They found a secret passage in the castle?"

Catrina laughed. "This old castle is full of them. Every time one is discovered, King Gregory orders it explored and then sealed off."

"Why would he do that?"

"Naturally, to prevent anyone sneaking into the castle," said the maid. "The passages to the outside are so the royals could escape in case of attack."

"Do all the passages lead out of the castle?"

Catrina bit her lip in thought. "I can't say for sure. I've never asked."

"Why would King Gregory want all the passages sealed? What if he had to escape?"

"I could never guess at the king's thoughts," said Catrina. "But it's no secret there are rebels in Fayterra who don't think he should rule here."

Krystal thought of Miraya and what she had said about Prince Jareth. Maybe these rebels were connected with him.

Catrina said something else, but Krystal had stopped listening. She thought it would be wonderful to find a secret passage herself. Escape would be so easy then. But she was certain the maid would find it odd if she walked around the castle feeling the walls.

"Princess?" Catrina had raised her voice to be heard. "Did you still want your bath?"

"What? Oh, no, don't worry about me if the men are busy," Krystal said. "Maybe tomorrow night they will be able to move the tub."

Catrina curtsied. "As you say, miss." She turned to leave.

"Where did you say the men had found the secret passage?"

The maid stopped to reply. "They found it outside, along an outer wall."

"Oh," Krystal said. "Good night, then. And thank you."

"Don't you want me to come back and help you dress for bed?"

"I can manage."

Talking to Catrina had improved Krystal's mood considerably. Tomorrow she would be able to go outside and see the gardens, but more importantly, she might be able to find a secret passage out of the castle. Though she hadn't had a chance to find a map yet, she wasn't about to pass up a chance to escape. If she came across a secret passage before looking at a map, she'd get away first and find directions later. Surely if she got far enough away from King Gregory, someone would be willing to help her.

∽

Krystal had already gotten out of bed when Lysabith brought

in the breakfast tray the next morning. Without help, she selected a simple blue gown, ate her meal, and got dressed. She opened her door the same moment King Gregory opened his. They met in the hall.

He smiled at her. "Good morning, my dear."

She frowned over the endearment but chose not to take issue. "Good morning."

"You look radiant in that gown." His eyes raked over her. "It suits you."

Krystal shivered from the heat in his gaze. "Shall we go?"

He offered his arm. "Of course."

She pretended she didn't see it and walked forward.

Gregory stepped in front of her. "You don't know where we're going. Let me guide you."

Though the king spoke as they walked, she paid little attention. Instead she searched the walls for a hint of a secret passage and tried not to think about what would happen if she failed.

The gardens took her breath away. From the high wall surrounding them to the walls of the palace, they were a rainbow of color. Tall trees, thick bushes, beds of roses and lilies—everything Krystal could think of, she found. Paths lined with small, round stones crisscrossed the entire expanse. It enchanted Krystal until she looked at Gregory and saw how he watched her.

"Why do you look at me that way?"

Instantly, King Gregory turned his gaze to something beyond her. When he looked at her again he had that hateful, condescending smile firmly in place.

"You are pleased by such simple things," he said. "I'm afraid I find that fascinating."

Krystal frowned at him. "You mentioned something you wanted to show me."

"Yes, follow me."

They walked deep into the gardens, far from prying eyes. There they found a small building Krystal thought looked like a miniature version of their stables back home.

"Do you keep horses here?"

"Not exactly," he said. "Come and see for yourself."

Nothing could prepare her for what she saw. The creature looked essentially like a horse, except shorter with a slightly longer snout. But it truly would have resembled a horse had it not been for the great, folded white wings protruding from its sides.

Gregory broke the silence. "She is yours. A gift. She has been reared here in my sister's gardens and is quite tame. Her name is White Lightning."

Krystal fought for words. "I don't know what to say."

He faced her. "Try, 'Thank you, Gregory.' I rather like the sound of that."

She looked at him. "Thank you, Gregory."

He stroked her cheek with his thumb. "That seemed simple enough, didn't it? You may ride her within the gardens, but I must ask that you do not attempt to fly her over the walls. The result would be perilous for both of you."

Krystal approached the Pegasus and slowly reached out her hand. White Lightning leaned forward, sniffed her fingers, and then blew on them. Krystal smiled. This spirited creature also had a good deal of gentleness. She had always been able to win an animal's trust.

"Are there many of her kind?"

Gregory shook his head. "I have only seen two, her and her mother. The mother had nearly died when they were found. The baby survived. She has been cared for well."

"This is so generous of you," said Krystal. "Why do this?"

"I am not a monster, you know," he said, suddenly abrupt. "I would shower you with gifts if you would but allow it."

"But I am your captive."

"I have a higher regard for you than that, my dear." King Gregory turned. "However, I must return to my duties inside the palace. Would you care to walk with me or remain here?"

"I will stay, I think, if it's all the same to you."

"I warn you again not to try to escape," he said. "I have men all over the grounds."

"I have already promised you that," she said.

He smiled at her. "You promised you wouldn't escape the castle. We aren't in the castle."

She thought for a moment he might be teasing her. She didn't know how to react. Before she could say anything he had walked away.

After he had gone, Krystal felt more comfortable getting acquainted with White Lightning. She found a brush and went over the gleaming white coat. She ran her hands all over the animal's strong body. She even dared to touch the wings.

"Would you like some exercise, my girl?" Krystal said to her.

White Lightning snorted. Krystal attached the halter and unlatched the stall gate. She had looked for a means of escape and King Gregory had practically handed her one. What could he do once they were gone? How could she not try?

"Would you like to get out of here?" she asked White Lightning.

White Lightning stood still while Krystal mounted her. She found it awkward in a gown, even more so because of the wings. First, she walked the Pegasus so she could accustom herself to the feel of the beast. Then Krystal gave a shout and White Lightning charged into the air.

Chapter 8

SHE FELT GLORIOUS FREEDOM at once. Girl and Pegasus rose higher and higher as the guards beneath them yelled, helpless to stop their flight. Just then, Krystal lurched as White Lightning seemed to hit something solid. Krystal could do nothing as they fell out of the sky and crashed to the ground.

King Gregory appeared at her side. "It is a magical shield," he said. "It keeps the Pegasus inside." He turned to his guards. "Make sure neither is injured and then bring the girl to me."

He returned to the palace. Three guards led the Pegasus away while two others took Krystal to their leader. She found herself alone in the king's study with him before she could recover. Gregory stood behind the vast desk, a glass of wine in his hand.

His eyes flashed brilliantly. "I did warn you, my dear."

"I just thought to exercise White Lightning's wings," Krystal said. She knew he knew she was lying. She folded her arms across her chest.

Gregory put down his glass and approached her. He took her chin in his hand and looked into her eyes. "I will accept your explanation for now. But understand, I am not a patient or particularly forgiving man. You are clever, but I will not be fooled again."

She opened her mouth to deny it, but he put a finger on her lips, effectively stopping her.

"Before you say another word, I will remind you of the dungeons and isolated towers of the castle," he said. "Your stay in Fayterra can be pleasant or desolate. The choice is yours."

Anger ignited and Krystal pushed away from him. "*Pleasant*? I don't find playing princess for you remotely pleasant! I'd rather be home than here with you."

He took a menacing step toward her. "Don't play me for a fool! Had I left you at your precious farm, you'd have run away at the first opportunity. You should fall at my feet in gratitude for saving you from your own impulsiveness! Six months on your own and you would have become a tavern whore just to survive."

Krystal slapped him soundly across the face. For a torturous heartbeat, they stared at one another. "I would never sell my body. I have useful skills. I would have been able to pay my own way."

King Gregory laughed. "Oh, yes, your precious skills. Your archery and sword play would get you killed in a real fight. A little girl shadowing her brothers does not become a warrior."

She reached up to slap him again, but he caught her wrist. Krystal looked in his eyes. The laughter had gone. He pulled her up against him.

"No," he said. "No more."

Krystal tried to pull away. She felt hot and cold all over; the air in the room became oppressive. For one insane moment, she thought he might kiss her. And then he did.

Frozen in shock and fear, she did nothing as he lowered his lips to hers. The kiss lasted the barest of seconds. Krystal pushed against him with all her strength and staggered back. She wiped her mouth with her sleeve. His eyes darkened with anger.

"How dare you!" she seethed. "I didn't say you could kiss me."

"I didn't ask," Gregory said in a hard voice. He stepped toward her.

Krystal backed up and put her hand out. "Stay away from me."

Gregory let out an angry roar and sliced the air with his hand. The wine glass behind him flew into the air and shattered on the wall across the room. Krystal watched the wine slide down the wall in shock. Gregory closed the gap between them and grabbed her arms.

He shook her roughly. "It is not your place to question me!"

The shattering glass alerted his guards, who were always just outside the door.

King Gregory pushed her toward them. "Get her out of my sight!"

Krystal gladly left with them. The whole afternoon threatened to crash in on her—the Pegasus, her short flight, the king's explosion, and then the kiss. Why had he kissed her?

A familiar face greeted her when she entered her room. The maid, Miraya, stood near the bed. The guard spoke to her.

"What are you doing here?"

"Cleaning," said Miraya.

"I'm sure you're finished," he said in a tone that suggested she had better be.

"Of course." Miraya curtsied to Krystal. "Good day to you, Princess."

"Wait," Krystal said. "I wish for her to stay."

The guard moved between them. "I'm sorry, Highness, but Miraya has many duties she must attend to. She cannot remain. If you need a maid, I will send for yours to attend you."

Krystal frowned at him. "Never mind."

The guard bowed to her and took Miraya's arm to lead her away. She looked back at Krystal as if she wanted to say something but then glanced at the guard and bit her lip. Krystal had no choice but to watch them leave.

The guard closed the door behind them. She heard the bolt slide home as she reached for the handle. She sighed and turned to the room. It looked exactly as it had when Krystal had left it earlier.

What had the maid been doing? Why did the guard seem so determined to keep them apart? Krystal walked around the room in the hopes of finding something unusual or out of place. It reminded her of checking her room back home to see if her brothers had been in there.

The thought of her brothers made Krystal homesick. She sat on the bed and tried not to think about how worried her mother must feel. What would Andrew and the others do to try and find her? If only she could get a message to them, to at least let them know she was alive.

Krystal doubted, in his present state of mind, King Gregory would grant any request she put to him. She knew she shouldn't have shouted, but he had an uncanny ability to anger her faster than her practiced calm could intervene. The control she had spent years cultivating, the control that had saved her countless times when dealing with Kayne, meant nothing now.

Logic told Krystal she'd have to try and get along with King Gregory. But her heart rebelled at this. She'd never been a good liar. Could she start now?

She heard the bolt of her door slide. Catrina entered with a tray. Krystal got off the bed.

"I have brought your lunch," the maid said. She put the tray down on the low table. "I've also been asked to help you select a gown for this evening's dinner."

"I'm surprised he is letting me attend," said Krystal.

"The king has requested you remain in your room until dinner. I will return in time to help you dress." Catrina crossed to the closet where she pulled out a gown of blue silk. "I think this will look best on you. It matches your eyes."

Krystal touched the skirt. "It's lovely."

The maid hung the gown on a hook. "This one was Queen Falina's particular favorite."

"She had exquisite taste," Krystal said.

Catrina nodded. "Of course you look lovely in her gowns too, Princess. It was so clever of King Gregory to think of using them again. I would think seeing someone else in his sister's gowns would be too painful, but I suppose it's different for a man." The maid moved to the door. "I'll be back in plenty of time to help you dress. Enjoy your lunch, Princess."

Krystal wanted to shout that she was certainly not a princess but instead gave the girl a strained, "Thank you," and let her leave.

Alone, she picked at her lunch and wondered what the evening would bring. How would King Gregory treat her? She dreaded seeing him again but knew it couldn't be helped.

Dusk came all too soon. Krystal sat while the maid combed and braided her hair and then wound it into an attractive knot on her head. She helped Krystal into the gown, and Krystal wondered if Queen Falina had preferred every gown to lace up the back.

Catrina stepped back as Krystal turned around. "If only you had a crown on your head. It would be perfect with this dress."

Krystal looked at herself in the mirror. "No wonder the queen loved this."

"Even without a crown you look like royalty. All eyes will be upon you tonight."

Krystal tried not to think of that or the knot that had started to build in her stomach as she walked to the dining hall. She paused just outside the doors, thinking it would be easier to go back to her room or simply run in the other direction. She suspected, though, if she failed to make an appearance, the king just might come looking for her. Feeling like a lamb in a den of wolves, Krystal took a deep breath and entered the room.

King Gregory did not make an appearance at dinner. Neither did Lady Fordyce. Though she half expected either one of them to walk through the door any time, Krystal managed to have a reasonably enjoyable meal. She still only had the sleeping Duke Milford for company, but it didn't bother her. She had started to find his soft snores soothing.

After dinner she walked back to her room alone with a candle to light the way. She paused at the king's study. There didn't appear to be anyone inside. Krystal looked down the hallway; it was deserted. She ducked inside.

Her single candle did not provide much light, but she'd been in the study often enough to know the king had a candelabra on his desk. Carefully she crossed the room.

A voice whispered from the darkness. "Falina?"

Krystal froze. "King Gregory?"

The candelabra flared to life, illuminating the king in his chair behind the desk. Krystal sighed; her bid to find a map had been foiled again. Did he never leave this room?

He seemed to have trouble focusing on her. "Krystal, it's you." He leaned forward jerkily and put his glass on the desk.

She understood. "You've been drinking."

The king rose on unsteady feet. "That's not entirely true. I've been getting drunk. What are you doing in here?"

Krystal thought fast. "I thought I heard a noise. It must have been you."

He started to move around the desk. "It must have been, though you must have the ears of a cat to have heard anything. It's a friendlier explanation than that you were snooping."

She backed away from him. "I should go."

"That dress," he said. "In the near darkness, I thought you might be a ghost come to visit me." King Gregory reached out and caught her hand. "I must say, though, that the reality is much more appealing." He caressed her with his eyes. "You look enchanting."

She tried to pull free. "Please let go."

Gregory put his other hand on her shoulder. "How do you manage to be so alluring?"

Krystal tried to get away from him, but his grip only tightened. She grimaced as his hand squeezed her wrist painfully. "You're hurting me. Stop it."

"No." His mouth settled on hers, sealing further protests.

They both turned at the sound of footsteps in the doorway. Lady Fordyce entered. Her eyes narrowed when she saw Krystal, but Krystal was too happy to see anyone to care.

"Am I interrupting?" Caprice sneered at Krystal.

She felt the king relax and pulled her hand free. "I was just returning to my room."

Krystal dared a look back at Gregory. He stared at her with a hot, almost hungry expression in his eyes. He looked as though he wanted to grab her. She darted away.

"Good night, Princess," said Caprice.

Krystal heard the laughter in her voice but didn't respond. Instead she rushed down the corridor to her room and went inside. Lysabith stood near the bed.

"Princess," she said when she saw Krystal. "Is something wrong?"

"I'm fine." She saw the bath waiting. "I'd forgotten the bath. Did I take too long?"

"The water is still warm," said the maid. She turned to leave.

"Wait," Krystal said. "Could you stay? I'd rather not be alone."

"Of course." Lysabith walked to her. "Did you need help?"

Krystal shook her head. "I would just like some company." She reached back and untied the dress, letting the laces loosen so she could wriggle out of it. Lysabith caught the gown before it hit the floor. Krystal stepped out of it and kicked off her shoes.

"Did you want to wash your hair?" asked the maid. "I could take it down for you."

"No, it's all right." Krystal slipped out of her undergarments and into the tub. She washed quickly and then accepted the towel Lysabith handed her. Krystal slipped into her nightgown and put on a robe before she unbraided her hair.

"Thank you for staying."

"I'm here to serve you, Princess," said Lysabith. "I will do what you ask, if I am able."

Krystal heard uneven footsteps in the hall and froze. She listened intently to them. They paused outside her door, and her eyes went to the door knob, but it didn't turn. The steps continued on. Krystal sighed with relief and looked up.

Lysabith turned away when their eyes met. "I'll have the tub removed."

Krystal watched her go and then pulled out her braid. She knew her behavior must have seemed odd, but she couldn't help it. For reasons she couldn't explain, a drunken King Gregory scared the life out of her.

The maid returned with two men before Krystal could work herself into a substantial panic. She watched while the men carried the tub away. Having done it for her mother, Krystal knew well the work involved when a person bathed, so she tried not to ask for a bath too often. She didn't get terribly dirty wandering around the castle.

Lysabith left last. She turned to curtsy to Krystal. "Have a good night, Princess."

Krystal wanted to ask her to wait, but she stopped. Instead, she nodded and let the maid leave. She knew she was letting her imagination run wild. She went to the bed and pulled down the covers. If she could go to sleep, she thought, she would feel better in the morning.

Krystal tossed and turned in the bed with no relief. Finally, she got up and poured herself a drink of water. She had left a candle burning by the bed, but blew it out when she walked back.

Sleep eventually claimed her and she dreamed. Krystal stood at the end of a dark corridor. At the other end she could see a light.

She walked toward the light and a figure of a man appeared, but she couldn't identify him. She felt a burning urgency to get to him and started to run, but she couldn't reach him. An evil, hideous laughter filled her ears.

Krystal woke with a start and sat up in bed. Darkness surrounded her, but she had the eerie feeling she wasn't alone. She searched the room but could see no one.

Her door stood slightly ajar. Krystal knew Lysabith had closed it. Had there indeed been someone in her room? She cursed herself for blowing out the candle; she had no way to relight it.

Krystal fumbled her way across the room to shut the door and then walked back again to the bed. She couldn't trust her eyes, so she lay still and listened for any sound in the room that might identify a presence. She only heard her own breathing.

At last she slept again, and when she woke, the morning sun shone through the window. She looked at the still closed door. Then she got out of bed and put on her robe to wait for breakfast.

Krystal sat down in front of her mirror and grimaced. She looked like she hadn't slept well. Her appearance didn't offend her vanity, but she didn't want any additional attention.

Her door opened and she turned but it was not a maid with her breakfast tray. Miraya shut the door quickly behind her. "I haven't much time. I can't be caught with you."

Krystal stood up. "Why not?"

Miraya smiled sadly. "King Gregory believes I talk too much."

"About what?"

The maid crossed the room. "Lysabith told me you seemed frightened last night when you returned to your room. Are you all right? What has happened?"

Krystal thought immediately of her encounter with the king. "Why do you ask?"

"Because you look half dead," Miraya said. "Something is troubling you."

She laughed shortly. "You mean something more than being taken from my home?"

Miraya nodded. "Yes." She looked closely at Krystal. "Something has happened."

"Are you magic too?"

The maid shook her head. "I can see it in your eyes. You are afraid, more now than the first time I saw you. Has the king done or said something?"

"Why should I trust you? Why should I trust anyone here? For all I know, you will repeat anything I say to King Gregory."

"If he finds out I'm talking to you, someone I love could die. I don't have time to play games with you. If you want help, I might be able to give it, but only if you trust me."

"Who will die?"

"That isn't your concern."

"I see. You want me to trust you, but you won't trust me."

Miraya frowned. She bit her lip. "My daughter," she said. "King Gregory has threatened her life if I disobey him. He knows I will always be loyal to Prince Jareth, but he refuses to let me leave the castle with her. He would let me go alone, but I won't leave Emelyn here."

Krystal sat down. "How old is she?"

"She will be four this winter."

"I'm sorry," Krystal said.

"You're right to be suspicious. There are many here who would do exactly as you think. They'd run to King Gregory with any tidbit of information, either out of loyalty or fear."

"Why aren't you afraid?"

"I'm terrified," the maid said. "Every night, when I'm able to see my daughter, I dread the time I have to leave her. But I can't sit by when I know you are in danger." She put up her hand when Krystal opened her mouth to speak. "But I digress. What happened to you last night?"

Krystal looked at the floor. "He kissed me."

She did not look up when she heard Miraya gasp. "The king?"

She nodded. "He'd been drinking." She explained what had happened.

Miraya sighed. "This is bad."

Krystal looked up. "What do you mean?"

"I can't explain everything now," she said. "We have to get you away from the king."

"I've been trying," said Krystal. "I've looked for other ways out of the castle, and then Catrina said something about secret passages, so I thought I might find one and use it to get out."

"That might work, if we can find one," said the maid. She moved toward the door. "I'll try to get back here soon. But I have to go before Catrina comes. She won't keep my secrets."

"Wait," said Krystal. "Why is it so important I get away from here? What do you know?"

"I know King Gregory well. I've seen his many sides." Miraya sighed again. "He wouldn't have gone through such trouble to bring you here just to rub it in Prince Jareth's face. I don't think he ever intends to let you go home."

"Because he kissed me last night?"

"If you're lucky, he wants to marry you," said Miraya. "He may just plan to keep you."

"Keep me?" The maid shot her a hard look and Krystal understood.

"I haven't heard him say it, but it wouldn't surprise me," said Miraya. "Before you came, he stared at the crystal sphere for hours at a time."

Krystal shivered as she thought of the way the king looked at her. Revulsion shot through her. She had no desire to be his queen, or his anything for that matter.

Miraya crossed the room and took Krystal's hands. "Never forget he is evil. He may show you kindness or tenderness, but he has a dark heart and is capable of horrible things."

Krystal nodded. "I saw him kill Bennett. I remember how cold he was afterward."

The maid nodded. "I have to go. I'll be back as soon as I can."

Krystal told herself that neither the king or his wishes mattered. None of it mattered. She would be long gone before the king could put any plan into action. She would escape; she had to escape. Now more than ever.

Chapter 9

FOR THE NEXT FEW DAYS, Krystal only saw the king at dinner. His absence did nothing to ease her mind, however, since he would only sit at the table and stare at her. She found it impossible to eat under those conditions, so she would sit and try to ignore him. It tortured her.

During the day, she roamed the castle. She wanted to go out into the gardens again but didn't want to approach King Gregory or enter the study. Instead she found ways to get around the castle without Catrina following her. The first day she told the maid she would stay in her room and then waited until Catrina left before sneaking out. The second day Catrina stayed in the room with her, so Krystal sent her on an errand just before lunch and left while she was gone.

The third day the maid proved craftier. She brought Lysabith along. Krystal understood her plan immediately and after breakfast selected a book off the shelf to read. She smiled brightly at Catrina as she sat in a chair and opened the book.

Waiting them out didn't work. By lunch Krystal had become impatient. Catrina had directed a thorough cleaning of the room, but neither maid had left all morning. When it became clear Catrina would send Lysabith to fetch the lunch tray Krystal closed the book.

"Lysabith," she said in an even tone. "Do you remember that wonderful hairstyle you did for me the other day?"

"Of course, Princess."

"Could you do it again?"

"Certainly," said the maid.

Krystal got up and walked to her mirror to sit down. "Thank you. I'm so tired of my hair hanging down my back all day."

Catrina stepped forward. "Wouldn't it make more sense, Princess, to have Lysabith fix your hair after lunch? You would be more prepared for dinner."

Krystal looked at her. "But I want it done now."

"Lysabith was about to go to the kitchens," said Catrina.

Krystal waved her hand. "You can do that."

Catrina had no choice but to obey, though she made it clear she didn't like it. After she had stomped from the room Krystal halted Lysabith's hand. She stood up.

"Didn't you want me to do your hair?" Lysabith asked.

"Forget that," said Krystal. "I just wanted her out of the room."

Lysabith put down the brush. "She won't be happy about this."

"I don't care," Krystal said. "Let's go."

"Where?"

"I have a sudden urge to explore the castle, maybe the gardens."

Lysabith looked worried. "Your lunch?"

"I'm not hungry," said Krystal. "Come on. Catrina can't object if you're with me."

Krystal opened the door slowly, half expecting Catrina to be waiting for her in the hall. When she saw no one, she motioned for the maid to follow her and left the room. They walked hurriedly toward the main doors. Krystal saw the guards standing there, and her hope plummeted.

The large guard she had met before stood there with a shorter blond man. They both bowed when she approached.

"Lysabith and I are going to the gardens," Krystal said.

"The king has not said anything about this," said the large guard.

"The king may have been too busy to tell you," she said. "He can't be expected to report to you every time I leave my room."

"He has ordered that you not leave the castle unguarded," said the shorter guard.

Krystal looked offended. "I have Lysabith."

Voltimande smiled at her. "She is hardly a proper guard for a princess."

"Then you come with me."

"But I have to stay here."

"Someone else can do that," Krystal said. "The king can hardly object if you guard me."

The two guards exchanged a look she did not understand. Voltimande bowed to her again. "Very well, Princess. I shall accompany you."

He opened one of the large outer doors and moved aside. Krystal felt the exhilaration of success as she led the way to the queen's gardens. She didn't know if she could trust her companions, but she had gotten outside without Gregory's knowledge.

She went first to see White Lightning. Lysabith stayed close to her but Voltimande fell back, putting a good distance between them. Krystal noticed he never let her out of his sight, though. She found it oddly comforting.

The Pegasus looked just as she had when Krystal first saw her. Krystal let White Lightning out so she could groom her. Lysabith offered to help, but the maid was too intimidated by the creature's wings to get close. Instead she hung back and held the grooming tools.

White Lightning shook her wings. Krystal thought of their ill fated flight. She looked up at the sky but could see no trace of the magical barrier that had sent them crashing to the ground. How would King Gregory know if it was there or not?

As though she'd conjured him with her thoughts, the king walked from behind a tree near the garden path and approached her. "Krystal, there you are."

She looked up at him. He looked angrier the closer he got to her. "Hello, King Gregory."

He stopped right in front of her. "I thought you had agreed to stay inside the castle."

"I didn't want to bother you," she said. "I came to check on White Lightning."

"A groom cares for her," he said. "I would have known if anything was wrong."

She gestured to Lysabith and Voltimande. "As you can see, I was well protected."

King Gregory turned to them. "I will deal with you two later. Go attend to your duties."

Krystal touched his arm. "They aren't in any trouble, are they?"

He looked at her. "Lysabith does her duty well, and Voltimande is one of my most worthy guards, but both of them know I didn't want you out here without me."

"But I insisted," she said. "They can't get into trouble for following orders."

"A king's orders take precedence over those of a princess," he said. "My people know that."

"You are intractable. If Voltimande is so worthy, why won't you trust him?"

He started growling. "This is not about trust. It's about obeying my orders." He took her by the elbow. "We're going inside now."

"Stop that," she scolded, pulling out of his grasp. "I need to put White Lightning away first."

Gregory glowered at her, but he did not stop her as she led White Lightning back to the stables. She took her time—knowing he stood out there did not inspire her to hurry. When she couldn't put it off any longer, Krystal took a deep breath and went to face him.

"If you've finished defying me, I'd like to take you inside now," he said.

"Why are you so angry? I couldn't leave her out here alone."

The king took Krystal's hand and started pulling her away. "I recall telling you I had a groom for that. I would have sent him out here."

"Why is it so important that I remain inside? And please stop dragging me. I *can* walk."

Gregory slowed his pace but did not release her. "I dislike explaining myself. Just now I am doing my best to control my temper, so I would suggest you not speak to me."

Krystal snapped her jaw shut. She did not want to anger him further. He reminded her of her brother Kayne, though she had learned how far she could push her brother and knew he would never actually hurt her. King Gregory didn't seem to have that kind of control.

He returned her to her room, where Catrina was waiting. Krystal saw the maid smile.

King Gregory faced her. "Catrina brought your lunch tray, and you had gone. She was looking for you when I found her. I needed to have a word with you, and she had no idea where you'd gone. I had nearly turned the castle upside down before I thought to look in the gardens."

Krystal gripped her hands together, thinking furiously. She ducked her head. "I'm sorry I worried you. Really, I only wanted to make sure White Lightning was all right, and then I meant to come back. I took Lysabith and Voltimande with me because I thought you'd approve." She'd said enough, so she bit her tongue to avoid ruining things.

Gregory took her chin and lifted her face. Krystal almost sighed with relief when she saw his expression had softened. "That wasn't so hard, was it? You apologize well."

"I don't want you thinking I was up to something," she said. "Now, what was it you wanted to speak to me about?"

"I have a little problem you may be able to help me with."

Krystal's mind raced wildly. "What could that be?"

"My men patrol the outskirts of the city," he said, "and on three different occasions, my patrols have been attacked by a large, black dog."

"Damen's here? He's in the city?"

"Not in the city, as yet," Gregory said. "Though I don't see that, if he so desired, I could keep him out. Five of my guardsmen have died already trying to keep him at bay."

Krystal could not bear the idea of the king retaliating against the dog. "Do you need me to go to him? I could perhaps talk him into leaving or going back into the forests."

Gregory brushed her hair over her shoulder. "You are not leaving the castle. What I need from you is an idea of what I can do with him. I am close to ordering my men to kill him."

"You can't do that!" Krystal came near to panic. "Damen is only here because I am. If you hadn't kidnapped me, he wouldn't be your problem."

Gregory gave her a stern, brooding look. His eyes darted from her to Catrina, who had backed away when Krystal raised her voice. He snapped a curt dismissal to the maid and waited until she had gone. Then he turned his anger on Krystal.

He took her upper arm in a painful grip. "I may occasionally tolerate your spirit when we are alone, but you may never question my motives in front of witnesses!"

Krystal tried to pry his fingers away. "Gregory, let me go! You're hurting me."

He released her with such force she stumbled a few steps backward. Immediately he closed the gap. "Krystal, my darling, I am sorry." He raised a hand as if to touch her shoulder, but she flinched, and he let his hand drop. "You can't know how difficult it is for me to keep my passions under control when I am around you. I wish I knew why your mere presence unsettles me so." Gregory caught her up in his arms. "Forgive me. I would never hurt you for the world."

She thought it best to say nothing.

His trembling hand stroked her hair. "Are you all right, then?"

She nodded. "What will you do about Damen?"

"I thought of the dungeons," he said. "Perhaps if he could be captured, I could have him put in the dungeons so he could not cause more trouble for my troops."

"He has never been caged," Krystal said. "He will resist."

"I either cage him or kill him. Which would you prefer?" The king waved his hand. "I believe I have access to some potions that may pacify him long enough for us to imprison him. It's a delicate balance, but it should be possible."

Krystal put a hand on his chest. "Please, try not to hurt him."

Gregory trapped her hand with his. "I will do what I can. But I will not risk human lives for your pet. I need my men more than I need a menacing monster roaming my kingdom."

"Please try." She tried to remove her hand from his grasp but could not. He continued to gaze at her, his face unreadable. "Gregory—Sire, I mean—please?"

He didn't immediately respond. Gregory lifted a finger to trace the outline of her lips. "I had no idea how beautiful a simple request could be coming from your lips." Cupping her face in his hand, he continued. "I find myself completely unable to resist you."

Before she could think of pulling away, Gregory took Krystal's shoulders in his hands and brushed her lips with a kiss. For once he demanded nothing; his touch remained gentle, and Krystal found it difficult to fight him.

"Gregory." This time her voice had an edge of panic to it. "Please."

Though his hands released her, his burning gaze held her riveted. "I wish I knew why it is so easy to completely lose my reason around you! I am not a fool, Krystal. But for some reason, I have this weakness for you. I know I should fight it, but when I am near you I find protest impossible!" He turned so she faced his back. "I don't know anymore if I even want to resist. My choice seems clear: either fight my attraction to you or make you feel about me as I do about you."

Krystal could not stand to hear any more. She backed away. "You can't mean that."

He took a step toward her. "You don't know anything, Krystal, but I promise you that you will. I will make you understand everything."

With that cryptic vow, he left her alone.

Krystal wished she could lock him out. She'd never asked for the king's attention. Life had been so much simpler when she'd only had to worry about Curtis Belvey. When Catrina entered her room to help her dress for dinner, Krystal balked.

"Tell him I'm sick," she said to the maid. "I don't care what you tell him. I'm not going."

Catrina curtsied. "As you say, Princess."

After she'd gone, Krystal put on her nightgown and got in bed. She suspected King Gregory would want to check on her, and he did. Two maids followed him, Catrina and a stranger. The stranger had beautiful golden hair braided down to her hips and round green eyes.

"This is Julienne," he said to Krystal. "She will be attending to your needs."

"Where is Lysabith?"

"I sent her back to her regular duties," said the king. "Julienne is more reliable." Gregory sat on the edge of her bed. "How are you?"

"It's nothing," she said. "I just need some rest, and I'll be fine."

"You're never sick," he said. "Should I send for the healer?"

How she hated that crystal sphere. "I'm sure I'll be fine tomorrow."

"Are you hungry? I could send Julienne for a tray."

"I'm fine."

He studied her face. She could tell he doubted her. Gregory put the back of his hand on her forehead, and she tried not to flinch. After a moment he withdrew his hand.

"You don't feel feverish," he said. "That's a good sign."

"I'd really like to rest." Her dismissal must have lacked bite because he didn't move.

"I'll have Julienne remain with you," he said. "She can get you anything you need."

"Thank you." Krystal rolled away from him and closed her eyes, hoping he'd get the point. She felt his weight leave the bed as he stood up.

"Good night, Krystal. Feel better."

She did not move until she was sure he'd gone. Then she rolled over. Catrina had gone as well, leaving Julienne. Krystal gave her a small smile and sat up.

"Do you need anything, Princess?"

She shook her head. "No, thank you. You can relax. I won't require anything."

"I'll be here if you need me." Julienne walked over to a chair and sat down.

Krystal soon felt awkward. As the evening wore on, a small seed of hunger began to gnaw at her belly. When she could stand it no longer, she sent Julienne for an apple. While she waited, she pulled back the covers and sat on the edge of the bed. When the door opened, Krystal thought Julienne had returned, but the king entered the room instead.

Gregory looked around with a frown. "Alone again?"

"I sent her for an apple."

"I see," he said and shut the door.

Chapter 10

KRYSTAL SIGHED. She'd tried to avoid King Gregory by skip-ping dinner but instead of seeing him less that evening, it seemed she would see him more.

"You appear to be feeling better," he said, approaching the bed.

"Thank you," said Krystal. "Did you just come to check on me?"

"I had to be sure you'd improved," he said. "I wouldn't have slept worrying about you."

"I seem to have caused you nothing but worry today." She pulled the covers back over her legs when she noticed he'd been staring.

Gregory frowned. "You didn't seem ill this afternoon."

Krystal's eyes darted up to his face, but he showed no hint that he wanted to discuss the kiss they'd shared. "It came on suddenly. I first had a headache and then grew tired."

"But you're better now?"

"Yes," she said.

"I'm glad." Gregory sat on the bed next to her and took her hand. "I've been thinking about what you said."

"About what?"

"About the gardens," he said. "I don't want you to worry about White Lightning, so I've decided to grant you time with her every morn-ing. You can go out after breakfast as long as you return to the castle for lunch. A maid and a guard will accompany you when I cannot."

Her heart sank a little. "Do you expect to have time to go with me often?"

The king squeezed her hand with his. "We should spend more time together."

It took all she had not to rip her hand away. Instead she made a show of adjusting the covers, an act that required both hands, so she could pull out of his grasp.

"And the afternoons?"

"You can still wander the castle if you wish," said Gregory. "This late in the summer it gets quite hot outside, so you should stay indoors."

"Of course it would be hot in those gowns you have me wear," she said. "If I had my trousers I'd be more comfortable."

"That is out of the question," he said. "Though I won't debate how a man can appreciate how you look in them, I can't approve of a lady wearing men's attire."

"What about Lady Caprice?"

"That is different," said the king. "Caprice has chosen a warrior's life. You have not."

"If you'll remember, I wasn't given the choice," Krystal said. "*You* chose for me."

"You'll see the rightness of it. I'm only looking out for your best interests, my dear."

Krystal bristled at his term of endearment. She took a deep breath to control her frustration. She didn't want to argue with him, but he made it so difficult.

"Why is it a lady has so few freedoms? I think I preferred being a farmer's daughter. At least then I could decide things for myself."

"I seem to remember it differently," he said. "Did you decide to betroth yourself to that village oaf? Didn't you have to sneak out of the house in those trousers because your brothers disapproved?"

Krystal felt her control slip. "Did you have that sphere watching me all day long? How much did you see? Did you watch me dress? Bathe? Sleep?"

King Gregory's hot gaze seared her. "Regrettably not. I think my sister had some sort of restricting spell put on it before she gave it to her teenage son."

She shivered at his tone. He'd mentioned Prince Jareth again. "People have no business spying on other people. It doesn't matter if you use magic or peer through a bedroom window—it's all the same."

"You'd use the power if you had it. The lure is irresistible."

"That's ridiculous," said Krystal. "I certainly wouldn't spy on others."

Gregory opened his mouth to respond, but at that moment, Julienne returned with Krystal's apple. When she saw the king sitting on the bed, she stopped and looked at Krystal.

"The king came to check on me," she told the maid. "I'm sure he was about to leave."

She felt his hot breath on her ear. "That is suspiciously close to an order." He stood up.

She shivered but forced herself to look at him. "Good night, sire."

He smiled at her. "Sleep well, my dear. I will see you in the morning."

Julienne sidestepped the doorway so the king could pass. After he'd gone, she approached Krystal and gave her the apple.

"Thank you," Krystal said. She looked at the fruit, having completely lost her appetite while sparring with the king. She put the apple on the table next to the bed and pulled up the covers. Something else Gregory said had made her think.

"Julienne," she said. "What do you know of Prince Jareth?"

"I know King Gregory doesn't care to hear the prince's name, and any of us caught uttering it face his wrath," said the maid.

"How convenient for Gregory," Krystal muttered. "Where is the prince?"

Julienne glanced at the closed door. She moved closer to the bed. "No one knows. He used to be kept in this room until about a year ago. King Gregory moved him one night."

"How does anyone know he's still alive then?"

"Servants hear things," said the maid. "We know there are men guarding him, and we know food is sent to him. I heard some of the rebels tried to follow the food cart once."

Krystal leaned closer. "I heard Prince Jareth is the rightful ruler of Fayterra. Is that true?"

Julienne nodded. "His father, King Emrik, was King of Fayterra and his father before him," she said. "There has been a Lochnikar on the throne of Fayterra for hundreds of years."

"Then I don't understand how Gregory claimed the throne," Krystal said. "Isn't his only tie through Jareth's mother?"

"At first he claimed stewardship—Prince Jareth was only twelve when he was orphaned," said Julienne. "But he stayed. Most of the nobility accepted him."

Catrina entered the room then and ended the conversation. Krystal wouldn't continue talking about Jareth in front of Gregory's spy. She didn't want to get another maid in trouble.

"I've come to check if you need anything," said Catrina.

"I'm fine," Krystal said. "Julienne has taken good care of me."

"Did you want her to stay through the night?" Catrina asked with a doting smile. "I'm sure she wouldn't mind making up a bed on the floor, just in case you need her."

Krystal smiled back. "That won't be necessary. I was just about to go to sleep."

"Good night, Princess," they said in unison. Krystal watched them turn to leave.

"Julienne, I wanted to thank you," she said. "You were most helpful to me."

Julienne smiled at her and nodded. Catrina shot them both a suspicious look. Krystal nodded to them, and they left the room.

Perhaps her own captivity slanted her viewpoint, but she hated the idea that Prince Jareth was his uncle's prisoner. If she had the power, she would set him free. The prince had faced years under his uncle's control.

But she couldn't rescue anyone while still a prisoner herself. Gregory's new attentions fueled her desire to escape. Krystal had even entertained the idea of storming out the kitchen door, though she had no idea where it led. For all she knew, she'd end up trapped in a dead end.

She fell asleep and dreamed again. This time she recognized Prince Jareth as he stood at the end of the hallway. He pled for her to hurry. "I'm coming!" she yelled, but she never reached him. Then evil laughter filled her ears, mocking her efforts.

Krystal shot up in bed. She'd left the candle lit this time, but it had either burned out or been blown out. She heard the sound of a click over her pounding heart and turned toward the door.

She saw a light from the hallway through the crack at the bottom of the door and a shadow move away. Someone had been in her room. He'd been coming into her room at night to what, watch her sleep? To steal? Why would he blow out the candle?

The shadow faded before she gathered enough courage to throw open her door and expose the person. Krystal lay back down, this time facing her door. She watched it as long as possible, determined that if the spy came back, she'd be waiting for him.

ᴄᴏ

Gregory appeared at Krystal's door just after breakfast for the next several mornings. They spent hours in the gardens. At first this tormented Krystal; she worried that if left alone with her, he would continue his advances to her, but he did not. He remained cordial and, apart from the occasional hot look in his eyes, gave no indication of reverting to his previous behavior.

Her frustrating dreams returned often. At times she dreaded going to bed. More than once, she awoke with the feeling that someone had been in her room. One night she put a low stool in front of the door, and the next morning it had been tipped over.

She spent the afternoons exploring the castle with either Julienne or Catrina. Krystal gave up on trying to find a secret passage out of the castle. She couldn't disguise her behavior from either of the maids, and the few times she managed to get out without them, someone always spotted her. Caprice Fordyce and even King Gregory himself once caught her attempting again to get through the kitchens to explore the area outside the door.

He had taken her back to her room and issued a warning. "I am beginning to regret giving you so much freedom. Regardless of whose care I leave you in, you manage to end up wandering around by yourself. If I have to, I will confine you to your room."

Krystal knew she had to reevaluate her tactics. She'd made the king suspicious of her, and now she had eyes watching her everywhere she went. Besides, she still needed to get into his study to find a map. She'd have to plan more carefully if she expected to escape.

Then King Gregory further complicated things. He'd taken to visiting her more and more after dinner, either walking her to her room and lingering or showing up without warning. She feared he would knock on her door one night while she bathed and had considered asking the maids to start delaying her baths until later.

One night, he carried a small wooden box with him. "I've brought you a gift."

This put Krystal on her guard. "Why?"

He held out the box to her. "I thought women loved to receive presents."

"I'm sure most do," she said. "But you have to admit, ours is not a normal circumstance."

"You've been my guest nearly three weeks now," said the king. "I thought we should mark the occasion. But there is another reason. Open the box."

Still suspicious, Krystal accepted the box and lifted the lid. Inside, on a velvet pad, was an exquisite jeweled necklace. As she lifted it out of the box, the necklace caught the candlelight and sparkled dazzlingly. Krystal looked up at the king.

"I want you to accept it as an engagement gift," Gregory said.

Krystal felt faint. "Whose engagement?"

"Yours and mine," he said, moving closer to her. He took the necklace from her hands and clasped it around her neck. "It suits you, just as I knew it would. Would you like to see?"

Krystal stepped away from him. "You cannot mean it."

Gregory frowned at her. "I intend to marry you."

"You would want an unwilling bride?"

He turned, offering her his profile. "I want *you*."

"I can't believe you would rather have a bride who will resist you than one of the eligible noblewomen who would love to be queen," said Krystal. "These are women of wealth, women of breeding—you would refuse them all for a farmer's daughter? It makes no sense!"

"I can't explain it." He turned, but she had moved away. He followed her. "My heart makes no distinction between a duchess and a peasant. As king, I *should* prefer a woman of wealth and breeding. Giving you a title didn't change your simple upbringing."

Gregory put his hands on her shoulders and forced her to face him. "I should not be swayed by your soft lips, your stunning blue eyes, or your silken hair. But I am blinded, entranced, by you. Giving you a title and land makes you an acceptable bride. No one can question a king marrying a princess. Your humble beginnings will endear you to the peasants."

He lifted a lock of her hair and let it slide between his fingers. "I like to think I'm not such a cold man. I told myself it would benefit me to take you as my wife. Even those loyal to Jareth would be won over by you. Sadly, that reasoning didn't last a full day."

Krystal stood hypnotized by his voice. She stared into his eyes. She couldn't move.

Gregory caressed her cheek. "At times I've felt I would die if I could not have you." He sighed. "Understand it? I cannot. Explain it? Impossible. Accept it? I can do nothing else."

Krystal closed her eyes as his lips brushed hers. She fought the lump in her throat. Every part of her screamed to run but his grip held her fast. He ended the kiss.

"You cannot force me to marry you," she said.

He did not pull away. Their heads touched. "I would rather not have to resort to force."

"Then please understand, I will never come to you willingly," she said.

"Never is a long time, my dear."

"I know my own mind!" She tried to pull away. "I won't marry you!"

His eyes bore into her. "I can give you all the love you could desire, if you but allow it. I could give you the world. So I cannot understand why you continue to resist me."

She tried to give him a command, but it came out as more of a plea. "Let me go!"

"Never!" he vowed before he crushed her into another kiss.

Krystal pushed against Gregory's chest with all her strength, though it did no good. She fumbled for the dagger he wore on his belt and brought the blade up between them.

He released her, a startled look on his face. "What are you doing?"

"I said no, Gregory," she said. "I refuse to be your wife."

He stepped toward her with an indulgent smile. "Put that down. You'll hurt yourself."

82

"You're the only one in danger of being hurt. Don't come any closer."

"This is absurd. Give me back the dagger, and we will discuss this like civilized people."

"No," she said. "When we simply talk, you don't listen. You need to hear me."

"Don't be ridiculous. I hear you."

She stepped back again. "No, you don't. You seem convinced time will change my mind. I refuse to accept your proposal. I will not be your queen."

Gregory moved in, his hand out to grab the dagger. "Stop this. You're acting like a child."

Krystal lashed out and gave him a warning cut. "Stay back."

Gregory pulled back his hand and watched as blood pooled on his palm. "You cut me!"

"I did warn you."

"You will regret that."

As he advanced, Krystal stepped back and waved the dagger again. He knocked the blade out of her hand and grabbed her wrist. Krystal fought to pull herself free, but he held her too tightly. He backed her against the wall and put a hand on her throat.

"I've killed men for less! What did you think to gain by pulling a dagger on me?"

He released her and retrieved his dagger. He pulled a cloth from his tunic and wrapped it around his hand. Krystal watched him without moving, desperately trying to control her anger.

"You assume too much," she said. "You touch me whenever you please. You announce I will be your queen without taking my feelings into consideration. You even kiss me without my consent! I want you to know that's unacceptable."

Gregory glared at her. "Unacceptable? Really? I didn't get much of a fight out of you the last time we kissed. You can't give a man such encouragement and then threaten him later." He stalked to where she stood. "As for your being my queen, I should think you'd be pleased someone is looking after you. I should think you'd want better than to bear some village idiot's brats and scrub his floors until you drop dead of exhaustion."

"That isn't your choice to make," said Krystal. "I should be allowed to choose my future. You didn't even ask me if I wanted to be queen; you made it a command."

He laughed shortly. "Did I offend you somehow by not asking you to be my wife?"

"No!" Krystal took a step toward him. "You could have come at me with cartfuls of roses and a trunk of jewels, and I'd still refuse. I don't want you."

"It's absurd to me you believe that you should have a choice," he said. "Where did you get the idea you could refuse the king of the land? You couldn't even refuse your brother the farmer!"

She felt like screaming. "What are you going to do when you have me at the altar, and I refuse to say yes? You can't make me say it, Gregory."

He grabbed her arm with his uninjured hand and brought her close to his face. "You have time to change your mind. You *will* marry me, or it will be the worse for you."

"What more can you do to me? You've done your best to strip away every freedom I ever had. How much worse can it get?"

Gregory pushed her away from him. "Let's just see how much worse it can get." He stepped back and gestured to the room at large. "I hope you enjoy looking at these four walls because you are no longer allowed to leave this room without me. And you can say good-bye to meals in the dining hall because you will take all your meals in here alone! I warned you before, Krystal. If you want to feel like a captive, I can certainly oblige you."

"So you'll lock me up just like you did Prince Jareth? Is that your answer for everything? If someone gives you trouble you either kill them or lock them away?"

"I will come to you every night after dinner," Gregory said. "I will ask for your apology then, and I will keep asking until you give it."

"You're in for a long wait," she said. "I have no reason to apologize to you."

He moved to the door. "We'll see about that."

Chapter II

KRYSTAL WENT TO THE DOOR after Gregory closed it and listened. Sure enough, she heard the bolt slide into place. Krystal turned around to look at her new prison. Strangely, it didn't look any different than when it had been her bedroom.

What had come over her? She'd been so careful not to anger King Gregory, to not to give him any reason to take away her freedoms, and then, in one moment, all that evaporated. Her hands still shook from fury. How could he assume she would willingly marry him?

The bolt slid, and Julienne entered. "There is a guard at your door. What happened?"

"The king has decided to make me a true prisoner after all," said Krystal.

The maid shook her head. "You must have angered him fiercely."

"I imagine so." Krystal looked at her. "Do you know who's outside? Is it Voltimande?"

"No, it is Nicholas. I don't think you've met him."

Krystal sighed. "Why did you come?"

"I told him I would help you get ready for bed. But really I wanted to check on you. The castle is buzzing. King Gregory is in a rage."

"I'm not surprised."

The maid moved behind Krystal to unhook her dress. "I hope I'm not being too nosy, Princess, but did you truly cut him?"

Krystal turned to look at her. "More fuel for the gossip?"

Julienne blushed. "I was only curious."

Krystal slipped out of the dress and slips and pulled on her nightgown. "I don't want people talking about me. I'd rather just forget it."

"Yes, my lady." Julienne gathered up the dress and moved to the door.

A few nights passed before the king visited one night after her bath. Catrina finished brushing out Krystal's hair and made a quick exit, leaving them alone. Krystal turned her back on Gregory when he arrived and did her best to pretend he wasn't there.

"Do I still get the silent treatment?" After she didn't reply he said, "Come now, Krystal. You know you're being childish."

She gave no indication she either heard or intended to respond.

Gregory sighed. "I suppose had I been a few minutes earlier, this conversation would be different," he said. "Would you still ignore me had I walked in on your bath?"

She couldn't help herself—she turned and glared at him.

"Ah, a reaction." He crossed the room to stand near her. "Do I get anything more?"

Krystal turned back to the wall, though she kept him in her peripheral vision.

"What a fun story to tell our grandchildren," he said in a tone that suggested the opposite. "Since you insist on being stubborn I will ask my question. Are you ready to apologize?"

She didn't move.

He sighed again. "I might as well be talking to the chair." Gregory turned and walked to the door. "I will wear you down, Krystal. You will give in to me."

After he had gone, she grabbed the nearest thing and threw it against the door. Her hairbrush hit the wood hard and clattered to the floor. She cried tears of frustration that night.

From that point on, King Gregory's visits varied in time. He'd come to her room later and later at night. She thought of his poor joke of showing up during her bath and started requesting her baths less often and later as well, determined to thwart him at whatever game he played.

Krystal did not spend the days sitting around waiting for Gregory to show up. She'd been watching, taking particular notice of the comings and goings of the maids. She noticed Julienne seemed to like Nicholas the guard; she often stopped to talk to him if she had a spare moment.

Krystal had thought about it and realized she couldn't sneak out of her room to look at the king's maps and then make it all the way to the kitchens to get out of the castle in the same night. She'd surely be discovered; besides, she knew Gregory would take his wrath out on the man who happened to be guarding her the night she escaped, and couldn't get the image of him torturing Nicholas out of her mind. She still hadn't seen Lysabith or Voltimande since that day in the gardens. So, she decided to focus on finding the maps to figure out where to go once she got away, and then she'd come up with a way of getting out of the castle without getting anyone killed.

The next night, Nicholas stood guard duty. Krystal made sure to stay awake until she thought the entire castle would be silent. Then she knocked on her door to get the guard's attention. She stepped back when she heard the bolt slide back.

"Did you require something, Princess?" he asked.

"I need Julienne." Krystal folded her hands and ducked her head. "It is a female matter."

Nicholas actually flushed. "Y-yes, my lady," he stammered. "I'll get her right away."

He shut the door and bolted it, and Krystal sat down to wait. She had to smile at his reaction to her supposed "female matter." Her brothers always reacted in much the same way.

Julienne arrived, and the guard let her in. She went immediately to Krystal's side. "Princess, what is it? Are you ill?"

"No," said Krystal. "What I really want is something to eat. I'm simply starved. Could you go get me an apple or something, please? I can't sleep."

The maid looked confused. "Of course, my lady. I'll be right back."

Krystal knew she'd have to wait for her to come back and then try to make her escape from the room. Julienne would hurry to the kitchens and back, but once she'd fulfilled Krystal's request she'd be more slow-paced and more likely to stop and chat with the guard.

Julienne returned with a fine red apple in a bowl. She poured Krystal a glass of water.

"Did you need anything else?"

"No, thank you. This will be perfect." She followed Julienne to the door. "I really appreciate you doing this for me. I know I must have pulled you out of bed."

"It's no trouble, my lady. I'm glad to serve you."

"Thank you just the same." Krystal positioned herself behind the door so Nicholas wouldn't see her. Julienne smiled at her one more time and left the room.

Krystal caught the door handle and guided it so that it didn't latch. Sure enough, Nicholas slid the bolt without looking at it; he was too busy looking at Julienne. Krystal put her eye near the crack in the door and watched them.

"Is everything all right?" he asked the maid.

"Yes," Julienne said. "Can I bring you something? You must be tired out here all night."

He smiled. "Things are better now."

Krystal rolled her eyes and had to stifle a sigh of impatience.

Julienne's eyes darted to the door and widened a fraction. Krystal froze; she'd given herself away. She started to open the door, prepared to be exposed, when Julienne took Nicholas' arm and turned him away.

Krystal didn't hesitate. She slipped out and backed down the hallway toward the darkness. She couldn't risk a candle, so she felt her way along the dark corridor until she came to the study doorway. She'd learned the castle layout well during her explorations.

No light had been left in the study, but she knew better than to assume it was empty. Krystal froze in the doorway and listened for breathing. She heard nothing, so she ventured a soft, "Hello?" Still nothing. She fetched a torch from a wall sconce and lit the candelabra.

She pulled the first desk drawer open with ease. It contained a bunch of scrolls and papers. She tried the next one but didn't find any maps. The third drawer didn't open as easily, but when she pulled hard it slid out to reveal stacks of what looked like personal letters.

All of them were written in the same delicate, loopy handwriting, and they all started the same way.

Dear Uncle Gregory. Krystal brought the letters closer to the light. Who wrote them? She scanned the first letter. It had been signed *Lovingly, Alana.* Krystal stared at the page.

She checked the others. All had been signed the same way. Krystal remembered Gregory telling her his niece had died as a baby. Why would he lie about that?

Krystal put the letters back in the drawer and closed it. She pulled the candelabra off the desk and used it to explore the room. Gregory didn't have room in his desk for maps. She walked to the table in the far corner of the room.

She shifted the papers across the top of the table and saw the corner of a map sticking out. Relief swept over her. Krystal put the candelabra on the corner of the table and dug out the map.

She found the castle easily enough. The map detailed Fayterra well, but didn't give her any indication of how to get home. A corner of the map was turned up, revealing another parchment underneath it. Krystal lifted it and found a second map hiding under the first one. On this map Fayterra was smaller, giving more room to the surrounding kingdoms.

Her excitement grew. She could now easily trace the path to her home kingdom. From there, she could probably find her village and farm. She went back to the desk to find a spare bit of paper. Gregory had sheets of paper for sending messages in one of the drawers. She drew a crude map that would serve her and started to let the first map fall.

Something caught her eye, and she stopped and lifted the map again. She snatched up the candelabra and brought it close. Krystal squinted to get a better view.

Someone had circled one of the mountains far behind the castle, near the sea. Next to the circle they'd drawn a series of crisscrossed lines. She didn't know what to make of it.

Krystal folded up her map, replaced the candelabra on the desk, and blew out the candles. Carefully, she opened up the study door and made her way back into the dark hallway. She felt her way along the wall slowly until she got close to her room.

It would have made things much easier if Julienne had still been talking to the guard, but Nicholas stood alone. She could barely make him out in the darkness; only the light of another torch down the hall on his other side silhouetted his body. She tucked the map down the front of her nightgown and moved forward. He would easily see her light robe even in dim light.

Nicholas stepped out from the wall. "Who's there?"

Krystal moved closer. "I am."

"Princess?" He glanced at the door. "How did you get out?"

"I walked. How do you usually get out of a room?"

"I will have to tell the king," said Nicholas.

"You do that," Krystal said. "Or better yet, I'll tell him. I'll tell him how I saw you so engrossed in your conversation, I didn't want to disturb you so I went to the kitchens myself."

"I thought Julienne brought you something to eat."

"I realized an apple would hardly satisfy me just after she left," said Krystal. "I opened the door to tell her, and you two were talking. I certainly didn't want to interrupt."

She watched him struggle as he came to the obvious conclusion. The only way he could save himself would be to keep her secret. She had a flash of guilt for deceiving him. It all seemed justifiable in the moment, but having to repeat her lies bothered her.

Nicholas closed his eyes in surrender. "At least promise me you will never do this again."

Krystal sighed. It had been so much easier to mislead King Gregory. "I promise."

"Will you please get back in your room now?"

She smiled. "Good night, Nicholas," she said and pushed open the door of her room.

She heard him grumble about the bolt and turned. He examined it closely before giving her one last look and closing the door. Krystal heard the door distinctly latch and the bolt slide into place. She'd actually done better sneaking around the castle than she'd hoped.

Krystal pulled the map out of her nightgown and looked for a good place to hide it. She ended up opening the trunk at the foot of her bed and putting it on the bottom under the clothes. Finally she got into bed. It had been a long night. However, her body refused to

cooperate with her desire for a good sleep. Krystal thought of Julienne and how she'd helped her get out of her room. She wanted to
know why the maid had been so helpful.

She also thought of the odd notation on Gregory's map, the circle
and crossing lines. Had Gregory made the marks, or had someone
else done it?

Sleep claimed her at last, and she awoke the next morning with
a new sense of purpose. She finally knew where she was going, and
now she only had to find a way out of the castle. She rolled out of
bed and dressed before breakfast. Julienne arrived with her tray just
as Krystal finished brushing her hair.

"Good morning, Princess," she said brightly, albeit somewhat
louder than necessary, as the guard shut the door behind her.

"Good morning." She glanced at the apple from the night before,
sitting on the table.

Julienne smiled and put the tray down next to it. "Can I tempt
you with breakfast?"

Krystal crossed to the table. "I might be a little hungry."

The maid leaned close. "I would imagine, as busy as you were
last night," she said in a softer voice. "Why didn't you tell me you
had something planned?"

Krystal understood. The loudly voiced pleasantries had been for
the benefit of the guard outside the door. "I didn't know if I could
trust you," she said in the same low tone. "For that matter, I still
don't. How do I know you aren't reporting everything I do to King
Gregory?"

"Because unlike Catrina, I have a brain and know a tyrant when
I see one," said Julienne. "And unlike Lysabith, I have enough back-
bone not to roll over to his every whim." She glanced back at the
door and then continued in a gentler tone. "It's *you* we weren't sure
about."

"We who?"

"The king calls us rebels," Julienne said. "There are about a dozen
of us in the castle loyal to Prince Jareth. At least, we're the only ones
willing to do something about helping his cause instead of accepting
King Gregory's rule."

"What do you do?"

"We have contacts outside the castle who carry messages to the rebels hiding throughout the countryside. If we hear of something important about the king or his plans, we let them know."

"King Gregory must know about you."

Julienne nodded. "We work hard not to call attention to ourselves, though sometimes it's difficult. The king himself motivates us. He is not compassionate to his enemies."

"What does all this have to do with me?" asked Krystal.

"It's become clear you don't want to be here. We'd like to help, if we can."

Krystal nodded in understanding. "So that's why you distracted the guard last night."

"Yes," said Julienne. "And that's why Miraya snuck in to visit you. It's especially risky for her, but she's said the sooner you're out of the castle the better."

"I can understand the need for spies. But if it's so dangerous, why stay? Surely you can leave if you want."

"The king is aware he has spies in his midst," Julienne said. "For that reason, he doesn't like accepting new servants or guards. Those of us who are here need to stay if at all possible."

They both jumped when the guard opened the door. Julienne curtsied to Krystal and turned toward the door. The guard stopped her.

"What's taking so long?"

"Princess Krystal asked me what would be offered for lunch," said Julienne in a cool voice. "I was simply going over the menu with her."

Krystal spoke up. "The soup, please, Julienne."

"Of course, my lady." Julienne swept past the guard. Krystal heard the bolt slide home.

As she ate, she thought about what Julienne had said. Gregory paid her so much attention that aligning with the castle rebels would be dangerous for her and for them. It might shed unwelcome light on their activities, or worse, expose them completely. On the other hand, it would be nice to feel like she had more than just herself to depend on for help. Still, Krystal decided it would be safer for all concerned if she continued to work on her own.

Now she had to figure out how to escape. She'd have to apologize to King Gregory. The thought didn't appeal to Krystal, but she needed her freedoms restored.

She resolved not to waste time. Krystal spent the afternoon trying to come up with just the right words to say. She wanted to avoid any discussion of his intent to make her queen. She didn't have the confidence she'd keep her temper if he brought up that topic again.

Julienne brought her lunch, but Catrina brought her dinner, and as it happened, Krystal had soup with both meals. She'd worked herself into such a state worrying about what she'd say to Gregory that the soup sat untouched. Krystal had only managed to eat the slice of thick bread.

When Catrina returned to collect the dinner tray she clucked in disapproval over the untouched food. "You hardly ate a bite. You'll waste away if you don't eat more."

Krystal turned to reply but her elbow caught on the tray as Catrina tried to lift it. The tray tipped, the bowl slid and the soup spilled all over Krystal's lap. She stood up quickly, and the bowl fell to the floor. Catrina dropped the tray on the table and covered her mouth in horror.

"Oh, my lady, I'm so sorry!" She handed Krystal a napkin. "I'll get this cleaned up right away. And you'll want a bath for certain."

"No," said Krystal. "I'm expecting the king to visit. There isn't time now."

"King Gregory went off to his study right after dinner," said Catrina. "I'm sure he'll be there a while. You have time for a quick bath, certainly."

Krystal looked down at her dress. As the soup soaked through her layers, it became uncomfortable. If they hurried, she'd be able to bathe before Gregory paid his visit.

Catrina returned and helped her out of her gown, so Krystal stood in her robe and waited for the tub to be filled with heated water. Catrina and Julienne cleaned up the floor.

Krystal worked herself into a frenzy of worry. In the confusion, she'd forgotten her carefully worded apology. She'd almost convinced herself the king would show up at her door while her room was still full of servants. After they'd left her alone, she resolved to take the fastest bath in history.

She'd nearly finished when Krystal heard Gregory in the hall. When his voice stopped just outside her door, she reached for her robe, barely managing to knot the belt as the door opened.

Chapter 12

ANDREW FROZE WHEN HE heard the barn door close. "Who's there?"

Douglas stepped into view. "It's me."

Andrew shook his head and put the saddle on his horse. "Don't try to stop me."

Bulging saddlebags were slung over Douglas' shoulder. "I didn't plan to."

Andrew frowned at him. "You're not going. I am."

Douglas sighed. "We've been through this. I'm the better tracker. Sadie's family may not let her return if they hear you've gone, and you know how good she's been for Mother."

"Sadie's family doesn't have anything to worry about," said Andrew. "I'm not going to back down from this. Krystal's my responsibility. I'm going to find her."

"We only figured out she didn't run away a few days ago," said Will as he approached.

"Where did you come from?" asked Andrew.

Will blushed slightly. "I was saddling my horse."

Andrew looked at his brothers. "It seems we all had the same idea."

"We don't know where to start," Douglas said.

"That doesn't seem to have stopped us," Andrew said.

Will shifted his weight. "Now what?"

"The two of you go back inside and let me go look for our sister," said Andrew.

"Why are you being stubborn?" asked Douglas. "We have a housekeeper cooking us the best food we've had in weeks. I thought we'd agreed you couldn't leave the farm."

"You, Kayne, and Will agreed," Andrew said. "I'm not going to let you use my place as head of the family to keep me from going. I have to go. Would Father have sent any of us to search?" He finished saddling his horse and led him out of the stall. "My leaving won't affect Sadie's position in this household. She goes home every night. There's nothing to protect."

The cool night greeted them. "Krystal is our sister too," said Will.

"We can't all go," Andrew said. "You have to stay here. I'll be back as soon as I can."

"Let him go." Kayne's voice carried from the doorway of the house. "He won't find her."

Andrew turned. Kayne shifted his foot as if to hide something, and Andrew noticed some saddlebags. He looked up at Kayne. Had he also planned to look for Krystal?

"Why don't you think he'll find her?" Douglas had asked.

"There's no trail," said Kayne. "The only clue we have that she didn't run away is that she took nothing with her. I'm still not convinced she's not just being clever."

"If she ran away, she'll be easy to find," Will said.

"And if she didn't, we may never know what happened," said Kayne.

All four brothers fell silent after that gloomy pronouncement. Andrew mounted his horse.

"None of you have swayed me. I have maps, some money, and food. I'll be back when I've found her or when my supplies run out."

"You could wait until morning," said Douglas.

Andrew smiled wryly. "And let one of you take off the moment I fall asleep? Take care of Mother, and don't forget to pay Sadie every week."

He turned his horse and disappeared into the night.

Chapter 13

KRYSTAL WAITED FOR GREGORY to give his usual greeting, but he only turned to shut the door. She couldn't hold her tongue any longer. "What are you doing?"

He didn't answer. Krystal backed away. The look in his eyes alarmed her.

"You're so beautiful," he said at last, and she understood.

"You've been drinking."

He shrugged clumsily. "It doesn't help."

"Help what?"

"I can't get you out of my head," He moved nearer. "And tonight, sitting alone with my drink, I asked myself why. Why do I fight my attraction to you? Why keep my distance?"

Krystal retreated. "Gregory, you aren't yourself. Please go."

"I'm not going anywhere." He lunged for her, but she kept out of reach.

She fought panic. "Go."

"I'm tired," he said. "It takes too much effort to resist you. Come to me. Yield to me."

"No," she said. "I will not be yours."

Too late she realized he'd backed her against the bed. Krystal tried to edge around it, but he moved too quickly. He caught hold of the sleeve of her robe, forcing her to stop before he pulled the garment right off her.

Gregory turned her to face him. He rubbed his thumbs across

her shoulders. So close to him, the scent of drink on his breath caused her to gag. "I wish I could define this power you have over me. No man wants to be the slave of a woman. Why do you consume me so?"

"If I knew, I would stop it," Krystal said, fighting to pull away. "Please release me!"

Gregory captured her mouth in a terrifying kiss. Krystal struggled against him but his strength overpowered her. He snaked an arm around her back and crushed her to his chest.

Krystal pushed against his shoulders with her hands. When that did nothing, she balled her hands into fists and hit him as hard as she could. She went for the dagger again, but he'd removed it. She felt his hand on her shoulder as he pushed back her robe, exposing bare skin.

"So lovely," he said, his voice a breathy whisper.

She pushed against him, hard. "Stop that!"

His eyes blazed. "Stop fighting me. Accept me, and this will go easier for you."

Krystal shouted at him. "I will never give in to you! Let me go!"

If Gregory replied, his words were drowned out by the sound of splintering wood. Voltimande came through the shattered door, not pausing as he crossed the room and took hold of Gregory. He pulled the king away from Krystal and shoved him back.

Krystal pulled her robe together. She stared at his face with wide eyes. "Thank you."

"We have to get you out of here." He bent down and scooped her into his arms.

Krystal saw Gregory move. She felt Voltimande shift her weight to free one hand and saw him halt the king's attack with one massive fist. Gregory flew backward like a rag doll, landing in her tub of water. He did not get back up.

Voltimande carried her down the hall. Krystal felt her body rebel. "You have to stop."

He shook his head. "I want to get you to safety before the alarm is raised."

"I'm going to be sick all over you if you don't put me down."

He hastily put her on her feet. Krystal narrowly missed his boots when she heaved. Without another word, he lifted her into his arms once more and they set off.

King Gregory must have recovered quickly, because before they could reach the castle entrance, they heard the sounds of pursuit. Voltimande changed directions.

"Where are you going?"

"We have to find another way," he said. "They're going to alarm the guards at the doors."

Krystal could hear their pursuers. "They aren't shouting for you. They're after me."

"They'll be after me soon enough."

"He'll kill you," she said. "He'll be livid you struck him."

"That won't matter if we get out of here."

Krystal realized what she had to do and she didn't like it. "If you take me away he'll come after me. He'll chase us down, and when he catches you, he'll kill you. Let me go back and you can get away."

She'd insulted him. "My mother would skin me alive if I left a woman in danger to save my own hide." He shook his head. "No thank you, Princess. I'd rather take my chances with King Gregory than face her wrath."

"You saved me," she said. "I'll always be grateful for that. But I'm afraid you don't get a vote." Krystal let go of his shoulders and pushed herself out of his arms. She dropped to the floor and came up on her feet.

Voltimande stopped and turned to her. "What are you doing?"

"I'm buying you time. I suggest you run."

"Don't do this."

She looked at him. "No one else is going to get hurt because of me."

Krystal took off at a run before Voltimande could grab her. She met up with their pursuers at an intersection of hallways and took off in the direction opposite Voltimande. As she'd expected, they followed her without hesitation.

As she ran, Krystal tried not to think how furious King Gregory would be once he got his hands on her or what he might do to her, though thinking along those lines kept her a few paces ahead of the guards. She couldn't know if she'd bought Voltimande enough time to escape when they finally caught her; she could only hope he'd gotten away.

The guards took her back to her room, where King Gregory waited. Lady Fordyce stood by his side. The king had been given a towel to dry off and a purple bruise had formed under his left eye. A guard knelt at his feet, the same guard who had been at Krystal's door earlier that day.

Gregory looked hard at the man. "The next time you need to visit the privy, be sure the man who replaces you is loyal to me!" He looked up and spotted Krystal. He spoke to the guard who held her. "I see you've found her. What about Voltimande?"

"We are still looking, sire," the guard said. "We should have him before long."

The king came to his feet. "See that you do."

Krystal looked at him as he approached. His expression made her wary, but at least the dunking he'd received appeared to have sobered him.

"I'm going to enjoy killing him," he said to her. "Once my men find him and drag him back to me, I will flay the flesh from his body, cut out his tongue, and then perhaps I'll let him die." Gregory raised his finger and traced her jaw line.

Krystal pulled away from him. "You'll have to find him first. He's long gone by now."

"Once I put my magic to work, I'll find him soon enough," said Gregory. "But just now you should be more concerned about yourself." He grabbed her chin with his hand. "What punishment is fit for you, my dear?"

"For what?" Krystal glared at him. "Should I be punished for resisting you? Or do you want to punish me for allowing a man twice my size to carry me off?" She tried to twist away from him, but the guard holding her gave her no room. "Before you came in here tonight, I'd planned to apologize to you!" At least that had been true.

His eyes widened a fraction. "And now?"

She felt his fingers caress her chin, and it startled her. Even now, in his fury, he seemed unable to stop himself. Krystal frowned at him. She had no desire for his affection.

"Now I want nothing more than to never see you again."

Gregory smiled, but it was not a friendly smile. "It's a pity you can't have everything you want." He looked at her guard. "Bring her and follow me." A guard handed him a single candle.

He led them through the castle and stopped at a closed door. "Behind this door is a long staircase that ends in your new prison. This is the only way in or out. Both doors will be guarded. If you can find an alternate escape, Krystal, you're smarter than I."

Krystal didn't bother to respond. King Gregory smirked at her and opened the door. The stairs spiraled upward, and by the time they reached the door at the top, Krystal had become winded. The chase through the castle certainly hadn't helped. The guard, watching the king, pushed her over to the bed at the other end of the room and left her there.

Gregory put the candle on the small table near the door. "You will remain here until your door can be replaced. I will continue to visit you each night, and I suggest you at least try for civility. In the morning, the servants will bring up your things. Sleep well, my dear."

They left her alone. Krystal looked around her new room. It had been sparsely decorated with a bed, a trunk, a table, and a single chair. A closet with hooks for clothes had been built into the wall, and she had one window.

She opened the door. The guard stood there. She shut the door in his face.

Krystal slept fitfully in the new bed. More than once she thought she felt Gregory's weight on her and woke up in a cold sweat. She took comfort in being alone—at least he hadn't come back.

Julienne brought up her breakfast tray. "We're to bring up your things," she said when she put the tray on the table. "I wanted to make sure you ate first."

"Thank you," said Krystal. "I need you to do something for me."

"What is it?"

"There is a piece of paper in the bottom of the trunk in my room. I need you to bring it to me. It would be bad if it fell into the wrong hands."

"I'll do what I can," said the maid.

"Thank you." Krystal pulled the blanket close. "It's cold in here."

"The towers get cool, but they warm up quickly. By this afternoon, I'll wager you'll be missing the morning chill." She grew serious. "I've only heard snatches of what happened last night."

Krystal motioned to the door. "Aren't you worried about the guard?"

"I'm more worried about you," said Julienne. "Did Voltimande strike the king?"

"He protected me."

"How did he get out of the castle?"

"I distracted the guards so he could get away, but I don't know where he went."

"So he saved you, and then you saved him?" Julienne smiled. "You have a good heart."

Krystal shook her head. "You wouldn't say that if you'd been there. I had no other choice. King Gregory wants his blood. I had to do something."

"I still say you have a good heart." Julienne put a hand on her shoulder. "I'll get that paper for you and bring it as soon as I can. Please let me know if there's anything else."

"Thank you," Krystal said again.

The guard opened the door. Julienne rolled her eyes at Krystal before turning around. "I was just leaving," she said to him as she passed.

Krystal did not expect to be hungry but ended up eating all of her breakfast. Servants arrived carrying her clothes just as she finished. Julienne brought in a pile of clothes Krystal recognized from her trunk. She threw Krystal a significant look.

"You can put those on the bed," Krystal said. "I'll put them away."

"Yes, Princess," the maid said. "I'll just go fetch the rest."

Krystal opened the trunk and made a show up folding the clothes and putting them inside until the last person left. Then she tore apart the rest of the pile looking for her map. She found it tucked inside the nightgown at the bottom of the pile and put it under the clothes she'd already placed in the trunk. Provided she didn't get relocated again, it would be safe there.

She couldn't get dressed until the maids finished moving her things, so she put her energy into helping organize the trunk and closet. At one point she simply positioned herself on the floor by the closet so she could put in the shoes.

Catrina brought up the last of the shoes, but she tripped over one of Krystal's feet and the shoes went flying, some landing on Krystal and others sliding into the closet.

The maid stammered her apology. "I'm so sorry. I thought I'd stepped over you."

"It's my fault. I stretched my leg out at the wrong moment. Don't worry, I'll pick them up. I'm down here anyway."

"I can help you."

"It's all right," Krystal insisted. "You go ahead. I can take care of this."

"Yes, my lady." Catrina curtsied and turned away.

Krystal found the matches to each shoe but one. She got on her knees and peered into the closet. The clothes that had been hung above her interfered with the light so she squeezed into the closet to find the lost shoe.

It had rolled against the back corner. She had crawled in so far as to be almost invisible to the servants in her room before she found the shoe. It rested against the closet's back wall and had rolled into some dust. Krystal supposed no one cleaned this far back into a closet. She certainly wouldn't if she could help it.

One of the stones in the wall looked odd, as though it sat in the wall without anything to secure it. Krystal reached her finger in and slid it along the gap between that stone and the one above it. A thrill of excitement ran down her spine.

"Princess? Are you all right?" Catrina had returned.

Krystal crawled out of the closet, errant shoe in hand. "It had rolled back pretty far."

Catrina held out a hand and helped her up. "You're covered in dust."

She looked down. "I guess it hasn't been cleaned in a while."

The maid almost looked insulted. "I'll have someone see to it right away."

"I'll do it," said Julienne from behind her.

Catrina looked from one to the other as though trying to figure out if they were up to something. "All right," she said. "Julienne can help you dress and then clean the room."

Everyone filed out, leaving Krystal and Julienne alone. Julienne sighed with relief.

"We're supposed to clean the throne room today," she said. "I hate that job, so this will be easy in comparison." Krystal had turned and gone back inside the closet. Julienne peered around the wall. "What are you doing?"

"There's something back here."

"Do you need help?"

"Even if I did, you wouldn't fit back here."

Krystal dug her fingers into the space around the stone and tried to grip it. She pulled, but her hands slipped off, and she hit her head on the wall behind her. Rubbing her head she sat back up.

Julienne had been watching. "Are you all right?"

"I'm fine. Let me try again."

This time she worked at getting a better grip, but no matter how hard she pulled, the stone wouldn't budge. She'd worked up a light sweat before giving up.

Krystal sighed. "I was sure there was something to this."

"I'm sorry," said Julienne.

Krystal sat back and studied the wall. Something about the wall didn't look right. She thought it might look different if she stood up so she put her hand on the wall to get to her feet.

Her palm was still sweaty and she slipped. Her hand slid down the wall as she fell, pushing against the odd stone. It moved under her hand, startling her. She landed on her knees.

Julienne gasped. "Are you hurt?"

Krystal didn't immediately reply. She looked down to see that the stone had recessed into the wall. She almost laughed with relief. All that energy she'd spent pulling when she should have pushed instead. She put her hand on the stone and pushed again.

A dull grinding sound started behind the wall. Thinking of the guard outside her door, Krystal scrambled out of the closet, nearly colliding with the maid.

"Grab a dress, quick!"

Julienne picked up a dress off the bed, a question in her eyes.

"Now hand it to me."

Just as she did so, the door opened and the guard stepped in. "What is that noise?"

Krystal looked at him. "I didn't hear anything. Did you, Julienne?"

"Not a whisper," Julienne said.

The guard looked at them. Krystal hoped it looked like they were busy unpacking. "I'm sure I heard something."

"Perhaps it was from downstairs," said Krystal.

Once he'd shut the door. Krystal dropped the dress and climbed back into the closet.

"What is it?" Julienne followed her.

Krystal stopped. "I think we found a secret passage."

A section of wall just large enough for a person to crawl through, had opened up in the back of the closet. Krystal had to find out if it was a secret room or an actual passage.

"I'm going in there."

"You don't have a light," said Julienne. "What if you fall to your death?"

"I'll be careful. Put some clothes under the blanket on the bed so it looks like I'm sleeping. If the guard comes in, just tell him I wanted to take a nap. I'll try not to be long."

"I should go," said the maid. "You don't know where it leads."

Krystal sighed. "Don't worry. This may get us out of the castle."

"Or it could lead straight into the king's bedchamber."

Krystal sobered instantly. She hadn't considered that. "There's only one way to find out."

"Just be careful. And hurry back."

Krystal smiled at her friend, got on her hands and knees, and crawled carefully through the wall. The idea of falling to her death didn't appeal to her, but the floor beneath her hands seemed solid enough so she stood up.

Julienne whispered through the opening. "Do you see anything?"

Krystal tried to look around, but no light permeated the space. "No. I'll feel my way."

She walked carefully along the wall, feeling not only with her hands but her feet as well. She'd completed a half arc when she stepped with one foot and found no floor. Carefully she felt along the floor. It dropped off just inches from where she stood; she edged her way closer and put her foot out to see if she felt anything. A step. Then another.

"I found stairs," she said softly, not knowing if Julienne could hear her or not.

She didn't hear a response, so she continued down the steps. Her eyes either started adjusting, or she imagined seeing the outline of the steps as she felt her way down. They wound around the outer wall of the tower and seemed to go on forever.

Just as Krystal worried she'd have to give up, the steps opened up to a landing. Across the landing stood a door and through the cracks around the door she could see light. Could it be daylight? Krystal crossed to the door and put her hands on it.

She felt warmth, as though the sun beat down on the door and warmed the wood all the way through. Her heart gave a great leap of hope.

She'd found a way out.

Krystal felt her way back up the steps, fearing she'd been gone too long. She climbed out of the closet and stood up. Julienne had been sitting by the bed; she came to her feet when she saw her.

"Did you find anything?" asked the maid.

"There's a door leading outside," said Krystal. "I'm sure of it. I could see the sunlight."

"Did you open it?"

Krystal felt like an idiot. "No, but I know it leads outside."

"It must open up to the gardens," Julienne said.

"That will be perfect," said Krystal. "We can get White Lightning as well."

"What are you planning?"

"I'm sneaking out of the castle. I'm going tonight, and you're coming with me."

Chapter 14

"OW WILL WE GET OUTSIDE the castle walls?" asked Julienne. "You know as well as I do that King Gregory's guards are everywhere!"

All I have to do is get White Lightning out of the gardens," Krystal said. "Then we fly."

"Have you ever flown her?"

"Briefly," said Krystal. "I'm sure we can hang on long enough to get away."

Julienne shook her head. "I can't go with you, but I know someone who should."

"Who?"

"Miraya and her daughter. King Gregory is already suspicious of her. If you can get both of them out of the castle, they can go where they can be safe."

"I asked her why she didn't just leave," Krystal said. "She might not want to go with me."

"I'll ask her, if you like. She won't be able to come up here and see you."

"If she can't even get past the guards, how will I get her to the secret passage?"

Julienne's face fell. "I hadn't thought of that."

But Krystal's mind had started working. "How much power do I have as a princess?"

"What do you mean?"

"If I ordered the guard to send Miraya to me, what would they do?"

Julienne caught on. "It depends on who is guarding you and what they know."

"Well, I'll have to try," said Krystal. "What's the worst that could happen?"

"They could not send for her and tell the king you asked for her."

"What could he do? He'd have no reason to guess I'm escaping."

"I'm not thinking of you," said Julienne. "I'm thinking of what he might do to her."

Krystal sighed. "He wouldn't think twice about harming her, would he?"

Julienne shook her head. "I want Miraya and Emelyn to be safe. This may be our only chance to get them away before King Gregory finds some excuse to justify getting rid of them."

Krystal agreed. "Anything I can do to inconvenience him will please me."

"I should go now," said Julienne. "I'll see you later."

"Be careful. When you talk to Miraya, be sure you aren't overheard."

"I will."

Krystal paced the room until Catrina brought her tray at lunch. She didn't want to eat, but she knew she'd need the energy later. Before she left, Catrina told her Julienne would bring in dinner, which Krystal hoped meant that Julienne had found Miraya. She acted as though it didn't matter and let Catrina go back to her other duties. Everything had to look normal to anyone who happened to come into her room.

Julienne brought dinner as promised. The guard apparently had his fill trusting them together, so he kept the door open, preventing them from talking. Regardless, Krystal took one look at the smile on Julienne's face and knew Miraya's answer. She smiled at Julienne to let her know she understood.

Krystal now felt her escape had purpose. Not only would she be able to get Miraya and Emelyn out from under Gregory's control, but she'd also reduce the threat to the rebels within the castle. If they didn't feel they had to watch out for her, they could go about their own business.

Krystal completely forgot about the king's nightly visits until after he opened the door. Her nervousness multiplied. How could she act normally around him?

"Good evening, my dear," he said.

Krystal frowned. "Hello, sire."

"I don't think you need to be that formal with your future husband."

Was he trying to get her riled? "That has hardly been decided."

King Gregory sighed. "Enough maidenly shyness. I didn't come here to fight with you."

" 'Maidenly shyness?' Is that what you think this is?"

He sat in the chair and motioned to the bed. "Sit down. Stop trying to pick a fight."

She glared at him but sat on the bed. "Why did you come here?"

"I told you I would visit you every night," said Gregory.

"I'm not up for sparring, Gregory."

"Then what *are* you up to?"

Did he suspect something? "What can I do locked up in this room all day?"

"I often wonder," said the king. "Did you have a good day?"

She motioned to the closet. "The maids and I organized my clothes."

Gregory looked. "I have ordered a new door made for your bedroom. It shouldn't take longer than a week, and then you can return there."

Krystal had no desire to see that room again. "This room is actually quite comfortable."

He frowned. "I didn't send you up here for you to enjoy it."

"I didn't say I enjoyed it. It's quiet, that's all. And I like the view." She frowned at him. "I can't say I enjoy captivity, no matter how nice the prison looks."

He dismissed that with a wave of his hand. "Your captivity is a state of mind."

"I suppose I'm imagining the guards on my stairs?" Krystal laughed shortly.

"You know what I mean." He reached out and took her hand. His eyes bore into hers. "I would be glad to treat you like an honored guest, if I could trust you to behave as one."

"I can't forget how I was brought here."

"You could, you know," he said. "I have potions that would help you forget. At times it's been tempting to slip you something, for your own sake."

Krystal shivered. "It bothers me that you would even consider doing something like that. Would you ask my consent or simply magic me unaware?"

"You seem determined to think the worst of me. I won't give you more ammunition."

"I wonder why I would think badly of you," she said, unable to keep the sarcasm from her voice.

Gregory looked darkly at her. "That's enough."

Krystal took a deep breath. She had to get a hold of herself before she said something completely stupid. "I'm sorry. I didn't sleep well last night."

"I didn't either," he said. "I guess neither of us is in the best frame of mind."

"I suppose not."

"So I shouldn't ask you if you've given my proposal any more thought."

She looked at him. "No, you shouldn't ask."

King Gregory stood up. "Perhaps we will have better luck tomorrow. Good night, Krystal."

He stepped in front of her and pulled her to her feet. "I'm going to kiss you good night."

At least he warned me, Krystal thought as his lips met hers. She stood still during the brief kiss, and when he stepped back she had to suppress a sigh of relief. The king left the room before she thought of anything to say.

The time had come. Krystal didn't anticipate any other visitors before morning so she could get ready for her escape. She slipped into a dark dress and tucked the map down the front. Then she climbed into the bed for a short nap.

∽

Krystal woke in the dead of night. She slipped out of bed and put on her robe to conceal the dress from the guard. Then she went to the door and opened it a few inches.

"I need you to fetch the maid Miraya."

"Why?" he asked.

Krystal tried to look embarrassed. "I'd rather not discuss it with you, if you don't mind."

"I'm not supposed to leave your door."

"Then go to tell the other guard to get her. I need Miraya."

"I'm not sure the king would approve. Why not just send for Julienne or Catrina?"

Krystal thought fast. "Julienne told me this evening she didn't feel well, and I know Miraya can help me. Please do as I ask."

"I think I should have Joseph alert the king as well."

She looked into his eyes and suspected he was testing her. "Go ahead. I'm not trying to be sneaky. I just need a woman's help. Please send for her."

She thought he would turn her down, but then he said, "I shall do so right away."

"Thank you. She can come right in when she arrives." Krystal then shut the door and went back to the bed. She pulled the covers up around her waist to hide the skirt of her gown.

Time ticked by. Krystal could almost feel it in her blood. If the guard did alert the king then they'd have precious little time to make their getaway.

After what felt like an eternity, the door opened and the guard stepped in. Miraya followed him and her daughter, Emelyn, followed her. Krystal suppressed her sigh of relief.

Miraya spoke. "I'm so sorry I had to bring my child, Princess, but poor Emelyn hates to be alone at night. She would have carried on something fierce had I left her behind."

"It's no matter. I'm sure you won't be long." She looked at the guard. "Please excuse us."

He bowed. "I'll be just outside the door."

Once he shut the door, Krystal sprang into action. "I don't know how much time we have. He mentioned alerting the king that I'd sent for you."

Miraya's eyes widened in fear. "What should we do?"

Krystal motioned to the table. "Grab that candle and follow me." She picked up the other lit candle and went to the closet.

They tossed some gowns out of the way before climbing into the closet. Emelyn watched them in silent fascination. Krystal worked the stone that opened the passageway. It slid open quietly, and she let out a breath of relief.

Miraya sent Emelyn through after Krystal and then climbed through herself. Krystal stood up and held her candle high. She hadn't seen this room in the light. It turned out to be more of a narrow hallway than a room.

"Look around," she told them. "There has to be a way to close the passage from this side. If Gregory finds us missing in the next few minutes I don't want him discovering our exit."

The candles didn't provide much light, but Krystal still found a stone similar to the one on the other side with the edges carved out from the wall. She pushed on it, and the wall reformed.

"Come on," she said. "I still think we should hurry."

Miraya grabbed her daughter's hand and followed Krystal to the stairs. Krystal looked down at the stairway and realized it had been to her benefit to not be able to see them the first time. They looked so steep in the light that she had second thoughts.

She wasn't alone. "These stairs haven't been used in years," Miraya said, clutching Emelyn tighter. "Are you sure we should do this?"

Krystal shook her head. "We don't have many other options. I'll go first. If either of you slip, I should be able to stop your fall."

"But who will stop yours?"

Krystal didn't reply. Instead, she set her mouth and lifted her candle. She could see the first turn the steps made as they wound down the tower. They descended slowly, cautiously, the faint light of the candles guiding the way. Krystal did well until a spider web brushed the top of her head. She slapped frantically at her hair and brushed off her arms. A tyrannical king she could face, but spiders horrified her.

At last they reached the bottom and the door that would lead to freedom. Krystal admired Emelyn—the child hadn't once complained about this odd nighttime excursion. Krystal handed the candle to Miraya and grasped the door handle. It turned in her hand. She gave them a smile and then tried to quietly open the door.

It didn't budge. Krystal pulled harder, but it wouldn't move. She lost her smile and put a hand on the wall to push while she pulled with the other hand. Nothing.

Miraya sighed. "Why can't anything ever be easy?"

"Then you wouldn't appreciate the reward," said Krystal. "My father used to say that."

"He was probably right, though at the moment I don't care."

Krystal nodded. "We'll both feel better once we're out of here."

"Is the door stuck?"

"Hush, Emy," said Miraya. "Let us think." She eyed the door. "What if it's been sealed?"

"It isn't locked," said Krystal. "The handle turns just fine but the door won't budge. We're in real trouble if it's been sealed shut."

"Should we go back?"

"I'm not ready to give up yet," Krystal said. "Help me look. Maybe there's a bolt or something keeping it closed."

Emelyn tugged at her mother's skirt. "Mama?"

"Not now, Emy."

"But Mama!"

Miraya sighed and looked at her daughter. "What is it?"

Emelyn pointed at the floor. "Maybe that board is keeping the door from opening."

Krystal looked at her. "What board?"

The child pointed again, and Krystal saw it. Across the bottom of the door, someone had made loops and slid a long, thick board through them to secure the door.

Miraya kissed her daughter's head. "You bright girl! You've found it."

Krystal knelt. "Help me move it."

It took both of them to slide the board free of the loops, and then their combined effort to push the door open. It had not moved for untold ages. Krystal peered around the door first. Sure enough, it had let them out right in the middle of the queen's gardens.

"The moon is out," Krystal said. "We won't need the candles anymore."

Miraya blew them out and took Emelyn's hand. "Now what?"

"We have to get White Lightning out of her stall and through the garden gates. Once we get around Gregory's magical shield, we can take to the skies."

The maid's hand shot out to grab her arm. "We're riding the Pegasus?"

"It's the fastest escape. Will it be a problem?"

Miraya shook her head. "I'll make sure it's not. It's just that I'm not fond of heights."

"I thought you could sit behind me with Emelyn between us," said Krystal. "Then you can wrap your arms around both of us and I can hold onto the mane. We'll be fine."

"I trust you," Miraya said. "Let's go."

Krystal led the way through the garden to White Lightning's stable and went in to fetch her pet. "Hello," she said. "We're taking a little trip."

Emelyn gasped when she saw the Pegasus. "Mommy, she's so beautiful!"

"Yes, she is," said Miraya. "Do you think she can carry us all?"

Krystal patted White Lightning's nose. "I know we'll be spotted by the sentries once we take flight, and I imagine the king will pursue us, but she should at least be able to get us far enough away that we can hide in the forest, and then she can rest if we're too heavy."

They walked the stable, and, checking first to see if anyone was around, Krystal led the Pegasus out. She mounted her faithful pet and pulled Emelyn up behind her. Miraya had a little more difficulty, but at last, the three of them sat across the animal's back.

Krystal bent down to whisper encouragement into White Lightning's ear. The Pegasus ran forward and stretched out her great wings. Krystal felt Miraya's hands grab her waist and glanced back. Her friend had covered Emelyn and buried her face into Krystal's back.

"Here we go," Krystal said as White Lightning's hooves left the ground. She tightened her grip on the mane and let the Pegasus carry them into the sky.

In a heartbeat, they heard shouts from below. Krystal glanced at the ground as it fell away and saw the sentries pointing and shouting. In seconds they'd cleared the castle walls and Krystal turned them toward the forest. White Lightning carried them quite a distance before she started tiring. Krystal looked for a place she could land and found a clearing near an outcropping of rock. She guided the Pegasus down toward it.

Miraya slid from White Lightning's back almost as soon as they touched ground. She fell to her knees and put her forehead on the grass. "Never again. I felt completely out of control."

Krystal slid to the ground and helped Emelyn off White Lightning's back. "You did wonderfully. Both of you did."

Miraya looked up at her. "We're free. How can I ever thank you?"

Krystal turned away, uncomfortable with the praise. "It wasn't my idea. Julienne decided it should be you."

"But you said yes. And since I have Emelyn, that's no small decision. I still thank you."

"We have much to do," Krystal said. "I have to get White Lightning rubbed down, and we need shelter and food and water. Then we need to make a plan of where and how to hide you."

Chapter 15

WE GOT OUT," said Miraya. "We can worry about the rest later. Emy and I will go look for shelter and water. You take care of the Pegasus."

"All right," Krystal said. "Let's get to work."

She had nothing to rub White Lightning down with except the skirt of her gown. The Pegasus stood still for her treatment, allowing Krystal to take care of her. While she did so, Krystal whispered praise to the animal for her hard work and fine flying.

"We're in luck," Miraya said as they returned. "There is a cave near here and a stream just over there."

They settled into the cave to sleep until dawn. White Lightning stood at the entrance.

Miraya whispered to Krystal. "I think Emelyn went to sleep right away. I wanted to ask you what your plans are now that you are free."

"I want to help you find a safe place. And then I'm going home."

"You miss your family?"

"I know they are worried about me. If I can ease their fears, I should."

Miraya sighed. "I understand. Will you fly home?"

"It would be faster. The map I have tells me what direction I need to go, but I don't know how long it will take me to get there." Krystal sighed. "It could be days or weeks, or even longer, if I go on foot or horseback."

"I wish the prince were free," said the maid. "He would know how long it would take."

"You care about him a great deal."

"He's my sovereign and friend," said Miraya. "If I could somehow free Jareth, he could organize the rebels and take his kingdom back."

"But in order to free him, you have to find the prison." Krystal thought of Gregory's maps and sat up. "I might know where it is."

Miraya sat up as well. "But how?"

"I snuck into the king's study to look at his maps in order to find my way home," said Krystal. "On one of his maps, I saw an area near the mountains that had been circled. Next to it was a series of lines. Now that I think about it, they looked sort of like bars, like a prison would have."

"If we can get that information to the rebels, they can free him."

"But what if that's not where he is?" Krystal lowered her voice when Emelyn stirred. "What if we send a bunch of rebels into a training camp for Gregory's guards?"

Miraya lapsed into silence. "Maybe we could go and make sure it's safe first and then tell the rebels."

"You speak of contacting the rebels like there's one behind every tree."

"It's not that easy," Miraya admitted. "I know only a few places where they might hide."

"So we could find Prince Jareth and then have no way of getting the message to them," said Krystal. "I don't like that."

"What do you suggest?"

Krystal hesitated. "Tell me about Jareth," she said to Miraya.

"I've told you—he's the rightful heir to the throne of Fayterra," said Miraya. "He is our only hope of overthrowing King Gregory. No one else has the power to challenge him."

"Does he want to be king?"

"No one has seen him in over a year," Miraya said. "But last time I spoke with him, he certainly did. Gregory rules without heart. He simply takes what he wants—what he believes the people should give. Jareth is just the opposite."

"It must have been difficult for him," Krystal said. "He grew up in the castle that became his prison. What if he has become hard, like Gregory?"

"Prince Jareth had his parents for twelve years. They helped foster in him compassion and other noble qualities. I'm not worried." Miraya sighed. "I know you don't know him as I do and that your experience in Fayterra hasn't been pleasant, but please believe me when I say Jareth is a good man. Politics aside, King Gregory will kill Jareth before he lets him take the throne."

Krystal bit her lip. "What would it be like to sit in a room waiting for death?"

Miraya was quiet for a moment. Then she asked, "Have you considered that you might not be safe if you go home? King Gregory knows where your farm is, and he's had you taken from there before. If you help us free Jareth, maybe the king will have other things to worry about than finding you."

Krystal realized that she'd had been naïve to assume that once she left Fayterra, the king's search would end. She had no doubt Gregory would come for her, especially after announcing his plans to wed her. The things he'd said about his feelings for her still echoed in her mind. Those were not the words of a man who would give up.

She rolled onto her side and put her arm under her head for a pillow. "Then I suggest we get some rest. We have a big day tomorrow."

"What are we doing tomorrow?"

"We are going to rescue a prince." She closed her eyes and prayed it would be true.

ॐ

Krystal awoke first the next morning. Moving to the entrance of the cave so she wouldn't disturb anyone, she pulled her map out of her dress. In the dim light, she studied the map to figure out their location. She didn't want to get lost trying to find Jareth's prison.

Miraya appeared at the mouth of the cave. "Good morning. How did you sleep?"

"I miss Damen," Krystal said. "He makes a wonderful pillow."

"Will he know that you've left the castle? Do you think he'll find you?"

Krystal folded the map and tucked it away. "I hope so."

"I think I'm going to see about breakfast," said Miraya. "Could you stay with Emelyn?"

"Of course," Krystal said. "But don't be long. I think we should move on as soon as possible. There's no telling how close Gregory might be."

Emelyn walked out of the cave before Miraya returned. She rubbed her eyes and looked around. "Where's Mama?"

"She went to go find you some breakfast," said Krystal. "She'll be right back."

Emelyn plopped down. "I liked flying, but Mama squished me so I didn't see anything."

Krystal smiled. "I liked flying too. We're going to fly some more after breakfast."

Miraya walked into the clearing, her skirt laden with goodies. "I have nuts and berries and some apples." She knelt before them and opened the folds of her skirt. "I can't carry water, so I'm afraid you'll have to get some from the stream."

The three of them ate their fill, drank from the stream, and took care of their personal needs before mounting White Lightning and taking to the air.

This time, though, rather than enjoying the freedom, Krystal felt vulnerable and exposed. She feared anyone with a reasonably clear field of sight could spot them. She tried to keep to the treetops in an effort to stay out of sight, but White Lightning didn't like that.

Krystal brought them back down when they'd neared the mountain. "I think we should give her a chance to rest before we take her closer," she said as they slid off her back.

Miraya nodded. She looked green and had her lips tightly closed.

"I'm sorry this is hard on you," Krystal said with sympathy. "I wish we had an alternative."

"We should stay together," said Miraya. "Don't worry about me."

"I tried to follow the stream," said Krystal. "It's just over there."

They went to the stream together, and Krystal made sure White Lightning got a drink. Afterward they found a place to rest. Krystal lamented not having a bow so she could hunt. Fruit and berries didn't feel like nearly enough for lunch.

As she lay under a tree, Krystal considered their options. While Miraya made a good point that they should stay together, she clearly hated flying. They also had Emelyn to consider, and no one could deny White Lightning would fly better—and longer—with only one rider.

Krystal sat up, unsure what to say. "I suppose we should get going."

As she'd thought, Miraya's shoulders sank a little. "Yes, we should."

Krystal looked at her. "What if you two stayed here? I could go on ahead and see if the mark on the map really is the prince's prison. Then I could return here. That way you don't have to fly. White Lightning is sure to carry one better than three."

"But what if something happens to you? Or the king finds us before you return?"

"We've covered quite a distance in the air," Krystal said. "I doubt he could catch up to us in less than a day. Even if his men rode through the night, we'd still have the advantage."

"I'm not sure I like this plan," said Miraya. "Anything could happen to you up there."

"I'll be careful," Krystal promised. "I will just fly out to the mountain, see if the prince is there, and come right back."

Krystal and Emelyn both watched in silence as Miraya struggled to accept the change in plans. At last she nodded. "Very well. We will be waiting anxiously for your return."

Krystal stood up. "Don't worry. I'll be back as soon as I can." She mounted White Lightning. When they took flight, Krystal noticed how much easier White Lightning gained altitude. She could see the mountains in the distance and turned the Pegasus in that direction.

As they flew closer, Krystal noticed the countryside became less hospitable. Eventually only a single path led through a canyon to the largest mountain. It looked almost like someone had built it that way. Just as Krystal thought the other side of the canyon would be the best place to stage an ambush, she flew right over one. A semi-permanent camp of guards had been positioned between the canyon and the mountain.

Almost immediately she heard shouts from below as they noticed her and White Lightning. She could tell by the color of their tunics they were King Gregory's men.

An arrow flew right in front of White Lightning's nose. Krystal banked right, away from them. They kept firing at her, so she tried to get White Lightning to climb higher into the sky, and her steed obliged. They gave the camp a wide berth and were soon out of range.

Krystal took several deep breaths to calm her racing heart. Once she looked White Lightning over to make sure she hadn't been hit, Krystal started to worry. If those men had any sense, they'd head straight to the prison to protect their prisoner. She wouldn't be able to come back later to get him. She'd have to rescue the prince now, before the men got there.

She urged White Lightning faster, keeping an eye on the path on the ground below so she wouldn't get lost. They landed in a small clearing not far from the mouth of a cave. Krystal made sure White Lightning would keep out of sight and then made her way to the cave.

Krystal reasoned there would be one or two guards at the prison itself. She picked up a sizeable rock and hid it in her skirts as she approached. Sure enough, she hadn't gotten ten steps away from the mouth of the cave when she heard a voice.

"Who approaches?" A guard stepped from the shadows and leveled a spear at her.

Krystal guessed playing helpless would work better than a frontal assault. "Oh, thank goodness I've found you! I've gotten separated from my group and I can't find my way back."

He looked doubtful. "Don't come any closer. How did you get past the men at the camp?"

She thought he'd wonder about that and pointed in another direction. "I came from that way. Please, won't you help me?"

The guard hesitated, but then lowered his spear. "I didn't know anyone could get through from that way."

"I can tell you it wasn't easy." She clutched at her heart dramatically. "I don't mind saying I've never been so frightened. You can't know what a relief it is to find you."

He puffed out his chest. "I'll do what I can, miss, but I'm sworn not to leave my post."

She moved closer to him. "Are you all alone here?"

"It's just me and the prisoner." He smiled. "It's nice to see a pretty face for a change."

Krystal ducked her chin and looked at him through her lashes. "You're too kind."

The guard turned around. "I can send a messenger pigeon to the camp asking someone to take my place so I can help you find your party. We'd also have the benefit of a horse."

Krystal followed him into the cave. "That would be so kind of you. You mentioned you had a prisoner here. It's not someone dangerous, is it?"

He chuckled. "Not at all. He's important, though. An enemy of the king himself."

She put a hand on her mouth. "The king must trust you a great deal to put you in charge of guarding him."

This guard must have been more starved for companionship than she thought. He stopped at the cage and looked back at her. "King Gregory assigns only his most trusted men to this post."

He bent over to unlatch the pigeon cage. Krystal lifted the rock she'd been holding and struck him on the back of the head. He turned back to her, a confused expression on his face. Horrified, she struck him again. He collapsed in a heap at her feet.

She found the cell easily enough. Inside, a young man with dirty blond hair and a short, scraggly beard rested against the wall. His eyes were closed as though he were sleeping. Krystal stared at him in astonishment. This was the face she'd seen in the crystal sphere all those weeks ago. This had to be Prince Jareth.

"Please," she said. "Please, wake up. We need to hurry."

His eyes flew open. He stared at her in astonishment as he slowly rose to his feet. "Are you a vision?" he asked in a hoarse voice. "Can this be real?"

"It's real enough," said Krystal. "And it will become even more real if we don't get out of here before the guard wakes up."

"Did you bring the key? The guard wears it on his belt."

"I'll be right back." Krystal ran back to where she'd left the guard and searched his belt for the key. She had to unhook the belt in order to get the key off and then ran back to the cell.

He still stared at her. "I can't believe you're really here."

Krystal put the key in the lock. "I suppose I should introduce myself."

"I know who you are."

She blushed and turned the key. The door creaked open. "We must go quickly. There isn't much time." She turned to leave the cave.

"I'm Jareth," he said as he fell in step behind her.

"I'd hoped you were, but even if you weren't I couldn't leave you in there."

"How did you find me? How did you get here?"

They reached the mouth of the cave, and Krystal led him around the rocks. "I don't think now is the time for questions. I'll explain after we get away."

White Lightning whinnied loudly when they approached. Krystal mounted first and then turned back and gave Jareth a hand up. Then she urged White Lightning to move.

"You'd better hold on to me," she said to the prince just before they took to the air.

He wrapped his arms around her waist. Krystal bit her lip as a warm shiver raced through her. White Lightning climbed into the sky, and Krystal directed her far away from the path in a large half circle that would keep them out of arrow range should they be spotted.

"I'd always imagined it would be like this," Jareth said. "I spent years dreaming of flying with this magnificent beast."

"She's a marvel, that's for sure," said Krystal.

"Where are you taking me?"

"I promise I'll explain later," Krystal said. "Right now please let me concentrate. I don't want to get us lost or shot."

"I'm sorry," said Jareth. "This is all just so unexpected."

"We'd have warned you if we could."

They'd gotten past the canyon, and Krystal turned the Pegasus back toward the forest. She saw the clearing shortly after that and looked for Miraya or Emelyn. Neither were visible. Krystal brought White Lightning down, and they landed gracefully on the grass.

Jareth let go of Krystal's waist and slid off the Pegasus. He lifted his arms to help her down. Krystal accepted his assistance. The moment he touched her, she felt warm all over. They stood for a moment staring at each other.

"I can't tell you how grateful I am." His voice still sounded rough from lack of use.

"It was Miraya's idea," Krystal said. "She said you're the only one who can stop your uncle."

"And I'm right." Miraya and Emelyn approached them. The maid sank into a deep curtsy before Jareth. "Highness, it is good to see you free."

He pulled her up and embraced her. "It is good to be free, my friend." Jareth released her and put his hands on her shoulders. "Tell me everything. Where are the people who have remained loyal to me?"

Miraya's face clouded with sadness. "I don't know. We haven't had contact in months."

"You did this on your own?" He looked at both of them in astonishment.

Krystal blushed. "It never would have been possible without White Lightning."

"As to that, I thought you were just going to look around," Miraya said to her.

"I made the mistake of flying directly over a camp of Gregory's guards," said Krystal. "I worried they'd give me away."

Miraya nodded. "But it was so dangerous. You could have turned back."

Krystal shook her head. "I didn't think we'd get another chance. And I'm sure by now they've realized he's gone. I suggest we move before we're caught."

Jareth looked at White Lightning. "There's no way she can carry us all."

"We'll go on foot," said Krystal.

Miraya took her daughter's hand. "But where do we go?"

"I have an idea," Jareth said. "My lieutenant and I spoke long ago about possible hideouts for him and his men. There's one not far from here. We can try there first."

Krystal looked at him. "And if we find no one there?"

He smiled grimly. "Then we keep looking."

Chapter 16

EMELYN HAD THE PLEASURE of riding White Lightning as the group walked through the forest. Miraya insisted the prince ride as well.

"Highness, you've nearly wasted away," Miraya said sternly. "We can't have you falling ill."

"She's right, you know," Krystal said.

Outnumbered, Jareth took his place on the Pegasus behind the little girl.

Darkness fell just as they reached their destination. Jareth looked around in the fading light and sighed. "They've been here, and recently too. But they must have had to move on."

"It's gotten too dark," said Krystal. "Let's make camp and try again in the morning."

Prince Jareth helped Krystal gather wood for a fire while Miraya and Emelyn foraged for food. He knelt to start the fire and glanced at Krystal.

"You might want to stand back," he said.

"Why?"

Just then, where his hand had been, a sturdy flame licked at the wood. Krystal couldn't help herself from jumping in surprise. He looked at her a bit sheepishly.

"I wasn't sure it would work," he said as he stood up.

Krystal looked from the growing fire to his face. "How did you do that?"

"I have a blood bond with the land. It's from my father's side. I haven't been able to access the magic for so long, so I didn't know if it would still work."

"Couldn't you use magic at the prison?"

Jareth shook his head. "My uncle put a spell on my cell to prevent me. He knew if I could call up that power I could escape."

Krystal frowned. "But doesn't Gregory have magic too? Where does he get it?"

"He has my father's amulet," Jareth said. "And my uncle has acquired potions and spells. With the amulet on, he is more powerful than I am without it." His hands clenched into fists.

Krystal could see how upset he'd become and turned the topic. "Isn't it a bit risky to start a fire?"

"The nights can get cold out in the open like this." His hands unclenched. "I thought we might be more comfortable once the chill sets in, since we have no blankets."

She sighed. "There are a lot of things I wish I could have brought with me."

"I'm not blaming you, Krystal. In fact I admire what you've done." Jareth smiled at her. "You can't know what a shock you gave me when you appeared at the door of my cell wearing my mother's dress. I was sure I'd started hallucinating."

"Your rescue wasn't well thought out either," she said. "Once the men at the camp spotted me on White Lightning, I knew I wouldn't get the chance to come back."

"You did it—that's what matters. I'm impressed."

Krystal smiled at him. "I'm learning quickly to be resourceful."

Miraya and Emelyn returned. Krystal noticed how tired her friend looked. They had to find shelter and decent food soon.

"I wish I'd found meat for that fire," she said as she sat down. "But Emelyn and I did find a strawberry patch. There's enough for us to eat our fill." She opened up the folds of her skirt to reveal a pile of strawberries.

Jareth held out his hand for one. "I don't remember what it feels like to eat my fill."

Miraya looked at him. "When you are king, I will cook you a feast every night."

He took her hand. "When I am king, you will never enter the kitchen again."

"King Gregory does as he pleases, which includes making servants of your friends." Miraya pulled away and offered a berry to Krystal. "He always will until you stop him."

Krystal accepted the strawberry. "Let's just hope you can."

Jareth sighed. "I'll have to, won't I?"

They fell silent as they ate. Once the berries had been devoured, each of them went to the nearby stream to get some fresh water. Krystal took White Lightning to the stream with her.

Miraya gathered some moss to make a bed for Emelyn. Jareth and Krystal sat by the fire while she soothed her daughter to sleep. Then she joined them.

"She is so tired," she said of her daughter. "But she doesn't want to miss anything."

"If we're lucky, there won't be anything to miss," Krystal said.

"We should be well protected here," said Jareth. "At least for one night."

"How long do you think it will take to find your men?" Miraya asked.

"I can't say. I hope we aren't far behind them. It all depends on how often they've had to move. I want to find them tomorrow. We need weapons to hunt. If I only had a dagger, I could carve a spear to use, but as it is, I couldn't even catch us a rabbit."

"You need meat more than we do," said Miraya. "They nearly starved you to death."

"Mama!"

Miraya's head turned. "I guess she wasn't as settled as I thought. Excuse me, please."

Krystal watched her fade into the darkness beyond the fire. "We're probably making too much noise," she said and moved closer to Jareth.

He nodded. "Krystal, there's something I need to say to you. I can't wait any longer."

She looked at him. "Is this about your uncle thinking you are in love with me?"

The prince's eyes grew wide. "He said that to you?"

"He said it the day I met him."

"I won't deny I have feelings for you. But I wanted to say something else."

Krystal blushed and ducked her head. "Oh."

"Can you ever forgive me?"

"Forgive you? For what?"

"If it wasn't for me and my crystal sphere, my uncle wouldn't even know you exist," Jareth said. "It's my fault you're here. I can't tell you how sorry I am for that."

"Gregory chose to do this," she said. "You aren't responsible for what he does."

"You have a good heart. It's one of the many things I admire about you."

She looked away. "You don't even know me."

Jareth touched her arm. Again, she felt that shocking heat his touch had caused before. Krystal turned back to him. For a moment, the intense color of his eyes in the firelight made her forget what they'd been talking about.

"I'm sorry I spied on you," he said. "In my defense, I was a young, lonely boy who had just lost his parents. But I'm not trying to make excuses." He pulled back his hand. "*You* are what kept me coming back. I marveled that even with all the responsibilities your family heaped on your shoulders, you still had your own hopes and dreams. Your courage impressed me. It inspired me to be more than just an annoyance to my uncle."

"You must have not seen everything through the magic sphere, could you?" asked Krystal. "You missed me buckling under the pressure of being the woman of the house at such a tender age. You missed all the times I broke down in tears of desperation and hopelessness."

"I didn't miss all those times," he said. "And I wished I could be there for you. It seemed to me you needed a friend's shoulder." He moved closer to her, an intent look on his face. "But you got up every morning. You did what was asked of you and more. That took great courage."

"What about you? I never could have survived all you've been through."

"I had no choice but to survive," Jareth said. "I have a responsibility to my people, not to mention the responsibility I have to generations of Lochnikars who have come before me."

Krystal smiled and looked at her hands. "I used to believe one king was the same as another. None of the kings of Brynne ever changed how my family lived. But now I understand how much difference one man can make."

"I wish you were back on your farm," Jareth said. "I wish you could get away from all of this."

"I can't go home now," said Krystal. "Gregory would come after me."

"I still don't really understand all that happened," he said. "You said my uncle brought you here. How did you get away? I can't imagine he let you go."

Krystal looked up at him again, unsure of what to reveal. "Your uncle had men kidnap me and bring me to Fayterra. They used some sort of artifact to teleport us, an experience I hope never to repeat. Damen managed to get through as well. I don't know where he is, but I'm sure he's looking for me by now."

"He's a bright animal," said Jareth. "I remember. What happened next?"

She told him all she dared about her time at the castle and Gregory's attentions. Jareth spoke up again when she mentioned the tower room and their escape.

"I know the passage," said the prince. "I'm surprised he hadn't found it first. He started sealing secret tunnels in and out of the castle as soon as he took power."

She nodded agreement. "Why does he go to so much trouble?"

"I think he doesn't want anyone to sneak up on him. Gregory hates the unexpected."

Krystal sniffed. "Doesn't everyone? I know I haven't had any good surprises."

"What about your brothers? Has Gregory mentioned them?"

"No," she said. "If they're even looking for me, I don't see how they could find me. From what I saw of the map, my home could be weeks away by horse."

"It's no easy journey," he agreed. "So what do you want to do now?

You say you can't go home. Are you planning to join the rebellion?"

She smiled at him. "I'm sure helping you escape is an adequate indication of my sympathies."

Jareth smiled back. "We'll be glad to have you. I know I would like having you near."

Krystal moved away slightly. "I don't know you. I'm not sure what you might expect of me, but I don't know what I'm able to give."

"I'd be satisfied with your friendship," he said. "Do you think that would be possible? Do you think we can be friends?"

Unlike his uncle, Prince Jareth radiated sincerity. "Yes," she said. "I'd like that."

Krystal turned to stare at the flames. He'd been right about the night growing cool. She could feel her back chilling, especially when the wind brushed by. Krystal thought again of how ill-prepared they were, but how could she have planned any better than she did?

Prince Jareth cleared his throat. "You should get some sleep. Tomorrow is sure to be another long day."

Krystal nodded. "What about you?"

"I'll keep watch. There is no way to know for sure how close my uncle's men may be."

"You can't stay up all night," she protested. "You need rest as well, if not more than I do. I didn't spend the last months in a dank prison cell, and you didn't spend them in the comfort of a castle bed."

"I got used to staying up nights," he said.

Krystal shook her head. "That's no reason to assume the responsibility to watch over us. At least let me take first watch. I'm not tired anyway. I'll wake you in a few hours."

"I'm not sure I believe you would. You'd stay up all night just so I could sleep."

Krystal smiled at him. "And how do I know you aren't planning to do that?"

He laughed. "What a pair we make. We can't even trust each other."

"It's a difficult problem," said Krystal.

"It's not practical either," he said. "It would be a waste of resources for both of us to stay up all night."

Krystal felt slight disappointment. She enjoyed talking to him. She rose to her feet. "Wake me when it's my turn."

"Of course. Good night, Krystal."

⁓

She awoke suddenly in the dead of night and lay still, listening. Her eyes could not focus past the fire but she felt a presence. She sat up.

Jareth had positioned himself against the log, his back to the fire. She couldn't see his face, but his chin appeared to be resting on his chest like he had fallen asleep. Then she saw a dark figure approaching the prince. As the figure drew closer, the firelight glinted across the steel of a sword. The man stopped in front of Jareth and leveled his blade at the young man's chest.

"You'd think a prince of the realm would know better than to light a camp fire in the middle of enemy territory," the stranger said. "Didn't your tutors teach you anything?"

Krystal's blood turned cold. She pulled her feet under her in a crouch and stealthily crept around the fire toward the stranger, hugging the darkness lest she be seen.

Jareth still hadn't moved or shown any indication of danger.

"Get up," the voice taunted. "Face your opponent."

Suddenly Jareth's leg swept under the man's feet, and the stranger tumbled to the ground. The prince leaned over him and pinned his arms to the ground. "I studied battle maps at my father's knee before I could walk. And I know my enemy when I see him."

Krystal stood up with relief. She intended to remove the sword from the man's hand when suddenly the stranger started to laugh. She froze in her tracks.

Jareth laughed and released his captive. "You have no idea how glad I am you found us."

The stranger sat up. "It is I who should be relieved. But how did you know it was me?"

"I established a magical perimeter," said the prince.

"I should have known better. Tell me, what has happened?"

Jareth stood and turned to Krystal. Though he had given no indication, he seemed to know she was there. She stepped into the firelight and faced the newcomer.

His eyes grew wide as he looked at her. He was nearly as tall as Jareth but had dark hair and was dressed all in black. She thought he might be slightly older than the prince as well, though he certainly looked young and fit.

"I never would have believed it." He turned to Jareth. "How?"

"My uncle wanted a new person to torment," he said.

The stranger turned back to Krystal and bowed low. "Allow me to introduce myself. I am Sir Calum Landen, knight and humble subject of Prince Jareth."

Jareth laughed. "Humble indeed. Calum has been my friend since we were boys in the castle. He has been coordinating the rebellion among my people."

Calum smiled. "King Gregory never would have believed I would be faithful to him. I had no place in the castle once he took control."

"If you're the leader of the rebels, what are you doing out alone at night?" Krystal asked.

"I never ask my men to do something I'm not willing to do myself," said Calum. "Occasionally I like to prove that to them. Besides, I wanted the exercise."

Krystal thought Calum's smile could charm the bark off trees. "Why come back here?"

"I like to keep the king guessing, so sometimes we return to one of our previous camps."

"I knew I had left my people in good hands," Jareth said.

"And now you've returned," said Calum. "But how did you escape your prison?"

Jareth would have replied had not a cry from behind made him turn around. Miraya flew past Jareth and Krystal and threw herself into Calum's arms. He embraced her, burying his face in her hair. Krystal looked at Jareth in confusion.

"Calum is Miraya's husband and Emelyn's father."

Krystal nodded with a smile. Miraya lifted her head to look at her husband's face.

"I had begun to wonder if I'd ever see you again."

"I never thought you'd get away," said the knight. "What miracle brought you to me?"

"I'll explain later." Miraya took his hand. "First, you must come see our daughter."

Calum brightened even more. "Emy is here?"

Jareth watched them walk away. "It appears we've ceased to exist."

"I don't mind," Krystal said. "It's good to see some happiness."

He nodded. "I'm sorry we woke you. You can go back to sleep if you wish."

Krystal smiled at him. "I'll do my best." She actually didn't have as difficult a time reclaiming sleep as she'd thought.

Chapter 17

THE FIRST THING KRYSTAL NOTICED was the delicious smell of cooking meat. Her stomach rumbled as she sat up. She arose and joined Calum at the fire where he sat tending the meat.

"Good morning," she said as she sat down. "That smells wonderful."

"I did some hunting earlier." He handed her a piece of meat.

"Thank you."

Calum grew somber. "I should thank you. You rescued my wife and daughter and then delivered Jareth from his prison. I owe you a debt I could never repay."

Krystal felt a hot blush creeping across her cheeks. "I didn't do it alone. Miraya helped me find Jareth's prison, and without Emelyn, we'd still be stuck in the castle."

He smiled. "Nonetheless, I'm convinced your coming to Fayterra has turned the course of this war in our favor."

"It wasn't my choice to come here," Krystal admitted. "Gregory kidnapped me. Since then, I've only done what I felt I should do."

"You are a rare woman, Krystal," said Calum. "You have my loyalty forever."

Krystal's blush deepened. She wiped her hands and stood up. "Are we leaving soon?"

"After everyone eats," Calum said. "Jareth should be back soon."

"Where did he go?"

The prince entered the clearing. Krystal stifled a gasp of surprise.

Jareth had bathed and wore a clean set of clothes. He'd even shaved. He looked almost too handsome to be real.

Her knees gave way, and Krystal sank back down on the log. She felt Calum's glance, but she couldn't take her eyes off the prince. She knew she must look like a fool and managed to close her gaping mouth.

Calum chuckled. "I had a spare change of clothes in my saddle-bags. The prince didn't look as though he'd seen clean clothes in months. I'd say he looks much better, wouldn't you?"

She managed a nod before Jareth reached them. "I could smell breakfast through the trees," he said. "Did you leave me any?"

"There's plenty to go around," said Calum. "I caught a rabbit coming out of its hole." Miraya and Emelyn came up from behind. Emelyn rushed to her father and put her arms around his neck. Calum took her in his arms and gave her a firm hug. "Good morning, my princess."

Emelyn giggled. "Krystal is the princess, Father."

Calum looked up at Krystal. "What's this?"

"King Gregory gave her a title," Miraya said. "She is the Princess of Avolonya."

Krystal found her voice. "It doesn't matter. I refused the title."

"Knowing my uncle, that wouldn't matter to him," said Jareth. "I'm sure he made it official without your assistance."

Krystal snorted. "It's nonsense," she said. "Let's talk about something else."

Emelyn bounded out of Calum's lap and sat next to him. Miraya sat at his other side. Calum passed around the rest of the rabbit. Krystal noticed with approval the large portion he offered to Jareth.

After they'd eaten, Calum put out the fire, and Krystal went to the stream to find White Lightning. The Pegasus stood almost where she'd left her. Krystal made sure to praise her well for being so obedient. The others joined her there, Calum leading a bay gelding by the reins.

He volunteered to have his wife and daughter ride with him, which left Krystal and Jareth riding White Lightning together. Jareth mounted first and gave her a hand up.

"He isn't fooling me in the least," the prince said with a nod toward Calum. "He just wants to spend some time with the women in his life."

"Wouldn't you?" Krystal smiled. "They've been separated for so long."

Jareth turned to her, gratitude in his eyes. "I forgot how it felt to be among friends."

"You never deserved imprisonment," she said.

"What I don't understand is why Gregory has brought you to Fayterra. Why now? It doesn't make any sense."

Krystal bit her lip. She thought of Gregory's vows of affection and his demand that she marry him. She knew she should probably share that information with Jareth and Calum, but she hesitated. It sounded ridiculous. *The king has vowed to marry me, a peasant nobody.* She kept silent.

They rode for the better part of the day. Emelyn began to complain of hunger, but her father promised her there would be food once they got to the camp. Krystal thought the little girl had been awfully brave and wished she had something to give her as a reward. But she didn't even see so much as an apple tree on their path.

"We're nearly there," Calum said at last.

He stopped his horse and put up his hand for Jareth to stop as well. Krystal looked around but could only see trees. She opened her mouth to ask what they were doing when an arrow flew from the trees and landed in front of Calum's horse.

Calum explained. "We post guards around the camp as an advance warning."

Jareth nodded. Calum turned back and called, "Show yourselves. It is I, Calum, and I have brought guests."

White Lightning grew nervous as men dropped from the trees around them. Almost immediately they started to whisper among themselves. Krystal didn't know if they whispered about the prince or the Pegasus. She waited to see what would happen next.

One of the men approached Calum. "We're glad to see you return safely. All is well."

"Good," said Calum. "Send someone ahead to have food ready. We're starved. Oh, and Robert, you may want to bow to your prince."

Robert the guard looked around. He gazed wide eyed at Jareth a moment. "Mercy, it *is* him! He's finally come to lead us."

Calum smiled. "Let us all celebrate the arrival of Prince Jareth and his brave rescuers."

The men all looked at Krystal, Miraya, and Emelyn—all three tired, dirty, and hungry. Krystal could feel herself blush deeply. Now, she imagined, they would all speculate on how two women and a child rescued their prince. Rumors would run rampant.

They rode still another half hour before reaching the rebel camp. As they rode she saw most of the shelters and structures were intended to be temporary. The camp could be cleared and deserted in a matter of minutes. She shook her head. No one should have to live like that.

Krystal had not expected there to be so many rebels. She saw mostly men, but there were some women and a few children as well. All of them stopped to watch the prince ride past. A small crowd had gathered by the time Calum stopped and dismounted.

Krystal slid off White Lightning's back first and walked over where Calum helped Miraya and Emelyn dismount. She stood with her friend while the prince faced his people.

Someone started to cheer, and everyone else followed suit. Jareth smiled at the crowd and gave them a halting wave. Krystal thought the attention might have embarrassed him.

Calum put up his hands. "We will celebrate the prince's return at dinner. For now, though, he is hungry and tired. Go about your business, but do so with new purpose. Soon we will put an end to King Gregory's tyranny."

Another cheer followed them as Calum led them away. Krystal could smell the food as they drew nearer, and her stomach reacted. The abundance of food at the castle had spoiled her.

"Miraya!" A woman ran forward and hugged Calum's wife. "I can't believe it's you."

"Laura!" Miraya returned the embrace. She turned to Krystal. "Krystal, this is my good friend. We've been apart for a long time."

Laura curtsied to Krystal. "I'm pleased to meet you." Then she turned to address them both. "When you're finished eating, I'll take you to get cleaned up. I'm sure you'll be glad to shed the dirt and leaves for some clean clothes."

Krystal looked down. Jareth's mother's gown had not fared well in the woods. It was now hopelessly stained and dirty. She regretted the loss of such a fine dress.

Jareth had stopped and now appeared at her side. "Aren't you hungry?"

"I just noticed how dirty I've gotten. Your mother's dress is ruined."

"It served a noble purpose," he said and put his arm around her waist. "Don't worry about it. Let's get some decent food in our bellies."

She allowed him to guide her into the tent. A few people sat around logs that had been brought in to serve as seats. A series of small pots simmered on low fires. Krystal guessed they used small pots rather than large ones because they'd be easier to carry.

"It's delicious," said Krystal as they ate. "How can rebels in hiding eat so well?"

Calum laughed. "We have help from villagers and farmers, and we have good hunters and skilled foragers. I think half of what's in this stew is from the forest. But I do miss fresh bread."

The prince closed his eyes. "I used to sneak down to the kitchens just to smell it baking."

Miraya nodded. "The smell will be even sweeter when you're in power again."

Jareth nodded in acknowledgment, but Krystal noticed he tensed when Miraya mentioned his regaining power. Did Jareth doubt himself? Did he doubt the strength of the rebels?

Miraya touched her shoulder. "Are you finished?"

Krystal looked down at her empty bowl. "Yes. Are you ready to get cleaned up?"

Miraya smiled. "More than ready." She lifted Emelyn and stood up.

Krystal stood and looked at Jareth. He remained deeply absorbed in conversation with Calum. She followed Miraya and Laura from the tent.

❧

The camp had been organized well. Everyone had an assignment, and Krystal was no exception. Men trained for battle and took turns standing watch or served as lookouts. Women cooked, washed, and mended. Three women watched the children while the others worked.

Jareth found Krystal washing clothes one day. She'd just hung up someone's shirt to dry when she heard him call her name. Krystal turned, her breath catching in her throat when she saw him. He looked more handsome than ever. She smiled as he approached. When he returned her smile, her heart did a little flip, Krystal frowned at her involuntary reaction.

"Are you all right?" Jareth asked, concerned.

Krystal recovered herself, smiling again. "Yes. How are you?"

"I'm fine."

The prince stared into her eyes a bit longer than necessary. He looked away quickly and cleared his throat. "You've been working hard."

Krystal smiled. "Are you just here to check up on me?"

"Not exactly. Actually, we have a problem, and I thought you could help."

"What is it?"

"I think my men have found Damen."

Krystal grew excited. "Are you sure? Where is he?"

He smiled. "Well, it's actually rather complicated. Some of our lookouts have been treed by what they call a large black dog. He won't let them down. They can only shout to some of our other lookouts about the problem."

"Take me to him, please."

"Follow me." He led her out of camp. "It's not far."

Krystal paused, put her fingers to her lips, and let out an earsplitting whistle. She looked at Jareth and blushed. "I know it's not ladylike, but it's effective. Damen probably heard it too."

"I'm impressed," he said and smiled. "I'm not sure I can do that."

She returned his smile and they walked on. Krystal hadn't gone ten steps when Damen stepped out of the trees before her. She gave a glad cry and ran to him, burying her face in his fur.

Her hand found wetness on his shoulder and her head came up instantly. "He's bleeding."

Jareth had not moved closer. "Is it bad?"

"I don't think so." Krystal examined it closer. "It looks like a scratch."

"That's my fault," said a voice behind Damen. She looked up at Robert. "We didn't know he was your pet at first, my lady, and when he attacked, we tried to defend ourselves."

Krystal wanted to be angry but she understood. "It's not important. He'll be fine."

Jareth took a step forward but stopped when Damen snapped at him. "He's not going to eat me, is he?"

Krystal smiled at him. "My brother Douglas always asked that. And no, I don't think Damen will eat you. He may take a bite or two, but no more."

The prince sighed. "Somehow that doesn't reassure me."

Krystal laughed. "Damen, come meet Jareth. I think you'll like him. He's a friend."

She didn't know who took more coaxing, the dog or the man, but at last Damen let Jareth stroke and pat his head. Jareth knelt in front of the dog, a true show of bravery in Krystal's estimation, and told him what a strong and handsome animal he was. After a moment, Jareth excused himself to speak to the men who had climbed from the trees.

She took Damen back to camp and cleaned his wound. It didn't need bandaging, so she took the opportunity to check the rest of his body over. She hadn't forgotten his dealings with Bennett, his men, and the rest of Gregory's guards.

Fortunately, he seemed none the worse for wear. Damen followed her as she went about her business in the camp and effectively scared away some of the children who had crowded around White Lightning. Krystal had become increasingly concerned about the Pegasus. Not only had she become a curiosity to the children, but some of the adults from the camp had started trying to pull out her wing feathers for luck. She resolved to speak to Jareth about the problem.

☙

Jareth found her at breakfast. "Good morning." He dropped to his knees beside her. "I wanted to ask you something."

His playful tone made her suspicious. "What is it?"

Jareth pulled a set of clothes from behind his back. "Would you like to spar with me?"

Krystal looked at the clothes. "Really?"

He shrugged. "It's the best way to improve your skill."

"I'll go change." Krystal took the clothes and hurried back to her tent. The pants fit her loosely and the tunic hung nearly to her knees, so she didn't worry that anyone would think her too scandalous. She pulled on her short, serviceable boots and returned to the prince's side.

Jareth smiled his approval. "You should have more freedom in those than in your skirt."

Krystal fairly beamed. "Thank you for this. What now?"

"I like to go for a run first," he said. "Would you care to join me?"

"Let's go."

Krystal followed the prince away from camp where he set a steady pace along a forest path. She kept up with him easily until he surprised her with the first short sprint. Once she got the idea, she was able to keep pace with him when he sprinted short distances.

Jareth stopped at a rose bush and smiled at her. She watched as he waved his hand slowly over a rosebud until it started to open. He coaxed the flower into full bloom and gestured to her. Krystal ran a finger along the soft petals and smiled at him.

"Is this more magic?" she asked.

He nodded. "Plants don't respond easily, but I've been working at this. So much of my power lay dormant during my imprisonment it feels good to exercise it, just like I exercise my body." Jareth took her hand. "It would be a shame to pluck the flower and bring it to you after it's done such work for me, so I wanted to bring you here."

"It's lovely." Krystal didn't pull her hand away.

"Should we head back? I want to spend some time on the field before it gets too busy."

She nodded. "I'd like to have as few witnesses as possible."

Jareth laughed. "I didn't mean it that way. You'll be fine."

Back at the practice field, Jareth handed her a dipper of water to drink and then a short sword. "Let's see what you can do."

"I haven't held a sword in ages—not since Bennett and his men took me," she said. "And even before then, I never had much training."

"You practiced the moves your brothers were taught more than they did," he said. "I know you worked late into the night when you wouldn't be disturbed."

"I'm still no expert."

He smiled. "I'm not asking you to be. Just attack me."

Krystal raised her sword. Jareth blocked her.

"That was good," he said. "Now try it without looking where you are going to slice."

She cocked her head. "You want me to attack you without looking?"

"I just want you to not show me with your eyes where you're going to aim. You need to keep your opponent guessing."

She tried again. "How was that?"

"Better," he said. "Now I'm going to attack you. Block me."

Easier said than done, Krystal thought as she brought her sword up to stop his swing. Her arm vibrated from the force of his blow. He brought the sword up again, and she watched, expecting the attack on the right, but he changed direction at the last moment, and she almost didn't deflect the blow.

Jareth pulled back. "Are you all right?"

"Yes." Krystal glanced to where some of the men stood watching them. She stepped closer to Jareth. "Are you sure you want to do this? We're drawing an audience."

He looked over. "Don't mind them. They're laughing at me anyway. I've been wasting away in that prison so long to some of them I'm like a tall Emelyn—no force behind my swing."

Krystal rubbed her upper arm. "I felt force enough."

He smiled. "We can build up our strength and practice our swings together. But if you'd rather do something else, I understand."

For the briefest moment, Krystal weighed sword fighting against laundry. The sword won. "I'm not going anywhere."

Jareth grinned at her and brought up his sword. "Have at me."

By the time Jareth called a halt to their practice for lunch, some of their spectators had stopped laughing at them. Krystal looked at him, grinning. She hadn't felt so good in months—since even before leaving home. She told him so.

"It worked out," he said. "I had wanted to point out to you that being unarmed doesn't mean you're helpless. I should have known you'd know that already."

Krystal shivered as Gregory flashed across her mind. "I'd feel better knowing I could defend myself even without weapons."

"I meant to ask, how is White Lightning handling the camp?"

Krystal sighed. "All these people make her nervous. The children keep coming around, and now the adults think her feathers are magic. I wish I had another place for her."

"Calum and I were just talking about the need to move the camp. If you're willing, you and I could take White Lightning to a safe place. Then we can meet up with the group at the new camp site."

"Is the king close to finding us?"

"His patrols are getting nearer," said Jareth. "If we don't move in the next day or two, his men will stumble upon our lookouts, which would give away our position."

"I don't understand."

"The forest is a great place to hide, if you know what you're doing. But it's much harder to hide such a large group of people. The reason the lookouts are positioned so far from camp is so they give as much warning as possible."

"What about this place for White Lightning? Why can't we hide the camp there?"

"It's not a practical hiding place for so many," he said. "But it will be perfect for the Pegasus. I'll speak to Calum, and we can leave first thing in the morning. Will that be all right?"

Krystal nodded.

℘

That night, Krystal set up a small camp near her Pegasus with Damen as company. After lighting a fire, she sat stroking Damen's fur.

"Do you mind if we join you?" Jareth's voice jarred her.

"Of course not." Krystal welcomed the prince, Miraya, and Calum.

"I wondered where you'd gone," Miraya said as she sat next to her.

"I just want to watch over White Lightning," said Krystal.

Jareth sat next to her, his friend on his other side. "Do you mind if I ask you some questions about your time in the castle?"

Krystal shrugged. "I don't think there's much I can tell you."

Jareth frowned. "Did my uncle treat you badly?"

She looked at him. "King Gregory had me kidnapped, but then he made me a princess and dressed me in finery. I couldn't make sense of it."

"I wish you could have seen the way he treated her," Miraya said. "I don't think he understood why she resisted his overtures of kindness."

"He brought you here for a reason," said Jareth. "I just wish we knew what that could be."

Calum spoke up. "That's obvious." He looked at Krystal. "He's made you a marriage offer, hasn't he?"

Chapter 18

"I WOULDN'T CALL IT AN OFFER so much as a demand." Krystal looked from Calum and Jareth and then lowered her eyes. She heard Miraya's gasp and continued. "He told me he would marry me the day before the coronation."

No one spoke for a long time. Krystal could not bear the silence and looked up at Jareth's face. He seemed to be waiting for her to do so and caught her gaze effortlessly with his eyes.

"I hadn't wanted to entertain that possibility." He smiled grimly. "I didn't want to believe he would see you in that way." He reached across the darkness and took Krystal's hand. "If it hadn't been for me, none of this would have happened to you."

She pulled her hand away. "I've told you before, you have no reason to apologize," she said. "You couldn't have known what your uncle would do. It's not your fault I'm here."

"I wish you had said something," he said. "What we've heard makes more sense now. My uncle is planning a wedding and has misplaced the bride."

"Not to mention his favorite prisoner is missing," said Calum. "No wonder he's frantic."

"Do we know for certain that he knows Jareth has escaped?" asked Miraya.

"One of the guards must have ridden to the castle to tell him," Jareth said.

The mention of guards brought Voltimande to Krystal's mind.

She had avoided asking about him, hoping she'd see him at the camp. But as the days passed, that hope quickly faded. She had to know if they had seen him.

She looked at Calum. "I've wanted to ask you about a guard from the castle."

To her surprise, he smiled at her. "Do you mean Voltimande?"

"How did you know?"

"I spoke with him the night my men found him. I thought it best that he spend some time away, so I sent him on a mission."

"What happened to him?" Jareth leaned into the light. "Why would he be on the run?"

Krystal did not want to discuss what had happened the night Voltimande came to her rescue. She looked to Miraya in a silent plea for help. Her friend nodded understanding.

"You know your uncle," Miraya said to the prince. "He was in a rage when he discovered Voltimande's true loyalties." She turned to Calum. "Where did you send him?"

"That's not important," said her husband. "He's out of Fayterra for a couple of weeks. That should be long enough for the king to find someone else to torment."

Krystal got the impression Calum was not telling them the whole truth. She didn't press him, though, for fear her own secret would also come out. "I think it's time to get some sleep." I'm sure we all have a long day tomorrow."

The knight smiled at her. "You have the easy part. We have to relocate an entire camp."

Krystal smiled back. She liked Calum's easy manner. "I don't envy you."

Jareth cleared his throat and stood. "I'd like to leave just after breakfast."

She nodded. "Of course. Good night, Prince Jareth."

Miraya took her hands and squeezed them. "Be safe."

"You too," Krystal called after them. She settled down to sleep, her back to Damen's. She thought of Jareth before falling asleep. Had she imagined it, or had his demeanor changed when she asked Calum about Voltimande?

Jareth found Krystal after breakfast the next morning. He held the reins to a handsome brown stallion, packed and ready. She looked up at him and smiled.

For a moment, his eyes bore into hers, and he reminded her of Gregory. But then he smiled, though it didn't quite reach his eyes. "Are you ready?"

"I just have to get my packs." She led the way to where her packs and White Lightning waited. She didn't have much by way of possessions, just the other set of clothes she had and a few personal items she'd collected while at the camp.

"Miraya packed food for us," he said as he helped her secure her things to his saddle.

"That was thoughtful of her," Krystal said, mounting White Lightning. There had been no need to whistle for Damen—he hadn't let her out of his sight all morning.

The prince mounted his horse. "We'll be able to move faster since we won't have to hunt. It will already slow us down to have only one horse for the trip back. I tried to get two, but Calum didn't have another to spare."

"Then we'll make do," she said. "Shall we go?"

"Follow me."

They made a strange procession—Jareth on a horse, followed by Krystal riding a Pegasus, and her large black dog bringing up the rear.

The prince seemed quite opposed to conversation, so Krystal spent much of the ride brooding at his back. At first she tried to justify his rudeness, but somehow his silence felt personal.

By the time he stopped his horse and dismounted, she'd worked herself into quite a state. What right did he have to be upset with her? Had she not been completely understanding and cooperative? It took all she had not to glare at him when he turned to her.

"I thought we could take a break," he said. "I know it isn't easy riding bareback."

Krystal slid from White Lightning's back before he could help her. "All right." She instructed her pets to wait and walked alone into the trees.

The prince had dug some food from his packs when she returned.

He handed her an apple and a chunk of dried pork. She took them without speaking and sat on the ground near a tree.

"We should be there by sunset," Jareth said.

Krystal nodded. She picked at the meat, feeding bits of it to Damen, not really hungry. Jareth seemed to be in the same state, at least from what Krystal could tell.

At last Jareth stood up and put his mostly uneaten lunch back in the pack. His boots came to rest in front of her, and she looked up. The sun shone on his back, casting his face in shadow.

"I have something to confess to you," he said.

"What is it?"

Jareth knelt to her eye level. "I asked Calum to tell me why Voltimande left the castle. He told me everything Voltimande told him about that night."

"And you're angry with me?" she asked. "Because it's my fault he was discovered?"

Jareth's eyes widened in surprise. "Nothing that happened that night was your fault. I'm furious with my uncle, though, and also with myself."

"Why are you angry with yourself?"

"I never dreamed watching you through the crystal sphere would in any way put you in danger," he said. "It's *my* fault. All of this is my fault."

Krystal lost her temper. "Stop blaming yourself for what your uncle does! You can't control him. From what I've seen, no one can. Stop playing the martyr, Jareth! Stop dwelling on what's happened and start figuring out what you're going to do about it."

She regretted her outburst almost instantly. He rocked back on his heels almost like she'd struck him. He said nothing for several heartbeats and just looked at her.

"I'm sorry," she said. "I shouldn't have said that."

"Yes, you should have." His sideways grin charmed her. "And you're right. I take myself too seriously sometimes. But I would do anything to keep you from harm. I'm having a hard time coming to grips with the fact that so much happened to you when I knew nothing about it."

"It isn't your duty to look after me," said Krystal. "No reasonable person can hold you responsible for anything I've been through. And I'm tired of having this conversation."

He took her hands. "I'll stop dwelling on it, but I can't forget about it. What happened to you is proof that I have to take my kingdom back. He's hurting people, and he's using my crown to do it."

"So why are we just sitting around here?" Krystal stood up. "The sooner we get White Lightning to safety, the sooner we can get back to your people. You have a great deal to do."

The prince stood also. "You're right, of course. But I wanted to apologize for being short with you earlier. I was never angry with you."

"I understand."

They continued on their way. Around sunset, just as he'd promised, Jareth stopped at a cave and dismounted. They'd ridden all the way to the base of a mountain.

"Is this it?"

Jareth smiled at her. "It doesn't look like much but trust me. I know you'll approve once you see it."

"I'm not seeing it now?"

"Wait here a moment." He disappeared into the cave.

Krystal dismounted and looked around. She felt exposed but not worried. Damen would alert her if anyone approached. Still, she watched the tree line while she waited for Jareth to return.

The prince didn't take long. Carrying a lit torch in one hand, he took hold of his horse's reins in the other. "Let's go."

Krystal led White Lightning and followed him. Damen brought up the rear. The cave opened up several feet inside.

"Where are we going?"

"It's just a little farther," he said.

When he stopped in front of a solid wall, Krystal wanted to snort in disbelief. *He must be lost,* Krystal thought. *And once we retrace our path back outside it will have gotten dark.* Jareth didn't appear at all concerned. He let go of the reins and ran his free hand over the wall in front of him.

"Here it is," Jareth said. "You might want to hold her." He stepped away from the wall and took his horse's reins.

Before Krystal could ask why, the cavern walls began to rumble and shake, causing bits of dust to fill the air. White Lightning tried to rear up, but Krystal forced her head down and held it. She looked at Jareth, who was trying to calm his horse, and did her best to believe the mountain wasn't coming down on top of them.

The dust cleared and Krystal gasped. Solid rock had opened, and light spilled out on them. She looked at Jareth, who smiled apologetically at her.

"I'm sorry," he said. "I would have warned you if I thought it would be so loud."

Krystal pulled her wits together. "What is this place?"

"It's a secret cavern inside the mountain," Jareth said. "My father discovered it years ago, and with a little magic and a lot of hard work, he created a haven for my mother. He meant it as a place we could go for safety, but when we needed it most, we couldn't get here. Now I'm the only one living who remembers it."

He pulled his horse through the opening, and Krystal followed him, leading White Lightning and Damen walking at her heels. She stopped almost immediately and gaped wide-eyed at their surroundings. The prince's secret cavern looked more like a private paradise. Its expanse sported all possible shades of green. Down the center ran a small stream that ended with a waterfall and a clear pond. Fading sunlight streamed from openings in the mountain far above their heads.

"It had to have taken more than a little magic to create this," she said.

Jareth shook his head. "Magic must have balance. If he'd tried to make this place using only magic, it would have created some kind of void somewhere else. A forest would have turned to desert, or a mountain would have collapsed in on itself, something like that." He smiled at her. "Besides, all the work he put into it made my mother appreciate his effort even more."

"But why not bring your rebels here? Surely they would be safe in this place."

"Don't think I haven't thought of it." Jareth looked around and sighed. "But it's really too small with too limited resources to sustain so many people for a long time. We'd constantly be going in and out for supplies and food, and that activity would draw attention."

He shook his head with regret. "I admit that there's a more personal reason I don't share this place. Coming here reminds me of my parents during happy times. I don't want that memory cheapened."

Krystal put her arm through his. "Back home I had my father's ring. When I held it, I could remember him wearing it. I could almost hear his voice. It's precious to me."

He looked down into her eyes. "I forget sometimes that you have a similar pain. It's one of the things that makes you so easy to talk to. That and your eyes, of course."

She smiled. "My eyes?"

Jareth nodded. "When you look at me with those luminous blue pools, so trusting and open, I find myself wanting to confess every deep desire of my heart. You've a dangerous weapon in those eyes, Krystal."

She blushed and looked away. "You're flattering me."

With his hand on her cheek, he gently turned her back. "I'm telling you the truth."

Krystal put her hand on his, intending to move it away, but when they touched, her heart leapt to her throat. "And tell me, Prince Jareth, how many poor girls have you enslaved with your eyes? I swear, a girl can't look into yours without wanting to hand over her heart."

The prince leaned in. "Be careful or you may give me hope."

She closed her eyes, thinking he would kiss her and that she would let him.

Chapter 19

DAMEN BARKED AND KRYSTAL JUMPED, her eyes flying open. She pulled away from Jareth and turned to her dog. He stood at her feet expectantly. She flushed. Part of her wanted to scold him, and part of her wanted to praise him.

She took a breath, hoping to steady her voice and her heart. "Should we turn the animals loose? I'm sure Damen is anxious to explore."

She heard the prince's sigh. "I'll set up camp."

Krystal's heart still raced, and she took another calming breath. She could hardly stand around and let him do all the work, but she wanted to avoid getting too near him.

Jareth had made a good start on the camp, so Krystal opened up the food pack to figure out what they could have for dinner. Miraya had been most thoughtful. She had packed food that needed no cooking. But as the light faded, Krystal thought they might want a fire anyway.

"Should we light a fire?" she asked. "It will be very dark without one."

Jareth agreed. "And it might get cold. This cavern doesn't get much direct sun."

"I'll go collect some wood." She walked away before he could say anything.

Krystal couldn't get over the beauty of the cavern paradise. White Lightning flew unhindered overhead. Damen joined Krystal and together they gathered firewood and returned to the campsite.

Jareth volunteered to start the fire with magic since it would be faster. Krystal divided up their dinner and started eating as she looked around at the campsite. The prince had thoughtfully provided her privacy for sleeping by draping a blanket over a tree limb and arranging her bedding under it.

Krystal couldn't bear the silence any longer. "Will the new rebel camp be far?"

Jareth looked at her. "We'll go in a different direction. From this point, we can reach almost any part of the forest within a day." He smiled. "If luck is on our side, we'll enjoy dinner with Calum and Miraya tomorrow."

She nodded.

"Now I'd like to ask you a question," Jareth said.

"What is it?"

"Have you thought of leaving Damen here along with White Lightning?"

Krystal smiled. "I have considered it. I want them to be safe."

Jareth took a long breath. "Have you considered staying with them?"

"I'd just be exchanging one prison for another," said Krystal.

"You'd be removed from the fighting, and I'd hardly call this a prison. You'd be able to come and go as you please. I wouldn't recommend it, but you have the option."

"Would *you* wait here to find out what happens?"

"That's different," said Jareth. "I can't stay in hiding and let my people fight."

"Nor can I hide while my fate is being decided. I have as much stake in this as you do."

"But you'd be safe," he said. "I can't guarantee your safety out there. And if you stayed here, you'd have the companionship of your pets."

"If you were in my position, would you stay here?"

"Yes."

She frowned at him. "You're lying. Why?"

Jareth looked away. "I don't want to worry about you."

"Then don't."

He turned back. "It's not that simple. I don't want my worry for you to preoccupy me, to keep me from focusing on my duties."

Krystal stood up. "You can't lay that responsibility at my feet."

Jareth stood too. "I just want you to understand that there are a lot of things that can happen to you out there. Our camp could be ambushed, and you could be recaptured. What do you think Gregory would do to you if he gets his hands on you again?"

"Are you trying to frighten me?"

He faced her. "You need to know how dangerous it is. I can't protect you and retake the kingdom. I'm only one man."

She looked up at him. "Then let me protect myself. I'm not helpless, Jareth. I've managed to survive all these years without your help. I think I can continue to do so."

He gave her a rueful smile and brushed her hair over her shoulder with his hand. "You are far too stubborn. But I had to try."

Krystal put her hand on his chest. "You have to stop worrying about me. I'm not going to throw myself in harm's way. But I must have a say in my future. Please understand that."

Jareth covered her hand with his. "I'm probably one of the few people who *can* understand. I only want you to be safe."

"I'll be fine." Krystal caught herself as she leaned toward him and stood straight. "There's so much more to worry about than one person."

He released her hand and stepped back. "You're right, of course. There isn't much time left to prepare an attack on the castle."

"Is that the only option? Attacking the castle is going to take a large force of well-trained men. We know Gregory is combing the countryside. Why not attack him outside the castle?"

Jareth shook his head. "We aren't strong enough yet. And it's impossible to know where he will be from one day to the next."

"What about the secret passages? If you could sneak a handful of men in at night, you could catch him by surprise and avoid a battle entirely."

"I don't know which passages he's found and sealed up," said Jareth. "I'm not even sure I know all the passages that exist. It's too uncertain."

Krystal sighed. "I'd have to guess Gregory doesn't come out of the castle often. He'd be more vulnerable, and he knows that."

"My uncle is an intelligent enemy. He's unlikely to make foolish mistakes, especially where his safety is concerned."

"If only we could lure him out for some reason. What do you think would entice him to leave the safety of the castle?"

The prince gave her a long look. "I'd hate to consider what that might be."

Krystal blushed. "Gregory wouldn't jeopardize his hold on the throne over a peasant girl."

"Since I refuse to use you to bait a trap, it's not worth arguing over," he said. "But I think you're wrong. My uncle doesn't suggest marriage to just anyone. He's serious about you."

Krystal regarded him a moment, considering his words. "But there has to be something else he'd value. What about your sister?"

Jareth's eyes widened. "What do you know of my sister?"

Krystal stepped back at the harshness of his tone. "I know she's alive and writing to your uncle. I found some letters while I searched his study for a map."

The prince relaxed. "I'm sorry. It surprised me that you knew anything about Alana."

"Gregory told me she'd died," Krystal said and recounted the conversation she had with the king that night in the portrait gallery. "I don't know why he'd lie like that."

"Some of my earliest memories are of Mother talking about Alana," said Jareth. "She didn't want me to forget about her. She wanted me to rescue her someday."

"Do you know where she is?"

"We've always known she's in Demarde, though it hasn't done us any good. Gregory effectively kept my father's troops from his castle. The only thing that works is sneaking in a single person to deliver messages."

"Have you tried to send her messages?"

Jareth sighed. "It doesn't do any good. The web of lies my uncle raised her on has kept her from seeing the truth. And I suppose I can understand that. It's easier for Alana to believe her family is gone than to think the man who raised her is a murderer."

Krystal nodded. "He's been with her for as long as she can

remember. I suppose she'd have to see his true character for herself before she could believe he has any evil in him."

"If only I could talk to her," he said. "Perhaps I could make her realize the truth."

"You can't force her to see something she doesn't want to see."

"You're probably right, but she's my sister. I can't just forget about her."

"I'm not suggesting you forget about her." Krystal sighed. "Who sends your messages?"

"Getting word to Alana was something Calum and I discussed before I left the castle," Jareth said. "Once Gregory moved me to the mountain prison, Calum started sneaking into Demarde to deliver messages to her. I hoped she'd send help, or better yet, come herself."

"But she hasn't." Krystal shook her head. "You'd think she'd be curious about the kingdom of her birth. I wonder what Gregory tells her about Fayterra."

"Whatever he tells her, it must be working because she hasn't set foot in Fayterra since our parents died." Jareth's shoulders slumped a little. "My worst nightmare is that I will succeed in conquering Gregory only to have my sister rise up against me with all of Demarde at her command."

"That would be awful," agreed Krystal. "How did he get hold of her in the first place?"

"He tricked my mother," said Jareth. "He'd already denounced my father as a false king, but after we were born, Gregory sent a message to my mother begging forgiveness. She said he asked to come in peace to visit her." Jareth shook his head. "She trusted him. But Gregory never intended peace. My mother used to tell me of the night she caught him over the cradle with Alana in his arms. She always said she lost her daughter and her brother that night."

"How horrible," Krystal said, thinking of her own brothers. "How could he do that to his own sister?"

"I don't pretend to know how his mind works," said Jareth. "Doubtless he had some sort of higher justification, the same way he dreamt up his ridiculous claim to my father's throne."

"Sometimes a person can't see the truth, even when it's right in front of him," Krystal said. "We're all susceptible to that flaw."

Jareth smiled. "My mother never recovered from that, so when Gregory killed my father in battle, it did something to her that couldn't be fixed. She tried to hang on for my sake, but the pain was too great." He sighed. "I wonder what will happen to Alana if she ever discovers the truth. Will the deception and betrayal prove too much for her as well?"

"That's an ugly thought," said Krystal.

"I can't let it stop me from doing what I know is right. Though in a way, I sound like my uncle when I say it like that."

"What other option do you have?"

Jareth looked grim. "None, though that hardly comforts me."

"All this speculation has worn me out." Krystal stood up. "I think I'll try to sleep."

Jareth nodded. "Let me know if you get cold during the night. I can build up the fire."

"I'll have Damen to help me stay warm," she said. "I should be fine."

Krystal called Damen to her and walked to her bed. Her dog settled down with her and pressed up against her back. She patted him reassuringly before falling asleep.

Something woke Krystal in the dead of night. She sat up, listening. Slowly she pulled the blanket back to check on Jareth. He wasn't in his bed, but she spotted him sitting at the fire with his back to her. He poked at the flames with a long stick. For a moment, she considered going to him. He let go of the stick and put his head in his hands. Krystal hesitated. Intruding now would probably embarrass more than comfort. She lay back down, wishing she could offer something that would help him, wishing she knew what that could be.

❧

Damen refused to leave her side. Krystal tried once more to stop him from following her as they left the cavern, but he refused to obey. She threw up her hands in defeat.

Jareth laughed. "At least there's someone around who is just as stubborn as you are."

Krystal frowned at him. "That's hardly a compliment, him being a dog."

"I think he worries about you. He's only just been reunited with you."

"And clearly he's not ready to let me out of his sight. Let's get going."

She felt a pang at leaving White Lightning behind, but Krystal knew her faithful pet would be safe in the cavern. It also meant, even though they now had just the one horse, that Krystal and Jareth would be able to set a better pace without the menagerie of animals. Krystal rode in the saddle behind Jareth with Damen keeping pace at their side.

The image of Jareth at the fire haunted Krystal. She wanted to say something comforting, but everything sounded hopelessly feeble when she thought of all he faced. Jareth must have been preoccupied too, since he had to backtrack twice on the way to the new camp.

They stopped for a drink and a quick bite around midday. Damen took off after a rabbit in a nearby bush while Krystal and Jareth sat across from each other on a flat-topped rock with their lunch.

"I don't want you to worry," he said. "I do know where we're going."

"I'm not worried about that," she said. "I only wish I could do more to help."

Jareth swallowed his last bite. "You're doing just fine." He stood and brushed his hands off on his pants. "We should move on. I don't want to lose too much time."

She walked over as he mounted the horse. "Do you think Damen will catch up?"

He reached down for her hand. "I'm sure he hasn't gone far."

Krystal grasped his hand and smiled. But his attention had centered on something behind her. She didn't want to turn around but did just the same.

King Gregory had found them.

Chapter 20

GREGORY SAT ATOP his horse on the other side of the clearing. His men stood on either side of him, crossbows at the ready. He had taken his nephew and Krystal utterly by surprise.

Gregory's fury washed over them. "Get away from her!"

"Hello, uncle," said Jareth.

Gregory didn't bother to return the greeting. "Release her, or my men will shoot you." Damen leapt from the bushes and wrapped his teeth around a soldier's hand. The man fired as he screamed, but the bolt went wild. One of the other soldiers tried to aim at the dog.

Without looking at her, Jareth tightened his grip on her hand. Krystal understood what he meant to do a second before he swung her up behind him. She wrapped her arms around his waist. Jareth dug his heels into the horse's sides, and they took off at a full gallop.

Krystal could hear Gregory's shouts. "Hold your fire, you fools! You might hit the girl!"

She half expected to feel a crossbow bolt in her back as they raced away. Krystal shut her eyes and buried her head in Jareth's back. She could hear the sounds of horses in pursuit but didn't dare look.

"We have to lose them!" Jareth called back. "I know this forest better than they do."

Krystal could only hope he was right. The jostling of the horse as they wove around the trees threatened to upset her lunch. The shouts behind them grew more distant.

Jareth slowed the horse. "We're going to have to jump."

"What?"

"Try to land in those bushes."

She opened her eyes in time to see a collection of rather uninviting bushes off to their right. Jareth pried her hands away from his waist. Krystal went down in the bushes and came up in time to see him land in front of her. The horse raced away.

Jareth pulled her to her feet and away from the path. They dove into some thicker brush as the enemy thundered past. The prince waited another several heartbeats before moving.

"With all these low trees, it should be a while before they notice the horse has no riders," he said. "We'll double back and take a different path."

He took her hand and pulled her away. They stopped several times to listen for horses or men. Krystal's heart leapt into her throat a couple of times when she thought she heard shouting.

"They can cover more ground on horseback," she said. "How can we keep out of sight?"

"There's a spot nearby too thick with trees for horses," the prince said. "If we can get there, we should be safe. Besides I know of a couple of places where we can hide."

They ended up needing to use both hiding places. At one point, Gregory got so close to them that Krystal could hear him threaten his men. "Find them, or you'll all spend time in the dungeon!" The second time they hid as a precaution. Jareth said he'd heard noises behind them.

Before long, Damen found them. He must have made the sounds Jareth had heard. Krystal checked him over for wounds but found nothing. Jareth urged her on; they had to move quickly.

The forest grew denser with trees and underbrush. Although it provided them with good cover, it also slowed their movement. At one point, they had to walk single file. Finally Jareth stopped.

"I think we've lost them," he said. "I'm sorry I pushed you off the horse."

"I'm sorrier we lost the packs," she said. "We're going to get hungry."

"We aren't going to be able to stop. I won't feel at ease until we reach the camp."

"We got away. That's what's important," she said. "We can't let him capture you again."

"Or you," Jareth said.

"Let's keep moving," she said. "I still feel exposed out here."

"Follow me," he said.

Krystal thought of their narrow escape. "You and Damen work well together."

Jareth nodded. "I admit, he's a good ally to have."

"He has an uncanny knack for being in the right place at the right time."

"You are fortunate in your pets," he said.

Krystal corrected him. "I'm fortunate in my friends."

He glanced back to smile at her. "Thank you."

The trees around them thinned, and they lapsed into silence. Soon darkness fell, but the prince did not stop. He used the light from the moon as it shone through the trees to guide them.

Krystal tripped over a root and grabbed his tunic to keep from falling. "You have the eyes of a cat. I can't see a thing."

"My bond with the land helps me sense the trees around us," he said.

"Gregory can't still be searching for us," she said. "Can't we stop for the night and continue on in the morning?"

"You forget Gregory has access to the land's magic as well," said the prince. "He may not have stopped searching."

Krystal tripped again and grasped at his hand. The minute her fingers closed around his, she could see the trees and ground as if it were day. Krystal pulled her hand away and everything went dark again.

Jareth turned to her. "What is it?"

Krystal rubbed at her eyes. "I'm not sure. Suddenly I could see. When I held your hand, everything became clearer."

"That's odd," he said. "Here, take my hand again."

She did and could see his face clearly. She pulled away and darkness enveloped them. "What's going on?"

"I don't know," he said. "But if it helps you to see then we can take advantage of it."

"It hurts a little," said Krystal. "My eyes aren't used to working like that."

She held on until her eyes couldn't take the strain any longer and then grasped the back of his tunic instead. The forest once again fell into darkness but the pain behind her eyes began to ease.

They encountered their first sentry shortly after that. Jareth announced himself and they were allowed to pass. They repeated the process with two more sentries before Krystal caught a glimpse of camp fires through the trees. She sighed in relief and exhaustion. They had made it.

Calum approached at the edge of camp. "We expected you hours ago. What happened?"

"My uncle stumbled upon us around midday," said Jareth. "I sent them after the horse while Krystal and I made our escape on foot. If we want to send someone now, we could probably retrieve the horse, and our packs."

"I'm not worried about that," said the knight. "The loss of one horse is worth your safety." He looked them over in the firelight. "You look exhausted. We'll talk in the morning."

Jareth grasped Krystal's arm. "Are you hungry? I know we missed dinner."

She sighed. "I'm more tired than hungry. I can eat in the morning."

He released her slowly, almost reluctantly, or so she thought. "Sleep well."

—"You too." Krystal followed Calum's directions to one of the women's tents and found a place to stretch out inside. She fell asleep before she thought to wonder where Damen had gone.

The next morning, Krystal awoke to a cold nose in her back. Damen had found her and had worked his way under her shirt. She rolled over and sat up. The dog nudged her hand in a play for affection, and she ruffled his fur.

The camp bustled with activity. She followed her nose to find the food tent. Spotting Jareth, Calum, and Miraya sitting together, she walked in that direction. Their voices floated toward her before they saw her.

"What do you think it means?" Calum asked Jareth.

"There is one obvious explanation," said the prince.

"Then why don't you tell her?"

Krystal stopped. Were they talking about her?

Jareth shook his head. "You didn't see her as I did that first day. Underneath all that bravery, she's frightened. She's been through a lot. I'm not going to jeopardize what may be my only chance to win her over because of my impatience."

"If you're right, she knows already," said Calum. "She just may not realize it yet."

"If she asks, I won't lie to her, but I don't think she's ready for me to blurt it out."

"How will you know she's ready if you don't talk to her?" Miraya said.

Jareth started to say something but then turned to where Krystal stood. "Good morning."

"Hello," she said.

Miraya got up and crossed to Krystal, taking her arm in hers.

"You must be hungry," she said as she led her away. "The prince said you haven't eaten since midday yesterday. Come on, I'll get you something." She led Krystal to a fallen log where she could sit and then went to fetch the food. Miraya returned shortly with a bowl of thick gruel.

"It's not much, but I did add a little cream and honey," she said.

"Thank you," Krystal said, taking the bowl and setting it in her lap.

Her friend lowered her voice. "There is just one thing I need to ask you."

"What is it?" Krystal asked between bites.

"How long have you been in love with Prince Jareth?"

Krystal almost choked as she tried to swallow. "I'm not. How could I be?"

"I'm not going to pretend you didn't hear us," said Miraya. "Last night, Prince Jareth told Calum you could channel a part of his magic when you held his hand. That would only be possible if you two had a bond of some kind."

"You're wrong," Krystal said. "Last night was unusual, but it doesn't mean I'm in love with him."

Miraya frowned at her. "I've seen how you look at him. You aren't fooling me. And just now, you said good morning to the prince, but

Calum and I could have been vapor for all the attention you gave us. Admit it—you have eyes only for Jareth."

Krystal gripped the sides of her bowl. "I barely know him. I admit, I *do* find him attractive, but that hardly constitutes love. It's too soon."

"Love knows no timetable," Miraya said.

"You're wrong," Krystal said again.

Miraya sighed. "A person can deny the truth, they can bend or twist it, but it doesn't stop being the truth. I'll wait until you're ready." She patted Krystal's shoulder before walking away.

As Jareth grew stronger so did his magic. She didn't try to test Miraya's theory by touching him when he used magic, but Krystal got used to seeing him light fires with magic or walk around in the dark. Though she still didn't understand the depth of his power, it interested her.

Krystal couldn't help but notice that Jareth had gotten stronger physically as well. The muscles in his arms and chest had filled out. He also had color in his cheeks, especially when he laughed.

She couldn't deny her attraction to Jareth. Nearly every time they touched, she felt like she'd been seared by flame. If he looked into her eyes for more than an instant, she'd lose her train of thought. She found herself making up excuses to be around him. His voice sent thrilling shivers up and down her spine. But did she love him?

Every morning, rain or shine, and whether or not the camp relocated that day, Krystal joined Jareth on his run. They would sit afterward and have breakfast together, and then he would take her to the practice field where they would spar with swords or shoot targets with bows and arrows. After a while, Jareth taught her some hand-to-hand fighting techniques, but she couldn't decide if he really wanted her to learn, or whether he liked knocking her to the ground. She got better, and pretty soon she knocked him on his backside almost as often.

After eating lunch together, Jareth would return to practice with the men while Krystal made herself useful among the women. She liked the afternoons she got to spend with the children best. Occasionally, they would pester a new bruise or cut she'd received that morning, but for the most part, they were more fun than trouble.

Under Jareth's guidance, her skill with the sword improved a great deal. One sunny morning near lunch time, they had stopped sparring and took a much needed break. Jareth drank water from a cup and then dumped the rest of it over his head. They sat beneath a tree to rest. He wiped his eyes and looked at her.

"You're doing much better," he said. "Your last attack almost had me."

Krystal smiled at him. "I'm still no match for you. Don't flatter me."

"You really are getting better. I suspect you go easy on me. I'd hate to cross swords with you when you really mean it."

She gave him a gentle push. "Then don't make me angry."

"Darling, I wouldn't dream of it."

She gave him a quizzical look. He clamped his hand over his mouth.

"I'm sorry. I didn't mean that. I mean, I didn't mean to say that." He sighed. "I'm not sure I know what I mean. Have I confused you yet?"

Krystal stepped closer. "We're friends. We can have affection for one another."

Jareth put a hand on her shoulder. "Of course we can. Thank you."

She put her hand on his. "And who knows? Perhaps we have the potential to be more than friends some day."

The look in his eyes grew intense. "I would like that very much."

She'd done it again—she'd looked into his eyes too long. Krystal felt her knees weakening. She glanced at his mouth and wondered what he would do if she kissed him. She wondered how it would feel to kiss him just once.

His hand tightened on her shoulder. "Don't do that."

Krystal sighed. "Don't do what?" She sounded distant, dreamy, even to her own ears.

"If you don't stop looking at me like that, I'm going to kiss you." Jareth leaned close to her face. "And then we'd both be embarrassed, wouldn't we?"

She looked into his eyes. "Would we?"

He gave her a heartbreaking smile. "I've begun to wonder."

Krystal smiled at him as he gently brushed her cheek with his hand. She saw Calum approach behind Jareth. The prince, without turning, greeted his friend.

"How did you know it was me?" Calum asked.

"Krystal's eyes," Jareth said. "She trusts you and it shows."

She smiled at Jareth. "I had no idea I was so easy to read."

Calum cleared his throat. "Highness, I have news."

Jareth looked at him. "What is it?"

"We spotted a carriage on its way to the castle. Its doors bear the arms of Demarde."

Chapter 21

THE PRINCE'S EYEBROWS shot up. "A coach from Demarde? Is it Gregory?"

Calum shook his head. "I doubt it. We would have known if he'd gone to Demarde."

Jareth stood up. "Come on. Let's interfere."

Krystal leapt to her feet. "I'm coming too."

He stopped. "You have the sword I gave you?"

She smiled at him to ease the concern in his eyes. "Of course. I'll be careful. Let's go."

Calum jogged ahead to alert the men to stop the carriage. By the time Krystal and Jareth arrived, the guardsmen had been subdued, and Krystal started when she recognized Voltimande holding the horses. He wore a Demarde uniform. Apparently he'd returned to Fayterra as part of the carriage escort. He must have delivered more messages to the princess.

Calum nodded to him in greeting, and Voltimande smiled at Krystal when he saw her. Jareth moved immediately to the carriage door, but a voice from inside stopped him.

He stepped back just in time. The door swung open. "What is the meaning of this?"

A beautiful girl stepped from the carriage and drew everyone's attention. She wore a traveling gown of the lightest green wool and had wavy blonde hair that fell to her hips. Her blue-green eyes took in the scene before her. Krystal noticed the hand on the carriage latch tighten, perhaps in fear, though none showed in the woman's face.

She picked out the leader of the group instantly. "Who are you?" she asked Jareth.

He appeared just as dazzled as everyone else. Jareth glanced at Calum before he replied. "I am Prince Jareth Lochnikar. But I suspect you knew that."

"You lie," she said. "I happen to know Prince Jareth is dead."

"You have been misinformed, I think," said Calum.

She turned to the knight. "And you are?"

He bowed. "Sir Calum Landen, Princess. I have known Prince Jareth since childhood."

"Then your friend is an imposter," she said. "My brother died as an infant."

Looking closer, it amazed Krystal that she hadn't recognized her immediately. Jareth shared the same face as his sister, though she had lighter hair and more delicate features. Krystal looked at the petite princess with a twinge of envy. Though Gregory had made her a princess, Krystal had never felt she looked the part. Now looking at a true princess by birth, Krystal felt gangly and inadequate in her dirt-covered trousers and old boots.

Princess Alana moved forward. "I insist you release me. My uncle is expecting me."

Jareth smiled at her. "He sent for you?"

She paused a moment. "Of course."

"I doubt that," said Calum.

"Are you calling me a liar?"

Jareth moved forward. "What my friend means is your uncle has spent a great deal of energy keeping you safely in Demarde. We find it difficult to believe he would suddenly send for you, especially when things are so turbulent in Fayterra."

She glared up at him. "Perhaps you are less of a threat to him than you believe yourself to be." Her glare swept the group. "You rebels will be dealt with easily enough."

Jareth stepped back. "Search the carriage."

"How dare you!" Princess Alana gasped. "You have no right to go through my things." She moved and exposed the sword she'd hidden in the folds of her gown.

Jareth was ready for her. He used his sword to block her swing and then grabbed her hand. "Temper, sister dear." He handed his sword to Calum and wrested hers from her hand.

Unarmed, she tore away from him. "Never call me that!"

Jareth reclaimed his sword from Calum and stepped back. He sheathed his sword and lifted hers to examine it. "You have excellent taste in weapons." His eyes moved to the hilt and his eyes shot back up to her face. "I remember this sword."

"Impossible." Princess Alana lifted her chin defiantly.

The prince shook his head at her. "This is a Lochnikar family sword, handed down for generations. How did you get it? It should be in the royal armory at the castle."

She met his gaze but refused to answer. Jareth's gaze darkened.

"Never mind," he said. "I can guess what happened. Our uncle has sticky fingers."

"That sword is mine," Alana said. "My uncle gave it to me as a gift for my sixteenth birthday. It was from my mother's side of the family."

Krystal saw Jareth's fist close around the hilt. "Your uncle is a liar and a murderer."

Calum's men had finished examining the carriage. "There is nothing here, Your Highness."

Krystal moved to Jareth's side. "What now?"

The prince didn't look at either of them but instead stared at the princess. They stood locked in that heated gaze for several moments. At last, Jareth stepped away.

"There is nothing more we can do here," he said. "Let's go."

Calum stepped toward the princess. "What about her?"

Jareth turned to look at her one more time. "Leave her. Let her go to her dear uncle."

"I'm not leaving without my sword," Alana said.

"You have no right to this sword," he said. "Gregory had no business giving it to you. I will keep this for now."

"You're the one with no right!" she spat at him. "I demand you return my things at once."

"Someday you will understand about Gregory," said Jareth.

"You know nothing about him."

"Ask him then," Jareth said. "Ask him about your brother and your parents. Watch him squirm as he lies to you. Ask him why he hasn't invited you here sooner. You *are* the princess of Fayterra, aren't you? Why have you never been here before?"

"How do you know I haven't?" Her defiance washed over them.

Jareth merely smiled at her as he backed away. "Ask him."

Released, Princess Alana's guards could only resume their stations and continue on their way—one man short. Voltimande took his place with Jareth's men. Krystal thought she saw a face peer through the rear window as the carriage rolled away.

She turned to Jareth. "Why let her go?"

"Do you honestly think I'd convince my sister of my sincerity if I kept her captive?" he asked. "She wasn't willing to come with us. I had no other choice."

"Do you think our letters had anything to do with her arrival?" Calum asked.

"Undoubtedly," said the prince. "We must have aroused her curiosity."

Calum smiled and rubbed his hands together. "Let's get back to camp. I'm sure Miraya will be interested in this new development. And we can hear what Voltimande has to say."

"You go on ahead," Jareth said. "We'll catch up."

Krystal lifted her head and looked askance at him, but he took her hand and walked away from the group. The men followed Calum. Once they were alone, Jareth released her hand but kept walking. She kept pace with him, her curiosity growing.

Jareth stopped and clasped his hands behind his back. "You're torturing me, you know." Krystal's eyebrows shot up. "I am? How?"

"Today, before Calum interrupted us, I could have sworn you gave me permission to kiss you." He brushed her cheek with his hand. "I promised myself I wouldn't pressure you. I don't want you to think you have to love me just because I love you."

Krystal sucked in a breath. "You've never said that before."

"Said what?"

"That you love me. I've heard it from other people, but that's not the same."

"I didn't want you to feel obligated."

"I just never guessed hearing it would matter so much."

Jareth drew her closer. "It matters? How much?"

Krystal put her arms around his neck. "This much, I suppose," she said and kissed him.

The forest around them evaporated. Jareth tightened his hold around her waist and took over the kiss. Krystal's senses reeled. Nothing had ever felt so right or natural to her before.

After what seemed like an eternity—but wasn't nearly long enough—Jareth drew back. She opened her eyes to his smile.

"That much, eh?" He laughed and kissed her again.

"Except now you're going to think I'm a terribly forward girl who goes around kissing devastatingly handsome princes whenever I feel like it."

Jareth laughed again. "You have my blessing, seeing as I'm the only prince around." He embraced her. "You have no idea how long I've dreamed of holding you. This is my paradise."

Krystal wrapped her arms around his waist and sighed. Paradise sounded just about right.

❧

Autumn hit in full force a few weeks later. Krystal and Jareth planned to check on White Lightning. The camp had moved again and would be much closer to the cavern, so they could go and return within a day. Calum approached as they prepared their horses.

"Try not to lose these this time," he said with a smile. "We're running low on horses."

Prince Jareth returned his smile. "We'll do our best."

A brisk autumn breeze whisked through the camp. Krystal pulled her borrowed cloak tightly around her. She hated the cold. She clicked her horse forward behind Jareth.

Damen had become more comfortable in the forest over the last weeks. He returned to check on Krystal often, but he spent most of his time out of sight among the trees.

They dismounted at the cave entrance, and Jareth led the way to the cavern's secret opening. This time it operated quietly without scaring the horses or Damen.

It relieved Krystal to find White Lightning flying in the air and not pining after them at the entrance to the cavern. "She seems content."

Jareth nodded. "I'm glad. I know you've worried about her."

She smiled. "Maybe a little."

They'd packed a cold lunch to share before heading back. Jareth removed the food and another bundle from his horse while Krystal spread her cloak on the ground. He handed her the food and put the other bundle on the grass next to him.

Krystal eyed the long rectangular package curiously. She'd seen him attach it to his saddle bag, but she hadn't asked about it at the time. Now her curiosity was piqued.

Jareth caught her attention. "Shall we eat?"

As she ate, Krystal came to the conclusion that this had to be the most ideal place for a picnic. She listened to the water as it flowed over the rocks in the stream and felt the surprisingly warm breeze as it danced across her cheeks. Sitting across from the man she loved made it just about perfect.

After lunch, Jareth relaxed on his elbow and toyed with a blade of grass. Krystal leaned against his chest and closed her eyes. Long, lazy moments passed before Jareth spoke.

"I have a confession to make. There's something I wanted to ask you," he said. "I brought you here because this garden has a certain sentimental attraction for me."

She sat up to look at him. "What is it?"

Jareth faced her. "You know I love you, don't you?"

She nodded.

Jareth smiled slowly. "It's funny, but I expected this to be more difficult than it is. I suppose that only confirms the rightness of it." He took her hands. "I know we've only been together a short while, but sometimes I feel as if I've always known you. I want to make that permanent. I want to marry you when all this turmoil is over. Please say you'll be my wife."

For the first time, Krystal faced an offer of marriage that didn't dismay or frighten her. "Of course I'll marry you." Had there ever been a moment of doubt?

Jareth pulled her to him and they shared a prolonged kiss.

"I love you so much," he said. "I promise, you will never regret this choice."

"I never could."

He kissed her again. "You haven't spoken of returning home for a while."

She nodded. "I've stopped thinking about the farm as home."

"I know it's not a ring," Jareth said, reaching for the package. "And I admit, I've never heard of something like this being given as an engagement gift, even in the barbaric ancient times."

Krystal recognized the sword he'd taken from his sister. "That's your family sword. Are you sure you want to give it to me?"

"You will soon be family," he said. "It's part of a Lochnikar family tradition. My father gave this sword to my mother, though for her, it was more ceremonial than practical."

Krystal gently grasped the hilt and lifted the sword. It had exceptional balance and felt surprisingly light in her grasp. "It's very well made."

"It has other qualities." Jareth motioned to the stone embedded in the hilt. "My father told me the sword is magical. It enhances its user's advantage in battle."

"How?"

His grin turned sheepish. "I don't know. I never thought to ask."

She smiled at him. "Thank you." Krystal put the sword down beside her.

"I did have another reason for giving you the sword." He smiled. "I know tomorrow is your birthday. I don't have anything else to offer as a gift, so the sword is serving multiple purposes. I'm sorry I can't give you more."

Krystal kissed his cheek. "Your love is the only gift I need."

"You are too generous, my darling." He sought out her mouth for a proper kiss.

"You're going to laugh at me," she said. "But I forgot about my birthday."

Jareth's eyebrows shot up. "I don't believe you. How can you forget your own birthday?"

Krystal shrugged. "I've been a little preoccupied."

Jareth moved closer. "I like the idea that I can cause you such distraction."

Krystal met him half way. "Perhaps I can do the same for you."

Her fingers wound into his hair as she threw herself into the embrace, body and soul. Blissful, thrilling moments blurred into one as they kissed again and again. Suddenly she felt his hands on her wrists, and he broke away. Krystal couldn't help but notice how his eyes had darkened and how intensely he stared at her as he loomed over her. Somehow she'd ended up on her back in the grass. Jareth's breath came in short gasps. He seemed pained when he spoke.

"Krystal, my parents taught me to treat women with respect. But for you, I have no resistance. I deeply regret having started this love play, for I did not see the effect until it was nearly too late. Your passion has nearly been my undoing. For this, forgive me." Jareth brushed her brow with a trembling hand. "Your purity is as precious to me as it is to you, and I pledge to preserve it until we wed. I don't want to do anything either of us may regret."

"I'm sorry," she said.

"I don't want you to be sorry." He offered her a timid smile. "We will just need to be careful. We've just learned how quickly we can lose control."

"I'll remember." She may remember that kiss until her dying day.

They said one last farewell to White Lightning before packing up to return to the rebel camp. Krystal tried once more to convince Damen to stay in the cavern, but he refused. She worried that he might come to harm wandering the forest. Evidently he worried about her as well because he wouldn't let her leave without him.

Krystal strapped the sword to her saddle and followed Jareth through the woods. She couldn't remember ever feeling so happy. She did worry about her family, though. She wanted them to know she was safe.

Jareth slowed the horses. "That's odd. We should have run into sentries by now."

"Maybe they just let us pass," said Krystal. "Do you think something's wrong?"

"I'm not sure." The prince pulled out his sword. "Stay close to me."

Krystal reached back and untied her sword. She kept her horse close as they continued.

He stopped abruptly. "Do you hear that?"

She listened hard but couldn't make anything out. "What is it?"

"It's faint, but I think it's swords," he said. "Can you find your way back to the cavern?"

"What are you going to do?"

"If my people are under attack, I have to help," Jareth said.

"If you charge into an attack, you could be captured, or worse," argued Krystal.

Jareth shook his head. "Go to the cavern and wait for me." He urged his horse forward.

Did he really expect her to obey? She dug her knees into her horse's sides and followed.

Chaos surrounded her. Fortunately she saw no children and only a few women. Calum and Jareth had announced some weeks ago that, if they were attacked, the women were to round up the children and spirit them away. Krystal had agreed at the time, having no intention to actually run from a fight. Others clearly felt the same way.

A soldier's sword sliced at her from the left. She blocked the swing and turned to face the attack. The soldier appeared battle crazed as his eyes locked on her sword. He raised his own weapon, and Krystal braced herself for the blow, but none came. His eyes widened and blood spurted from his mouth. Krystal spun her horse out of the way. As he fell, she saw the crossbow bolt in his back. She looked for her savior, and when she saw him, her jaw dropped.

King Gregory put the crossbow away and turned his horse toward her. Krystal looked around but had nowhere to run. If she stayed on her horse, he'd be upon her in an instant.

Krystal let out an ear-piercing whistle for Damen. She slid to the ground, putting her horse between her and the king just in time. Then she whistled again.

She found Jareth, who was still on his horse. Calum fought on foot at his side. Gregory's men surrounded them. She saw a soldier raise his crossbow. He had Jareth in his sights.

Krystal ran toward the man and hit him on the back of the head with the flat of her blade. As he fell forward, she leapt over him and kept running. She had to get to Jareth.

Gregory's horse rode into her path. Krystal slid to a stop and looked up at the rider. The king glared down at her. She took a step back to keep out of reach. He leaned down and stretched his hand to her anyway, only to draw it away sharply when Damen tried to close his jaws on it.

She could have cried in relief. Damen had heard her. Krystal watched Gregory work to control his horse. She put one hand on Damen's shoulders and felt the fur there on end. Her pet growled menacingly at the king.

The battle had turned away from them. She looked back toward Jareth. He had maintained his height advantage atop his horse but he, Calum, and the men who fought with them were being pushed back. Damen snapped his jaws again as Gregory tried to draw nearer to Krystal. She looked from Jareth to Gregory and back. She knew what had to be done.

"Go, Damen," she said. "Protect Jareth!"

Chapter 22

GREGORY SPOKE. "Come with me, and I'll call off my men." Krystal blinked. Could she trust him?

"I speak the truth. If you come with me, I'll let him live, for now."

With a deep breath, Krystal stepped toward the horse and rider. She turned her sword and handed it to him hilt first. He secured it and then held out his arm to her.

She let him lift her up in front of him. He wrapped one arm around her waist and winced as his armor bit through her tunic. At this point, she hoped Gregory would turn his horse to the right and leave the battle quietly. Instead, Gregory turned his horse to the left in order to expose her to Jareth.

Krystal's heart flipped as Jareth locked eyes with her. His anguish tore at her soul. She saw Damen bite the sword arm of a soldier who threatened the prince. Calum shouted to Jareth as he moved forward to stop him from confronting Gregory.

She shouted the first thing that came to mind. "I love you!"

Gregory's arm cut into her as he tightened his hold. His body stiffened. The king bellowed across the clearing. "Men, to me!"

His soldiers started to fall back in order to protect the king's retreat. They would keep any of the rebels from stopping him.

Gregory did not speak during the long ride back to the castle. Krystal sat before him on his horse, her nerves humming with anticipation. She held as still as possible. If she moved even a fraction, his armor dug at her belly.

Once inside the courtyard, the king dragged her off the horse's back and pulled her by her arm into the castle. Krystal did not resist him. She thought it safer to let him do to her what he wanted. She kept seeing the look on Jareth's face in her mind's eye.

Gregory dragged her to the dungeon entrance. He pulled open the heavy, reinforced iron door and forced her inside. Krystal stumbled as her eyes adjusted to the semi-darkness. Gregory didn't stop until they stood before a dank dungeon cell.

Gregory threw her away from him. "This is where you belong. This is what all traitors deserve."

Krystal recovered her voice with a vengeance. "I never claimed allegiance to you."

"Do you have any idea how I felt when I saw you together?" he demanded. "Even without touching you, he was closer than I've ever been to you. I wanted to kill you both with my bare hands." He stepped closer. "I still might, if for no other reason than to put me out of my misery."

"Then why don't you?" Krystal took a step toward him.

Gregory glared at her a long, silent moment. "I've enough ghosts by now. I'll not give you that power over me."

His words gave her pause. "I love Jareth. You can't stop that, whatever you do to me."

He came close enough to strike her. "I vow to make you forget your infatuation with that child! You will stay here and contemplate your fate, Krystal. *I* control your destiny now. You would do well to remember that!" Gregory stepped back and slammed her cell door.

He turned away but she called after him. "You can't control my heart, Gregory! *You* would do well to remember *that!*" The clanking of the heavy door was his only reply.

Alone, Krystal sank down to the pile of straw that would serve as her bed. She couldn't think of Jareth anymore. It hurt too much. After she'd cried all the tears she had, Krystal collapsed in the straw and slept.

❧

The sound of the heavy dungeon door woke her. Krystal stood up to see who had come. If Gregory thought he would find her broken and miserable, she had a surprise for him. But instead of the king, she saw a somber-faced Julienne rounding the corner of the stairs, bearing a tray.

"I wish I could say I'm glad to see you," Julienne said. "I've brought your breakfast."

"Is it morning then?" Krystal's dungeon cell had no windows to indicate time of day.

"It's very early," said Julienne. "The king is still asleep. He's given no orders about feeding you, but he hasn't expressly forbidden us to do so. I thought I'd take advantage of the early hour and make sure you get at least one meal today."

Krystal laughed without humor. Morning brought her birthday. She'd spend it in a dungeon. She accepted the tray Julienne pushed through the hole in the bottom of the door.

"Thank you," she said. "How has it been here since I've been away?"

"Those first days were horrible," the maid said. "I've never seen the king so close to madness. He ordered the men guarding you thrown in here for allowing you to escape. After they found the secret passage, I thought he'd let them go, but he didn't. Then we heard of Prince Jareth's escape. When the prison guard described the girl who had hit him over the head, King Gregory killed him on the spot. Was it really you who freed the prince?"

"I had to," Krystal said. "He was slowly starving to death. No one could have left him there."

"Countess Fordyce convinced the king to release the men he'd put in the dungeon. She said they needed all the men they had to search for the prince."

"At least they didn't die as well."

"The king was frenzied for weeks," said Julienne. "He hardly ate and almost never slept. He didn't calm down until Princess Alana arrived." She laughed. "She asked him what had happened to the door of your old room. I've never seen the king at a loss for words like that."

"Has she been asking him a lot of questions?"

"I don't really know," Julienne said. "I did hear her say once that she needed to know more about Fayterra, since it would be her home someday. I left the room before he replied."

Krystal smiled. Maybe Alana had taken her brother's advice after all. "So Gregory has stopped randomly killing people?"

"One time his group came back with one soldier dead. King Gregory said the prince had killed him, but others in his party whispered he'd done it himself."

"I wonder if that was the day he found us in the woods. We barely got away." It made sense to her.

"I don't know what day he saw you."

"I guess it's not important." Krystal slid the empty tray back to Julienne. "Tell me about the princess. What do you think of her?"

"She's kind," said Julienne. "She spends her days sketching and painting."

"We saw her," Krystal said. "Jareth's men stopped her carriage on its way here."

"The prince and princess met?" Julienne gasped. "I would have loved to see that."

"She called him a fake, a pretender to the throne," said Krystal.

"The king forbade us from speaking of the prince," Julienne said. "Though some of us may have accidentally left a few mementos of his childhood lying around."

Krystal found a true smile. "Has she said anything?"

"Not that I've heard, but she may yet. Now I must go. I don't want to be discovered here."

"Thank you again."

"I'll return if I can. Good-bye."

Krystal leaned against the wall. Her stomach ached on the outside as well as the inside. She checked her flesh where Gregory's armor had cut through her clothes. She traced the dried blood across two slashes with her fingers. The cuts didn't feel deep and hadn't bled much. The layers of clothing had shielded her from more serious wounds.

It became unbearably warm inside the dungeon as the day wore on, and the heat made her sleepy. She woke when someone used a lit torch to illuminate her cell.

"You look terrible." She recognized the king's voice.

"So sorry to disappoint," she said. "I must have left my hairbrush in my other cell."

He sighed. "I get no pleasure seeing you like this."

She laughed. "Of course you do. You wouldn't be here if you didn't."

"I came to check on you."

"Did you think less than a day in your dungeon would break me?"

"Stop being confrontational. You're behaving like a child."

"I *am* a child."

"No, you aren't!"

Krystal laughed again. "Then what am I, a seventeen-year-old grandmother perhaps?"

"Stop it. You're trying to anger me on purpose."

"Is it working?"

He evidently chose to ignore that. "I came to give you the terms of your imprisonment."

"There are terms?"

"You must be punished, but if you show proper contrition then I will release you."

"What constitutes proper contrition? Do I prostrate myself and kiss your boots?"

"This is serious! Do you have any idea how many people died because of you?"

She pretended ignorance. "No one drops dead because a prisoner escapes, Gregory."

"I have to maintain order and discipline among my people," he said.

"So I must pay for the people you murdered?"

She jumped when he hit the door with his fist. "Do you *want* to rot in here? Because I can easily arrange it."

"I don't want anything from you. Just leave me alone."

"I honestly wish I could." The torch light receded with his boot steps.

Krystal resumed her position in the straw and closed her eyes. Why did she work so hard to infuriate him? She should give him the contrition he wanted and get out of the dungeon. But then, she'd always been a terrible liar.

༉

She must have slept again because a sudden light in her eyes jolted her awake once again. Immediately she thought of the king and said the first thing that came into her mind.

"Are you back to gape at your prisoner some more?"

"I know you." This time a woman spoke. "I've seen you before."

"Princess Alana?" Krystal sat up.

"You have the advantage. You know my name, but I don't know yours."

"I'm Krystal."

"You were in the forest with that man who claimed to be Prince Jareth."

"No, I was in the forest with the man who *is* Prince Jareth."

"That's impossible," said Alana.

Krystal sighed. "A wise woman once told me that denying the truth doesn't make it any less true, princess. Does your uncle know you're here?"

"I'm sure Uncle Gregory wouldn't think anything of my visiting you."

Krystal groaned at her aching muscles. "Why did you come?"

"I thought I recognized you," Alana said. "It's been bothering me."

"Now that you know, I'm sure you'd like to go back to your beauty sleep."

"I suppose I should." Alana stepped back from the cell door.

"Wait," Krystal said. "I'm sorry. I don't mean to be rude. Can I ask you something?"

"I suppose."

"Have you asked Gregory about your family?"

"My uncle is a busy man," said Alana. "I see no reason to pester him with questions. My br— That man you follow is wrong. My uncle would never lie to me."

Darkness enveloped Krystal as the princess left, but this time she smiled. Despite what she'd said, Alana did have doubts. She'd almost called Jareth her brother.

Krystal's entire body ached. She barely moved when Julienne

snuck her more food and a full water skin. She thanked her friend and hid the water under the straw before collapsing.

The dungeon had cooled considerably over night. Krystal retrieved the cloak she'd discarded the day before and wrapped it around her, but it didn't help. She still shivered.

She'd become ill. Krystal huddled under her cloak miserably. She could think of a hundred things that would be better than getting sick in the dungeon.

King Gregory did not make an appearance in the dungeon that day, but Princess Alana returned that night. Krystal lay in the straw, too weak to move. She heard tension in the princess's melodic voice, but she could only wish the girl would get to the point and leave her to rest.

Alana asked about Jareth. "This man who claims to be my brother, what is he like?"

"He's an honest, caring man," Krystal said. "He wants only the best for his people."

"My uncle does as well."

"Then he needs to tend to his people in Demarde and leave Fayterra alone."

Alana did not comment. "He is very troubled. I'm not sure what to do for him."

Krystal tried to roll over and groaned with the effort. She'd gotten overly warm again. "Why are you telling me this? Am I not the enemy?"

"I have no enemies," Alana said.

Krystal laughed. "I used to think the same thing."

"It's strange for me to be down here talking to you, but you seem so open," said Alana. "It's been . . . difficult to get my questions answered since I arrived."

"Do you sense your uncle is hiding something?"

"If he doesn't tell me something, I'm sure it's for my own good," Alana said.

Krystal sighed. "I'm sure it makes you feel better to believe that."

"Are you all right? You seem out of sorts."

"I'm in a dungeon cell," said Krystal. "Isn't that enough reason to be out of sorts?"

"No, I mean apart from that," said Alana. "Are you ill?"

"Perhaps a little."

"Should I fetch someone?"

"Who would care if a prisoner falls ill?"

"Prisoner or not, you should have care," Alana said.

Krystal thought to dissuade her. "I'm sure it's nothing. All I need is sleep."

Even in her haze, Krystal could tell she hadn't convinced her entirely. "If you're certain, then I shall leave you to rest."

☙

Krystal's eyes felt glued shut. She couldn't open them. She heard voices, though they sounded far away. Gregory's voice, then Julienne's. Or was it Princess Alana's?

"Why did no one tell me?" Gregory sounded angry.

"We didn't know, sire," said the woman's voice. "She didn't answer me this morning when I spoke to her, so I used a torch to look into the cell. She was just lying there. I sent someone for you immediately."

Krystal felt the ground rock beneath her. She tried to steady herself but couldn't move. Gregory spoke again. "She could have died in here for all any of you noticed."

"But, sire, you ordered us to stay away."

"Stop defending your stupidity and go fetch Gerta. I'm taking her to her old chambers."

The rocking had turned almost rhythmic. Krystal couldn't open her eyes to see what caused the motion, but it started to turn her stomach. Just when she thought she couldn't stand it any longer, she felt herself falling. She landed on something soft.

Gregory spoke. "You foolish girl. Don't you know what would happen if I lost you?"

You never had me, she wanted to say, but she couldn't make her lips move. Krystal drifted again; she didn't know for how long. Then she heard another voice.

"You'll be in my way if you don't leave," a woman spoke abruptly. She sounded older and wise.

"I'm not going anywhere. Work around me."

"At least turn around while I get her out of these filthy clothes."

Krystal felt the brusque, efficient movements and tried to help, but she still couldn't move. Cool air hit her skin, and she started to shiver. She felt sudden warmth on her hips and chest, but her belly still chilled.

"She's been cut, and it looks infected."

Gregory said, "She couldn't have been injured in the battle. What made these marks?"

"It's unimportant now," the woman said. "I have to clean the cuts and apply my salve or she'll never get better. Stand back and try to stay out of the way."

"Heal her, Gerta. You must."

"I'll do my best."

Krystal felt the sting on her belly and wanted to cry out but couldn't. Her mind drifted away again. She couldn't hold it. She was plagued by nightmares of desperation that she couldn't escape. She couldn't wake up enough to forget them.

She remained trapped in the endless nightmares for days. She saw people she loved slaughtered and her family's farm decimated. Gregory kept Jareth forever out of her reach.

At last she opened her eyes. A candle burned on each side of her bed. Gregory sat in a chair next to her, his head on his chest. He'd fallen asleep watching over her.

Chapter 23

WHEN KRYSTAL WOKE, her mouth felt like cotton. She yearned for a drink but couldn't even sit up. She moved to lift her hand and found her fingers intertwined in Gregory's.

She tried to pull away, but he opened his eyes when she twitched. "You're awake. Your eyes look clear. How do you feel?"

"Thirsty," she said in a weak croak.

He poured a glass of water from the pitcher beside her bed and lifted her head. The cool liquid trickled down her throat. It felt wonderful.

Gregory lowered her head to the pillow and put the cup on the table. "Better?"

"Thank you." Her voice sounded clearer.

"You should rest. Gerta will come to check on you in the morning."

"Will . . . you . . . be here?"

He smiled at her. "I won't leave your side. I'd do anything for you."

"Then let me go."

His eyes clouded, but he did not reply. She fell asleep.

☙

Krystal awoke to a room bathed in sunlight. She recognized the room; it had been her first room when she arrived in Fayterra. She tried to sit up.

"Be still," Princess Alana said. "You shouldn't try to move just yet."

Krystal turned her head. "What are you doing here?" At least she could speak again.

"My uncle left with the healer," she said. "I wanted to make sure you were all right."

"How long have I been ill?"

"Uncle Gregory carried you out of the dungeon four days ago."

"Has he been here all this time?"

"Nearly," Alana said. "Gerta assured him you would recover today. He's sleeping."

"So he had you sit with me?"

"Not exactly. He's actually forbidden me to attend you."

Krystal raised her eyebrows. "I see how well you obey."

Princess Alana blushed. "Do you need anything? Are you thirsty or hungry?"

Krystal let her change the subject, for the moment. "Water would be lovely."

"The entire castle has been worried about you." She poured a cup of water and held it out to Krystal. "Do you need help?"

"I think I can manage." She grasped the cup and brought it to her lips. It didn't quite match the feeling she got from her drink the night before, but it soothed her throat. Her hand started to tremble; Alana took the cup before it spilled. "Thank you. Can you help me sit up?"

Alana arranged the pillows so Krystal could lean on them and then helped her into a near sitting position. "Is that better?"

"Yes, thank you." She felt her belly through her nightgown.

"You're bandaged," said Alana. "It might feel tight, like a corset, if you sit too long."

Krystal nodded. "I can feel it."

"The cuts have almost healed."

"How would you know that?"

Alana bowed her head. "The healer found me in here. I asked her. She told me her special salve had cleared up your cuts in no time. The fever just had to run its course."

"I must be alive," Krystal said. "I ache too much to be dead."

The princess's head came up. "You shouldn't joke about death. It's no laughing matter."

Krystal thought of Alana's past. "You're right. I'm sorry."

Alana smiled. "I didn't mean to be harsh."

"I have to ask why you kept coming in here if you knew it meant disobeying your uncle."

"My room is right next to yours," said Alana. "We share a wall. While you were so ill, you mumbled, sometimes shouted, in your fitful sleep."

"And you heard me?"

The princess nodded.

"What exactly did you hear?"

"I heard the truth," Alana said. "You were right about my uncle. I have to help my brother defeat him."

"I'm still dreaming," Krystal said. "This is another one of those horrible dreams."

"I'm serious," said Alana. "I want to join Jareth and the rebels."

Krystal frantically searched her mind for any memory of her illness-induced nightmares. What had she seen? What had she said? She couldn't remember a thing.

Alana seemed encouraged by her silence and continued. "The things you said in your dreams are things you believe, and it convinced me. A conscious person can choose to lie, and that's what my uncle has done my whole life."

"He lied to you, but he's still the man who raised you," Krystal said. "And he must have done a decent job for you to have turned out as you have."

"How could he be both nurturer and tyrant? And why tell me my brother is dead?"

"Gregory has his reasons."

"What can we do to help Jareth?"

"I'm not sure," said Krystal. "Doing so is much more difficult from inside the castle."

"I'm sure we can think of something." Alana sighed. "I wish I could talk to my uncle about it. I'm used to talking my worries over with him."

Krystal shook her head. "I must warn you against it. You'd be risking the lives of a lot of people if you tried to be honest with him now."

Alana lowered her head. "I won't say anything to him."

"I'm sorry," Krystal said. "I know this has to be difficult for you."

"It's nothing compared to what my family has faced," Alana said, shaking her head. "I don't even know what happened."

Krystal opened her mouth to tell her what she knew but stopped as she heard the door open. Both she and Alana turned in time to see King Gregory enter.

Alana pulled away from Krystal and stood up. "Good morning, Uncle."

"What are you doing in here?" he asked.

"It's my fault," Krystal said. "I was so desperately thirsty."

"I heard her call for help," said the princess. "I had just asked her name when you came in."

Krystal smiled at her. "I'm Krystal."

"*Princess* Krystal," said Gregory, with a distinct note of irritation in his voice. "Princess Alana of Fayterra, this is Princess Krystal of Avolonya."

Alana looked back at her. "I am pleased to meet you."

Krystal suspected the king might expect some reaction on her part. She widened her eyes.

Gregory stepped forward. "She must be weary. We should let her rest."

"Of course, Uncle."

He led her to the door. "Why don't you go on?"

Alana stopped. "I can wait for you."

Gregory shook his head. "I'll just be a moment." He closed the door on her protest.

Krystal frowned when he turned to her. "She seems healthy to me."

"Excuse me?"

"Alana," said Krystal. "For a person who died as a child, she seems the picture of health."

"I told her to remain in Demarde. I want her as far from Fay-terra as will be safe for her." He sighed. "Young princesses don't feel inclined to obey my instructions. You certainly don't."

Krystal shook her head. "I won't bear that responsibility. These are *your* lies."

"And you've never lied to me?" he said, his eyes piercing.

What could she say to that?

"I had planned to wait to introduce you. Alana's arrival has unsettled me, and I wish to reconsider certain things before you spend more time with her."

"She knows I'm here," said Krystal. "What are you going to say to her?"

"That you are recovering from your illness and cannot have visitors," Gregory said. "I will explain that to Alana. Her innate compassion will dictate that she stay away from you."

"And I will remain alone in here? For how long?"

He frowned at her. "I don't think you should question my requests. You don't have to be alone. I could dine with you some evenings."

Krystal fought the urge to roll her eyes. "What about Julienne? Can I have my maid back?"

"I don't think so," he said. "I'm not sure I should reunite you with anyone who may have been instrumental in your previous escape."

"If Julienne had known anything of my escape, why wouldn't I have taken her with me? We get along well together. Is her companionship so much to ask?"

Gregory nodded. "She can return as your maid. Now, I have a request to ask of you."

"What?"

"Do not tell Alana about her brother."

"Doesn't she know Jareth is alive?"

He frowned again. "I see no point in telling her about him when his life won't last the year."

Her love for Jareth wouldn't let her stay silent. "You don't know that."

"Just promise me."

"I won't tell her," Krystal said.

"Thank you, Krystal, for being cooperative about this." He turned toward the door. "I will see you for dinner. Alana is waiting for me."

"You don't need to have dinner with me," she said. "I'll probably be asleep."

"I will return." He paused in the doorway. "There are things I'd like to discuss with you."

Dread settled on Krystal as he shut the door. She couldn't imagine that going well.

Julienne entered shortly after Gregory had left. "I've been worried about you."

"I've worried about you too," Krystal said. "Did he punish you at all when he found you'd been sneaking me food?"

The maid shook her head. "He's been too busy fretting over you." She looked around. "This place looks and smells like a sick room. What do you want to do first? Are you hungry or would you like a bath?"

"I suppose I could eat a little something."

"I'll go fetch some soup," said Julienne. "We can move you to the chair so you can eat. I can at least get this bedding changed." She walked to the door.

Krystal nodded her agreement. She leaned back and closed her eyes to wait.

The maid returned with a bowl of warm soup and busied herself straightening the room and changing the sheets while Krystal ate. Krystal decided she did want to bathe after all. Julienne had to help her, but once she had finished and put on a clean nightgown, she felt much better. Julienne dried Krystal's hair while they talked.

"Tomorrow I'll have some maids help me with your clothes," the maid said. "Once you feel better, you will want warmer gowns to wear."

"I didn't realize I had anything else," said Krystal.

"King Gregory saw to it."

"He plans for everything." Krystal sighed. "I wish he'd stop it."

"I don't think you'll get that wish."

"I would think I'd be sent back to the dungeons once I'm well. He told me I wouldn't be allowed out unless I showed remorse."

"I'm sure he'll explain when he returns."

"That's what worries me," Krystal said.

King Gregory entered her room just as Krystal had finished a light dinner. She'd considered feigning sleep when he arrived but didn't want to appear cowardly. She returned his greeting as he sat down in the chair.

"You look much better," he said.

"I told you, Julienne takes good care of me."

"We need to discuss the future. I won't put you back in the dungeon."

"So I won't have to apologize for doing what was right?"

He looked at her darkly. "I will not discuss with you what has happened in the past. I wish to offer you a clean slate. We will forget what has transpired."

She could not conceal her shock. "You want me to simply forget what you did? You had me kidnapped. You imprisoned me in this castle."

Gregory waved his hand. "We must both make concessions here, Krystal. I am willing to forget your deceptions and your escape from the castle. We need to look to the future and not dwell on the past."

Krystal sighed and looked at her hands. So much had happened that she could not forget. But she needed to buy some time so she could think of a way to help Jareth.

"I can try."

"Thank you." He seemed to relax a little. "I would like us to be cordial to one another. I don't want to have to worry about an undercurrent of hostility between us."

Krystal wondered if she had the self-control to maintain cordiality with him. "What about my restrictions? Will I have the freedom to roam the castle and the gardens?"

He fixed her with a pointed gaze. "Will you try to escape? Need I remind you that you came with me willingly this time?"

"I accepted your offer to save Jareth's life."

"I could restrict you to this room with a guard posted at your door. I could give you freedom to roam the castle with a guard following your every move. Or I could give you unrestricted freedom to go where you please with no supervision." He leaned forward. "But I won't give you leave to make a fool of me again. I'm not going to give you all the freedom you may desire if it means you will run away. The choice is yours."

Krystal knew she couldn't leave the castle yet. She couldn't promise Alana help and then leave at the first opportunity. She doubted she and Alana could escape without White Lightning. And regardless of what he said, she knew Gregory would watch her every move. She had to stay, possibly until Jareth attacked with his men and took his throne back.

"I promise I won't try to escape," Krystal said.

"Excellent," Gregory said. "I have one more thing to ask you."

"What is it?"

He leaned forward. "In a few weeks, Fayterra will hold its annual Fall Festival. It's a costumed gala with plenty of food, dancing, and games. I'd like to take you."

"I've never been to a festival. I don't know how to dance."

"Dancing isn't difficult. I'd be happy to show you."

Krystal didn't have to think about that. "I don't need all that attention."

He reached out and cupped her chin. "I'd give you the world if you'd allow it."

His eyes captured her. "The world isn't yours to give."

"Give me time." Gregory released her chin. "You can dine with us in the dining hall when you've recovered." He smiled again. "I think you will like Alana. She is very much like you."

Krystal lowered her eyes. "I'm sure I will."

The king started to rise but then stopped and took her hands in his. "I want you to know nothing has changed. I will not stop trying to win your love. And I will marry you."

Her heart sank. "Will nothing dissuade you?"

"You are the only queen I will accept. Good night, Krystal."

Krystal resolved to a solitary goal: to somehow help Jareth regain his throne. She did not have physical strength and couldn't openly challenge the king. She didn't have the power to convince the castle folk to obey her orders. But Krystal *did* have a power over Gregory. She could either make such a nuisance of herself with escape attempts, or she could somehow convince him she'd had a change of heart and wanted to marry him.

She blew out one of the candles by her bed and settled into her pillows, wishing she could talk over her worries with someone. Alana troubled her. Perhaps, if she could remember what she'd said during her delirium, the princess would be easier to believe.

Krystal had the most pleasant dream about Jareth while she slept. When he kissed her, she felt it all the way down to her toes.

She bolted upright in bed and looked around the room. She was alone. It had been no more than a realistic dream.

Her room had cooled considerably. Krystal burrowed under her covers and looked longingly at the fireplace. It had to be late; no one would come if she called. She didn't think she had the strength to get the fire going, even though it had already been stocked with wood.

"Oh, light yourself," she said with a small wave at the fireplace. Krystal almost laughed then. Apparently she'd resorted to talking to fireplaces.

The roar of flame made her jump.

Krystal sat up in surprise and stared at the fire. She looked stupidly at her hand, examining it in the firelight. It looked the same. The room had already started to warm up, and she felt too sleepy to worry about anything just then. Krystal settled into the covers and fell asleep.

ↄ

King Gregory allowed Alana to visit Krystal daily. Her strength returned quickly, and the more she spoke with Alana, the more Krystal trusted her. The worry she'd felt at first had eased. Krystal remained suspicious of the fire and asked Julienne to be sure it didn't burn out through the night again.

As they planned and schemed, Alana volunteered to keep Lady Fordyce occupied. They agreed that they needed to keep Gregory from being able to effectively delegate responsibilities as much as possible.

Chapter 24

JULIENNE BROUGHT THE COSTUME for the Fall Festival. "The king spoils you."

Krystal had to agree. The magnificent purple velvet gown trimmed with silver and gold had a stiff white collar at the back of the neckline and a full and heavy skirt. She held it up.

"It's beautiful."

Julienne laughed. "It is a gown fit for a queen."

"I would have to agree." Gregory stood in the doorway. "But one thing is missing."

He held a large wooden box. He opened it and Krystal's breath caught.

"Oh, Gregory. I couldn't."

"You must. It's part of the costume."

"But they are so exquisite!" she said. "I could not wear something so valuable."

"When you are queen, trinkets such as these will seem common place." He took her hand and led her to the chair. "Come, I will put them on you."

She sat and let him place the decorative sapphire necklace around her neck. He put the crown on her head. Julienne came forward. "There is one more part." She held a golden mask.

Krystal held it in front of her face. "I don't recognize myself."

"Which is what makes it the perfect costume," said the king. "You look lovely, my dear."

"It is a grand costume, Gregory," she said. "I'm grateful for the use of it."

"I'm going to kiss you good-bye," he said. "Try to behave."

She let him kiss her. "Good-bye, Gregory."

❧

The entire castle buzzed with plans for the Fall Festival. When Gregory arrived at Krystal's door to escort her, she had been washed, dressed, and decorated to a nearly painful point. Though the yards of fabric seemed heavy to Krystal, the deep royal colors of the gown suited her coloring well. Julienne assured her she looked beautiful. Gregory seemed to concur.

"You look glorious," he said.

"As do you." She meant it. He wore black trousers and boots that matched the cloak that hung over his arm. His tunic and shirt shared the same fabric and colors of her gown.

They rode the short distance to the village in silence. The reason for the carriage became obvious when they arrived. A great deal of pomp and circumstance heralded the arrival of the king. Gregory seemed to savor all of the attention, but it embarrassed Krystal.

She could not retain the emotion for long. She saw tables full of sweets and foods, games of skill to play, and a band of minstrels playing for the vast number of people who wished to dance. Men, women, and children—all in costumes—laughed and danced all around her.

She clutched Gregory's arm. "It's wonderful."

He smiled down at her. "You have yet to experience it. Come with me."

Gregory took her to the games booths first, where he had her toss rings onto bottles to win a prize. She proved quite skilled at the game and won a band of silk ribbons. Next they tasted some of the foods offered. And finally they danced. Krystal couldn't help but laugh as he swung her about. Even there with the king, she felt free and content.

As the hours passed, women and children seemed to melt away, leaving a predominantly male crowd. The noise grew louder. King Gregory announced their return to the castle.

Krystal eagerly watched out the window as the village faded away into the darkness. When the last lights of the fires disappeared, she sighed and rested back onto the cushions.

King Gregory had been watching her, his eyes fervent. Krystal closed her eyes to shut him out. He didn't seem the least bit concerned to be caught staring at her. The carriage rolled to a stop in the courtyard, and he helped her out.

"It's cold tonight, once away from the festivities," he said as they entered the main hall. "Could I entice you to my study for something warm to drink?"

Krystal agreed, but soon his "warm drink" was a rather large goblet of wine. A knot formed in her stomach as she watched him drink, and it wouldn't go away. The euphoria of the night slid away, leaving behind only a grim reminder of the last time he'd been drunk. He handed her a glass.

"Actually, Gregory," she said, "I find myself overtired. I've had an exciting evening. Perhaps I should just return to my room."

"You haven't even taken a sip," he said. "Come, just a little. You will feel better."

Not likely, she thought to herself. "I really would rather go to bed." Krystal placed the glass on the table. "Good night, Gregory."

She swept from the room before he could say another word.

Chapter 25

A NDREW ARRIVED IN THE VILLAGE near the castle in time for
Fayterra's Fall Festival. Smells of roasting meat wafted through
the air. His stomach growled.

As he ate, Andrew looked around at all the splendor. Festivals
at home had not been this excessive. One particular couple caught
his eye. They'd dressed as king and queen. Either the man wore the
costume extremely well, or it wasn't a costume. His queen, however,
caught Andrew's eye. Behind her mask, even from so far away, he
could see her wide smile.

His sister, ever on his mind, sprang up again. The woman could
easily have been Krystal. He looked around. Many of the women
could be his sister.

He sighed. He still didn't know why he'd traveled so far from
home. The journey had cost him his horse. How could Krystal possibly be here?

Andrew walked around amid the crush of people. He stopped
one or two and asked the same questions he'd asked at every village
since leaving home. *I'm looking for a girl. She'd be a stranger to you;
she has long brown hair and blue eyes. Have you seen her?*

Just then, Andrew spotted some guardsmen standing near the
dancers. They wore the uniforms described to him as the Fayterra
Royal Guard, the same uniform reportedly on the body some villagers had found buried in the woods of Brynne. Impatient, he strode
in their direction.

Without warning, two masked men looped their arms in his and began pulling him in the opposite direction. Andrew struggled as they pulled him back from the festivities and into the shadows.

"Release me!" he said. "What is this? Are you robbers?"

One of the men laughed. "No."

"Who are you? Tell me!"

"There isn't time for that," the other said. "We need to get you away from here."

"I'm not going anywhere with you." Andrew continued to fight them. "Let me go."

A third man appeared from the shadows, and Andrew's world suddenly went dark.

஧

Andrew woke when he landed on the grass. He closed his eyes and listened to the low voices nearby. They had not bound him. Standing seemed a bit beyond him.

"Calum, what are you talking about?" A new voice asked that question.

"Him, sire."

Andrew couldn't help himself. He looked up. A tall young man stood before him with long blonde hair and a confused look on his face.

"How did you get here?" he demanded.

Andrew looked at him. "Who's asking?"

"Watch your tone," the one called Calum said. "This is Crown Prince Jareth of Fayterra. You will show him respect."

With difficulty, Andrew stood. "I am to respect a prince who has an innocent man grabbed off the street and assaulted only to be dropped at his feet like a dog?"

Calum stepped forward, but Jareth halted him. "It was poorly done of you, Sir Landen. You could have explained yourself to him."

"I could not," said Calum. "Gregory had attended the festival. Sire, *she* accompanied him."

Jareth released him. "She did? Did she look all right?"

"She looked fine." He continued in a meaningful tone. "They seemed happy."

Jareth turned suddenly and angrily punched a tree.

Andrew snapped. "I'm tired of being ignored. I want answers, and I want them now!"

The prince turned on him, eyes burning. "You want answers? You were brought to me to save your life! I have no doubt that your blabbing all over the village would have reached the ears of the king. And if he hears you are in Fayterra, you're a dead man!" He then stalked away.

Calum stood with Andrew, who fell silent now. "He's not usually so brusque. Jareth is under a good deal of strain."

"What is going on in this backward, mixed-up kingdom anyway?" Andrew asked in a more subdued tone. "And why did he seem to know me?"

The knight sighed. "You're looking for your sister, correct?"

Taken aback, he nodded. "Yes."

"Prince Jareth knows exactly where she is," Calum said.

"How does he know Krystal?"

"He is engaged to her."

"What?"

"To understand about your sister, you must first learn the history of this kingdom," the knight said. "If you sit down, I'll explain everything. But first, what do you know of magic?"

Andrew sat. "Magic is the stuff of stories."

Calum smiled at him. "Not anymore. This explanation may take longer than I thought."

❧

Andrew couldn't think of what to say. He sat with the paper before him. Finally he wrote: *I have found Krystal but we cannot return yet. Keep the farm running. I will explain later.*

He folded the paper and handed it to Avery, who waited nearby. As the messenger walked to his waiting horse, Andrew looked up at Calum.

"I want to help. If defeating the king is the only way to get my sister back, I want to do what I can to make that happen."

Jareth approached them. "What skill do you possess with a weapon?"

"My father taught me the blade," he said. "I brought my sword. I also hunt with the bow and brought that as well."

"Do you practice?"

"When I can," said Andrew.

"There is a field over the hill where the men train by day," Jareth said. "Why don't you get your sword? We'll go see how rusty you are."

Andrew got to his feet, frowning. He took a couple of steps closer to Jareth and stopped. "I am not one of your subjects. You cannot order me about like everyone else out here to do your bidding. Your politics mean nothing to me. I only want my sister safe."

Jareth stepped up. "If you want to help rescue Krystal, you will do everything you are told. If you aren't willing to do that, you can go hide out on your own until this is all over. Or you can catch up to Avery and take your message home yourself."

Krystal's eldest brother and her betrothed stood toe-to-toe for several moments. Neither spoke. Neither would back down.

At last Andrew sighed. "Very well. I will do you as you ask. My sword is in my pack. Excuse me." He retrieved his weapon and returned to Jareth.

The prince moved closer. "I don't want to have to worry that you will cause problems."

Andrew frowned at him. "I told you I would do as you order. Besides, I can't imagine you'd behave much differently if you had a sister in trouble."

"I do," said Jareth.

"What do you mean?"

"My sister is in the castle with Krystal," Jareth said. "But unlike you and your sister, Alana doesn't even know who I am."

Andrew's frown deepened. He didn't want to feel sorry for this arrogant young prince, but just the same, he felt a pang of sympathy. He changed the subject. "Am I to prove my skill to you, or should I go practice with your men?"

Jareth looked him over. "First show me what you can do." He drew his own sword.

Andrew brought the sword up and swung at Jareth. "Why doesn't your sister know you?"

Jareth blocked him. "My uncle stole her when we were infants." He attacked. "Calum tells me Krystal is betrothed to a man from your village."

Andrew dodged the blow. "His name is Curtis Belvey," he said. "I arranged the marriage, and Krystal wasn't happy about it."

Jareth smiled and swung his sword again. "I imagine she wasn't."

Conversation gave way as their attacks became more earnest. Andrew soon felt sweat drip down from his forehead. Jareth certainly had skill with the blade, and he hardly looked winded.

In another moment, the prince had knocked the sword from Andrew's hand. "I concede. I guess this is what I get from sitting at a desk most days."

"You aren't inept," Jareth said. "You just need practice. I told your sister something similar when we crossed swords."

"You sparred with Krystal?" Andrew could not quite contain his shock. "Why?"

Jareth dug his sword into the ground and leaned on the hilt. "Do you want the real reason or what I told her?"

"Both," Andrew said.

"I told her it would do me good to practice with her to regain my strength after my long stay in prison," said the prince. "In reality, I just wanted to spend more time with her."

"I don't need to hear you were chasing after my sister."

Jareth frowned. "I'm not going to conceal from you that I love your sister. Krystal means more to me than you can imagine. I should think you'd be glad to hear it. There isn't anyone else more committed than I am to seeing her free again."

"Yes, there is," said Andrew. "And I'm right here."

Chapter 26

KRYSTAL PICKED AT HER BREAKFAST before Julienne arrived to help her dress. She chose her gown with care. The black gown with silver trim fortified her. She fastened every button up the front to her chin and let Julienne brush out her hair until it shimmered. Resolved that she could not put it off any longer, Krystal left her chambers to find the king.

She found him in his study. "I wondered if you had time to talk."

"For you, I will make the time." King Gregory crossed the room and closed the study door. Taking her hand he led her to a chair and sat opposite her.

"This is hard for me," she said. "I don't know where to begin."

"I can wait."

Krystal stared at the fire in the hearth while she composed her mind. The weather had turned cold, and a fire burned in nearly every room of the castle. Spurts of sunshine warmed the daylight hours some, but she found herself shivering nonetheless.

"I know we are supposed to move forward, but I have to say this. This isn't easy for me to admit, Gregory, so I'm just going to come out and say it. I've been wrong, about so many things." She looked at him. "If Jareth truly cared about me, he would have done anything to keep me close to him. I've begun to think you care about me more than he does." She let her eyes fall to her hands. "And I can't deny any longer that something between you and I has changed."

King Gregory started to stand but sat clumsily on the edge of the chair instead. He opened his mouth then closed it. He leaned forward. "Did you just agree to marry me?"

She looked up. "I don't know. You haven't asked me yet."

"Don't move." Gregory hurried to the desk and opened one of the lower drawers. "I've had this for a while now, waiting for just the right moment." He rushed back to where she sat.

"My beloved Krystal," Gregory said. "Will you marry me?"

Krystal looked him in the eye and lied through her teeth. "Yes."

He pulled a gold ring out of the box. With a smile, she let him slip it onto her finger.

King Gregory rose and took her into his arms. "Shall we seal it with a kiss?"

"Naturally," she said.

Before when he had forced kisses on her, she had not responded, but now she could not afford that luxury. Fortunately, the door opened and Lady Fordyce walked inside.

"Your Majesty," Caprice faltered when she saw them. "I didn't mean to intrude."

Gregory looked up at her. "What do you want, Countess?"

"You asked me to give you a status report of our troops this morning. I'll return later."

Gregory stopped her. "Krystal has just agreed to be my bride."

Krystal watched the cascade of emotions the king's words caused. In a mere moment, Caprice paled, her face contorted, and finally she settled her features into a smile.

"You have my congratulations and my best wishes," she said. "King Gregory, I will speak with you later about the troops."

"Of course." After she had gone he turned back to Krystal. "Now, where were we?"

Krystal put a finger gently on his lips. "I believe we were somewhere around here."

Princess Alana walked in then. Caprice had left the door open in her haste. "Good morning, Uncle Gregory." Her voice trailed away as she took in the scene before her. "Uncle?"

At the sight of his niece, Gregory released Krystal so suddenly she almost fell. He recovered quickly enough to catch her and pull her back into his arms.

"What is this?"

Gregory answered her. "Krystal has agreed to be my wife."

Alana paled. "How wonderful! Uncle, you didn't tell me you were courting anyone. Nor did my new friend mention this to me."

The king shifted uncomfortably. "I am a grown man, my dear. Surely you can't expect me to discuss such matters with my innocent young niece. It is long past time I sought a queen, and with the issues in this kingdom nearly settled once and for all, I can't see a better time to wed."

"And I'm sorry to not have discussed this with you," Krystal said, trying to play the part. "I just couldn't think what to say."

"It's fine," Alana said airily when she really looked ready to bolt. "I suppose I'll return to my chambers."

Krystal pulled out of Gregory's arms and stepped forward. "I'll go with you."

The king put up a hand to stop her. "Krystal, that isn't necessary."

"I'll be back in a few minutes. I promise I won't be long."

Alana seemed to struggle with her next words. "Congratulations, Uncle."

Halfway to her room Alana's face regained its color. "I sounded like a blithering idiot. I didn't expect that to be so hard. What made you do it now?"

"I'm not sure," Krystal said. "Time is so short. Surely Jareth will attack soon."

Alana embraced her. "We are lucky to have you." She then turned and went to her room.

Krystal had no choice but to return to Gregory. She knew he'd be suspicious if she took her time. As his future bride, he expected her to *want* to be with him. She walked back to the king's study.

Lady Fordyce had returned. "They are still camped outside the village. Sixteen of Vandior's mercenaries died during the journey." She looked at the door as Krystal entered. "Fourteen due to rebel attacks, and there were two stupid enough to try to desert."

"Will Vandior be joining his men?"

"No, sire." Caprice did not elaborate. Her gaze still centered on the doorway.

The king followed her eyes. "Hello, my love."

The countess excused herself. "I will speak to you when you are free, King Gregory. Right now I have an appointment. Princess Alana requested to see me."

After she had gone, Gregory pulled Krystal into his arms. "Let's plan a party. I want to tell the whole kingdom you will be my bride."

The perfect distraction. "That sounds wonderful," she said. "Will we have time? There is so much to do. I will need a wedding dress, for starters."

He smiled. "I've taken care of that already."

Krystal fought to keep her disappointment from showing. "How? When?"

Gregory stepped away and sighed. "I guess it's time I confessed. I engaged a seamstress to make your wedding dress before you came to Fayterra. She finished it some weeks ago."

Chills coursed through her. "Will I get to see it?"

"You will." He closed the gap between them. "I wanted to present it to you as a gift."

Krystal smiled up at him. "You are so considerate. Thank you."

"We should have the engagement party as soon as possible," Gregory said. "I still want to marry you as soon as I am crowned king of Fayterra, and the coronation is fast approaching."

She nodded; she knew Jareth's deadline well. "I've never planned a party before."

"Alana can help you," he said. "It was part of her education."

"I'll be glad for her assistance."

He leaned down and kissed her gently. "I don't want you to worry about anything. You will learn the duties of a queen. Right now, I just want to enjoy having you near me."

"I love you too," she said. Desperate to change the subject, she reached out and placed her hand on his chest. "Tell me something."

Gregory inhaled deeply. "Anything."

"How old are you?"

His eyes widened. "Why?"

"It's not unusual for me to want to know a little about the man I'm going to marry," Krystal said. "You'd have to admit, though we have spent a measure of time together, we don't know much about each other. At least I don't know much about your past."

Gregory seemed uncomfortable. "We agreed to leave the past behind us."

"Your age is hardly a past event." His hesitation confused her.

"What is so important about a number?" He released her. "I've never believed a person's physical age should matter in important things. We should just forget it."

"What's wrong?" A sudden thought hit her. "Are you embarrassed?"

"No," he said. "I don't feel it should be important, that's all."

She smiled playfully. "Just tell me. I promise it won't hurt."

He smiled. "You can be so persuasive."

"So you'll tell me?"

"I'll think about it."

She raised her hand to toy with his hair. "Your age can't be such a secret. There have to be others who know how old you are. I can just ask your niece."

He captured her hand in his. "I hadn't thought of that. You would, wouldn't you?"

Krystal batted her eyelashes at him but said nothing.

The king sighed. "Forty."

She blinked. "I'm sorry?"

"I am forty years old," he said. "I will be forty-one in the spring."

"That wasn't so hard, now was it?"

"You have no idea." He looked down at her. "As for the rest of it, there isn't much to tell. I have no family, save Alana. No parents or distant cousins to present to you."

"And you know mine," she said. "The farm is all I knew. We're boring."

"Not boring," he said as he squeezed her. "Uncomplicated."

Krystal wanted to laugh. Her life had never been so complicated. "That sounds nice," she said instead. "I'd like a quiet life."

Gregory put a finger under her chin. "Not too quiet, I hope. I have an expectation of sons. Perhaps a few daughters, as well."

His hold on her changed as he kissed her. Krystal wrapped her arms around his neck and kissed him back. She pulled away when he deepened the kiss.

"I hope I can trust you to behave yourself," she said.

His eyes darkened with passion. "So do I." He reached for her, but Krystal skirted away.

"Perhaps I should go talk to Alana about the party."

Gregory gave her a pained smile. "Perhaps you should. I will see you at dinner, my love."

She smiled at the door. "Of course, darling."

ↀ

Krystal found Alana. "We're to plan an engagement party," she said when the princess opened her door. Krystal noticed Lysabith behind her. "Should I come back later?"

"No, come in," Alana said. "Lyssa was just leaving."

The maid smiled at Krystal and walked to the door. Krystal stepped out of her way. "There's more. My wedding dress is already made."

To her surprise, Lyssa stopped and nodded. "That's true. I knew the lady who made it."

Krystal caught it. "Knew her?"

"It's a sad story," said Lyssa. "She died before delivering the gown to the castle."

"But Gregory has it."

Lyssa nodded. "He must have sent someone after it. I expect it's a beautiful dress. My friend went to considerable trouble and expense to make it."

"Thank you, Lysabith," said Alana. "You may go." She shut the door after the maid.

"Why does my blood run cold at the idea of this woman's accident?" asked Krystal.

"I feel it too," said Alana. "Do you think Gregory had something to do with it?"

"It is convenient for him that she died before he could pay her. He now has the gown."

Alana shook her head. "I don't want to speculate. Tell me about the party."

"He wants an engagement party," Krystal said. "And it has to be fast."

"But you'll need a new gown! And planning a party takes time."

Krystal smiled at her. "You have a plan."

"I believe I should go speak with my uncle. This party needs more time to be perfect."

"And lots of interruptions."

Alana moved to the door. "Exactly."

ຕາ

Krystal dressed for the king that night. Julienne protested that the gown she chose was intended for summer, but Krystal wanted it for the neckline. She would stun him to distraction if she must. After one last, fortifying breath, Krystal went to the dining hall.

King Gregory met her at the door. He eyed her bare arms and frowned.

"Don't you think you'll be cold?"

She looked up at him through her lashes. "I shouldn't be."

The king bent and kissed her cheek. He sighed. "Come, let's get you seated."

There had been a reorganization of the placements at the dinner table. The king placed his fiancée in the seat formerly occupied by Lady Fordyce. Princess Alana took the seat on Gregory's other side across from Krystal. Caprice glowered at Krystal as she took her place further down the table. Krystal glared back and placed her hand on the king's arm. He looked adoringly at her and kept his eyes on her throughout dinner.

Krystal fought the panic that rose within her and plastered a smile to her face. The performance took its toll; she could hardly eat a bite. Gregory and Alana spoke of the upcoming party.

"I doubt you will find my celebration difficult to plan at all," Gregory said. "Though I do agree that Krystal, and you as my niece, should have new gowns for the occasion."

"But it can take weeks to sew a new gown!" Alana smiled at him. "There will be fittings, and second fittings, and that's not including the shoes. Why, sometimes a cobbler takes as much time with a pair of shoes that a seamstress would take on a gown."

"You worry too much," said the king. "I have a team of seamstresses and cobblers. For them, this work will be simple."

Krystal couldn't resist. "Does one of your seamstresses happen to be the woman who made my wedding gown?"

Gregory frowned. "No, that woman died."

She shot Alana a look. "That's shocking. Was she old?"

"Not particularly. She wrote asking for more money but was killed before my reply reached her."

"How terrible," said Krystal. "How her poor family must suffer."

"Don't dwell on it," he said. "These things happen."

"Uncle, how long do you think the planning should take?"

Gregory looked down at his niece. "I think two weeks is more than enough time."

Alana's face creased with worry. "That's so soon. Are you certain?"

"I am." Gregory's tone left no room for argument.

Chapter 27

KRYSTAL SLEPT LATE on the morning of the engagement gala. The flurry of preparations over the last two weeks had exhausted her. She had just finished bathing and dressing before Alana knocked on her door.

"I can't believe we did it," Alana said after Krystal let her in. "I wish Uncle Gregory had given us more time."

"We did our best. I've never pretended to be so helpless in my life."

Alana smiled. "You did wonderfully. I thought the many times you changed your mind about your gown was inspired."

"The real surprise is that Gregory still wants to marry me after all that," said Krystal.

"You did get annoying," Alana agreed. "I confess that once or twice I wanted to clamp my hand over your mouth."

"It's almost over."

"Has there been any word from Jareth?"

Krystal shook her head. "There's almost no time before Gregory's planned coronation."

"And your wedding." Alana sighed. "I wish I knew what was going on out there."

"So do I."

Getting ready for the engagement party took the better part of the day, but when Krystal looked at her friend, she thought it well worth the trouble. "Alana, you look exquisite."

"I pale in comparison to you," the princess said. "My uncle's jaw will hit the finely polished floor when you enter the ballroom."

Krystal couldn't help but feel that she walked toward her doom as they walked to the ballroom together. Her feet felt heavier with every step. Princess Alana kept up a nervous chatter as they walked. Krystal clasped Alana's hand briefly for strength before they were announced.

"Princess Krystal of Avolonya and Princess Alana of Fayterra."

King Gregory, resplendent in his finest clothes, strode forward to greet them. His crown glinted in the torchlight. "Alana, you look lovely." He took Krystal's hand. "And you look simply perfect." The king led them away. "Come and let me introduce you to some people."

It amazed Krystal as she looked around that she recognized some of the faces present. The Grand Minister stood away from the crush of people, surveying the event. Across the room she could see the tall head of the Elder Patriarch. She instantly worried if Gregory had seen him.

King Gregory introduced them to several people, all of whom Krystal had never met before. At last she saw a familiar face.

"Count Alexander," the king said. "You remember Princess Krystal?"

The young man bowed. "I could never forget such a lovely lady. May I offer my congratulations to you both?"

"Alexander, may I present my niece, Princess Alana?"

The handsome man stared at the princess for a long moment. Krystal could feel the heat radiating from him. Alana met his stare. Finally he took her hand and kissed it.

"A true pleasure, Princess," he said. "King Gregory, might we speak privately a moment? I'd like to talk with you about a problem my father is having."

"I think the ladies can entertain themselves a moment," said Gregory. "I won't be long."

"Good evening, Princess Krystal."

Krystal turned and smiled her first true smile in a long time. "Alana, may I present Leodegrance Severin, the Elder Patriarch? Sir, this is Princess Alana of Fayterra."

Alana curtsied to the Elder Patriarch. "I am honored, sir."

Though Krystal couldn't explain it, she felt safer around Brother Severin. They had only met briefly, but she found herself wishing this time he would stay.

The tall man smiled. "The pleasure is mine, Princess." His eyes suddenly had an odd look to them. "Will you be visiting your uncle long?"

"I'm lonesome for family," said the princess. "I'd like to stay."

"Family is vital to our happiness."

"Indeed," Gregory said. He had left Alexander standing alone in his haste to return.

Brother Severin's brown eyes sharply glanced at the king. "Yes." He looked back at Krystal. "Have you been here all this time?"

"Princess Krystal has become something of a permanent visitor," Gregory said. "If you will forgive us, I must introduce the princesses to the other guests."

She could barely spare Brother Severin a nod before the king steered her away. Puzzled by Gregory's behavior, Krystal tried to speak to him, but he only hushed her inquiries and led her and Alana to an older gentleman and his wife. The lady happened to be conversing with Caprice Fordyce, who looked positively mutinous in a hastily selected and poor fitting gown.

"Charles, how nice to see you. And Gretchen, you're looking well." He turned. "Princesses Krystal and Alana, allow me to introduce you to the duke and duchess of Eldor, Charles and Gretchen Almaine."

"A pleasure, ladies," the gray-haired man said with a bow.

Gretchen curtsied. "They're so charming, King Gregory."

"Yes," said the duke. "However did you come by them, old man?"

Gregory laughed. "Alana is my niece, and Krystal is my bride to be."

The couple offered their sincere congratulations. Krystal could tell the king thoroughly enjoyed introducing her as his. She noted his obvious omission of the fact he'd kidnapped her but supposed she could not argue with him now.

"We do hope to be seeing more of you dear ladies," Duke Charles said. "Now, though, I must introduce my wife to the Elder Patriarch. Please excuse us."

"May I come?" asked Princess Alana. "I'd love to speak more with that man. I find him fascinating." She walked away with the couple before her uncle could protest.

Gregory turned to his left and faced his Captain. "Krystal, I'd like you to meet . . . uh, I'm terribly sorry, what was your name again?"

The lady's face flushed. "Caprice, sire."

Her king started. "Lady Fordyce? I hardly recognized you."

Caprice scowled. "You ordered me to wear a gown, Majesty."

"Yes, well, you look nice. Excuse us, won't you?"

"You really didn't recognize her, Gregory?" Krystal asked after they'd moved away.

"Not at first." He looked down at her. "Dance with me. I want an excuse to hold you."

He led her out to the center of the floor, and the music began. Krystal had to admit, despite everything, she enjoyed dancing with the king. She felt so graceful in his arms. She could almost forget everything but the music in her ears and the floor beneath her feet.

Exuberant, she looked up at him. King Gregory's eyes darted around the room as they moved. She was surprised to see him frowning fiercely. In his distraction, he nearly steered them into another dancing couple. His eyes flashed green fire.

"Gregory?" she said. "What's wrong?"

He looked down at her and sighed. "You are so ravishing. Even though we are betrothed, most of these men are openly staring at you." Gregory smiled without humor, almost sadly. "I knew this would happen."

"They are curious, that's all."

"And you are delightfully naïve," he said. "You have no idea how lovely you look."

Krystal chose not to reply and turned her head to locate Alana. The princess stood near the refreshment table next to the Elder Patriarch, who spoke with Count Alexander.

Without warning, Brother Severin stepped back and the count bowed to Princess Alana. Krystal smiled as her friend allowed him to lead her in a dance.

Gregory must have noticed her smile. "Tell me what amuses you, love."

"Count Alexander seems taken with Alana," Krystal said. "They're dancing."

"Alexander always had an eye for beauty. I always found it strange that he visited Lady Fordyce."

This surprised Krystal. "He was charmed by Caprice?"

"He often came to see her. Perhaps they exchanged sword techniques."

"Perhaps." Krystal searched the crowd for the countess and found her standing alone, watching the dancers.

While he allowed Krystal to dance with other men, Gregory stood nearby, watching their every move. It unnerved her. She quickly began to lose her good spirits. He danced with her most often himself, but when she tried to point out his behavior, he denied it.

"I am only looking out for you, my love," he said.

"How can I come to harm at a party?"

He did not answer her.

Count Alexander, who had frequented the dance floor with Alana, interrupted them. "Might I cut in, Your Majesty?" the count said. "Your niece would like a rest, and I have yet to dance with your charming fiancée."

"Of course," said Gregory. He stepped back to allow the count to take Krystal's hand and then led Alana off the dance floor.

"Hello again, Princess Krystal," said the young man. "Are you enjoying the ball?"

"Yes," she said. "You seem to be enjoying Princess Alana's company."

Alexander smiled. "She is a charming, lovely girl. I find myself fascinated by her."

"She is my dearest friend," Krystal said.

"The king is watching us," he said.

Krystal sighed. "He has been doing that all night."

"You don't seem pleased."

"Would you like being the bug in a glass jar? I wanted to enjoy myself tonight; I wanted to forget things." Her words trailed off as she realized she was speaking to a man she hardly knew.

His tone sounded gentle. "What did you want to forget?"

Krystal regarded her handsome young dance partner with suspicion. Though she had seen him with Alana most this evening, she wasn't sure if he could be trusted. What if she opened her heart to him, and he betrayed her to the king? Gregory would be furious.

"Perhaps it would put you at ease if I told you about myself," he said. "As a small boy, my parents brought me to Fayterra to live. I was among a group of youngsters who grew up in the palace with the prince. We were here when King Gregory assumed the throne, and some of us continued to live in the castle until our parents called for our return home."

"Why are you telling me this?"

He leaned in. "I want you to know Jareth is a friend," he said. "I have always been loyal to him, even to the point of spying for him. I know him well. He would not like this game you play with his uncle. I've already proven myself to Alana. Must I prove myself to you as well?"

"Keep your distance," Krystal said. "Gregory is possessive."

Alexander straightened. "It's little wonder. I've never seen him so consumed."

"What did Alana tell you?"

"She confided you were in league with Prince Jareth and that he plans to attack the palace."

Krystal sighed. "She didn't leave much out."

"What of your engagement to King Gregory?"

"It's a ruse," she said. "I only told him I would marry him to distract him from planning against Jareth's impending attack."

"I'd say it's working," he said. "Here he comes."

Gregory stood behind Krystal. "Excuse me, Alexander, but may I cut in?"

"Certainly, sire. Princess, thank you for the dance." The young man bowed and walked away.

Gregory began his tirade when the count stepped out of earshot. "I know the man likes beautiful women, but not *my* beautiful woman!"

Krystal looked up at him, exasperated. "Count Alexander is a gentleman. He was only being polite."

"Ha!" the king snorted. "Men can't be friendly with you, Krystal. You are the type of woman who is either hated or desired. You may as well learn to live with that."

She sighed. "You speak nonsense, Gregory. No woman is as you describe."

He remained unperturbed by her argument. "You are utterly without guile, Krystal."

"We both know that isn't true." She looked away. "I see Alana has gotten her second wind."

"Yes, and Alexander seems to be paying her exorbitant attention," said the king. "I should speak with him of his intentions toward my niece."

Krystal had to agree. "You had probably better."

Each dance drew them closer to the time when the king would formally introduce Krystal as his betrothed. Tradition in Fayterra called for a toast of wine, so when the goblets were filled, Gregory brought Krystal to stand with him at the entrance to the balcony. The Grand Minister moved to stand one step below him and, at his beckoning, the Elder Patriarch. Brother Severin stood close to Krystal as Gregory and the Grand Minister conferred.

"I must say that it is with misgivings I would wed you to the king," he said. "He is not the man for you, Princess. There are certain aspects of his character you do not know."

"On the contrary, Brother Severin, I know him better than most."

Those keen eyes regarded her closely, and he said nothing more.

The herald's trumpet silenced them, as well as everyone else in the hall. "Presenting King Gregory Gildresleve of Demarde and Fayterra."

Gregory held up his hands. The clocks chimed midnight.

"My people," he said, "it is my honor to stand before you this night." The twelfth chime ceased. "Well, morning then."

Polite laughter rose from the crowd.

"As you know, I am at last going to take a wife. Ladies and gentlemen, I present my betrothed, Princess Krystal of Avolonya."

The crowd cheered as he took Krystal's hand and brought her to stand next to him. She looked out at all the faces, Jareth's people, and hoped they would understand. With all her heart, she wished Jareth could be the one standing beside her.

One of Gregory's guards burst into the room. "Prince Jareth is attacking the palace!"

Gregory whirled and pushed open the balcony doors. Krystal followed him. She could clearly pick Jareth, Calum, and Voltimande out of the melee before the king dragged her inside.

"Caprice!" the king said. A guard handed him a sword. "Take Krystal and Alana to their chambers and then find me! Alana, where's Alexander?"

The princess shook her head, eyes wide. "I don't know. He rushed out."

Lady Fordyce spoke up. "Sire, I am not dressed to fight!"

"Then change into suitable clothes and find me." Gregory pulled Krystal up against his body and kissed her hard. "I swear I will return for you!" He tore out of the room.

"Come with me," Caprice ordered the princess, pushing through the panicking guests. Alana and Krystal followed her. She shut them into Krystal's chambers and ordered them to wait there. The moment the door closed, Krystal began unfastening her gown.

"What are you doing?"

"I'm going to Jareth. I have to help him." The gown fell to the floor.

Alana shook her head, eyes wide in fear. "We can't! We should stay here."

"I will not hide in my room while the castle falls apart!" The slips fluttered to the floor.

The princess stood still a moment, as though wrestling with something. Then she seemed to come to a decision. "Very well. Let's go."

Krystal slipped on another gown. "You are staying here. I wish I had my pants."

"No, I'm not." The princess turned to leave. "Wait for me. I'm going to change."

Krystal didn't have time to argue. "If you don't hurry, I will go without you."

Alana returned as she pulled on her boots. She wore a serviceable blue gown and carried something in her arms. "Take this. I think you'll be able to put it to better use."

Krystal took the blade that had been a gift from Jareth. The sword glinted in the firelight. "Thank you," she said. "I'd wondered where it had gone."

Alana smiled. "It wasn't mine to keep. It's only right you should have it."

"Thank you," Krystal said again. They opened the door and stepped into the hall.

Before they could move, they heard footsteps pounding down the hall. Caprice rounded the corner before them, dressed as normal, sword in hand.

Chapter 28

I TOLD YOU TO STAY IN YOUR ROOM," Lady Fordyce said to the two young women.

Alana stepped forward. "And not help my brother regain his throne?" She advanced angrily. "We will assist Jareth, the *rightful* king, and rid his domain of you rebels!"

Lady Fordyce seethed at them silently a moment. "You lied about everything. You deceived both the king and me. You are both traitors." She drew her sword. "Come, Krystal, let's see if you have any skill with that weapon in your hand. After I have killed you, I will execute your sneaky little princess friend."

"You're mad!" Krystal said. "You would never attack the king's niece!"

"King Gregory will thank me for disposing of a traitor," she said. "Stand guard! In my sovereign's name, I command you to fight!"

Krystal didn't consider retreating. Her friend drew back into the doorway of Krystal's chamber. She caught a glimpse of Alana's horror stricken face before Caprice called out again.

"Now we will see how talented you really are, *Princess*." She saluted Krystal with her blade.

Krystal copied her. "You know who the rightful king is, Caprice. I will do everything in my power to help Jareth."

"Your struggles will be in vain! You will never leave this spot!" She brought her sword up with a yell.

Krystal blocked her sword, her teeth rattling as the blades met.

Caprice broke away and came from the right for another attack. Krystal moved back, prepared, but the lady feinted left and opened a deep gash on Krystal's right arm. Alana cried out as blood soaked the sleeve of Krystal's gown. Krystal glared at Lady Fordyce. A cold, calm feeling washed over her.

"First blood was yours," she said, transferring the blade into her good left hand, "but last blood will be mine."

Dimly, Krystal realized that something more than her own skill was keeping her alive. Caprice swung madly in her wild anger, but Krystal kept her head enough to prevent meeting Caprice's blade with flesh. Sometimes it even felt as though the Lochnikar sword fought on its own. Despite all this, Krystal found herself tiring, and soon the more experienced Lady Fordyce knocked the weapon from her hands.

Caprice threw her own sword away and drew a dagger with a triumphant laugh. "Come closer, traitor, so I can kill you."

Krystal smiled without humor. "Come and get me."

The countess lunged. Krystal fell to the ground, Caprice on top of her. They struggled for her dagger until Krystal managed to kick her away. They rolled apart. Krystal tried to gain her feet but felt her skirt catch. She looked up. Caprice had knelt on the fabric, her eyes gleaming wickedly. She raised the dagger and thrust it downward.

Alana cried out again as blood flowered across Krystal's midsection. Lady Fordyce smiled. Krystal fell back onto her elbows, eyes on the dagger. With her skirts twisted around her legs and pinned by Caprice, she couldn't move.

"Now you know why real warriors don't wear gowns," Caprice said as she raised her dagger once more.

Krystal expected to feel the blade pierce her chest. Instead, something shot over her head. Caprice saw it too late. Woman and weapon collided, and the steel cut deep into her chest, the force of the blow throwing her backward. Lady Fordyce died before she hit the floor. The stone of Krystal's sword glowed bright as it rested in the fallen woman's body.

Krystal stared, unblinking, at the scene before her. Then her stomach lurched unpleasantly, and she turned to regard Princess Alana's white face.

For a moment Alana couldn't move. "The sword," she said in a weak voice. "Legend says the powers within the stone always protect the sword's master. I didn't give any credit to the tales, though I'm glad in this instance to be wrong."

Krystal nodded. "As am I."

Alana stepped over the body and knelt by her side. "How bad is it?"

Krystal put her hand on her middle. "I'm not sure. It burns like fire."

"Let me see." Alana reached over to pull Krystal's hand back. "This might hurt a bit; I'm sorry." She did what she could to stem the flow of blood. "Can you walk? I think the healer should see this. Or you could wait here while I go get her."

Krystal glanced at Caprice's body. "No. Help me up." She had to see Jareth. It just didn't feel like she would be all right until she did. "We need to find your brother."

Alana pursed her lips. "I really think you need to take care of your injuries first."

Krystal tore a bit of her skirt and pressed it to her wound. Using the wall, she pushed herself to her feet with the help of her friend. Krystal nodded her thanks and started to walk forward.

Her body, however, refused to accommodate her. She faltered after a few steps. The petite princess could not support her, and Krystal slid to her knees. Her brain clouded.

"Alana?" Krystal's breath came in snatches. "I think I'm in trouble."

They heard boot steps thunder down the corridor. Krystal raised her head when Alana gasped. King Gregory stood there with a handful of his men.

The shock of seeing him there momentarily overrode her pain. It didn't make sense; not enough time had passed since Jareth's attack had begun. The bloody sword in his hand was evidence that he'd engaged his enemy. Krystal met his eyes but saw only surprise and concern. Wouldn't he be worried if he had to flee from Jareth's assault?

Alana spoke to him. "What are you doing here?"

King Gregory ignored the question. Instead he passed off his sword and slid to his knees before his fiancée. "Krystal, what has happened to you?"

"Lady Caprice," said his niece. "She attacked us."

The king's eyes flicked to the body of his fallen lieutenant and back again. "Why?"

Krystal ignored them. She wanted to ask about Jareth but felt somehow Gregory's apparent unconcern about the attack spoke volumes. He had blood on his tunic and pants. Was it Jareth's? Dare she ask? Another wave of dizziness hit her, preventing any questions.

Gregory caught her as she pitched forward.

"She's been wounded, Uncle," Alana said. "I'll go fetch the healer."

"No, you will stay here and explain this to me." The king turned to his men. "Go tell Gerta she is needed in the Rose Room; it's nearest. Tell her Princess Krystal is in mortal peril."

Gregory lifted Krystal into his arms and gained his feet. "Come with me," he ordered Alana.

He placed Krystal on the bed in Alana's chambers and began to examine her injuries. She moaned as he prodded the wounded area, but she didn't open her eyes. She didn't have the strength, it seemed, to see and hear at the same time. At the moment she wanted to hear.

"Fetch some water," he said.

Krystal heard Alana pour water into the basin from the pitcher. She felt the pull of fabric as Gregory carefully cut Krystal's dress away from her wound with his dagger. He then wet a cloth and dabbed at the area for a better view. Krystal bit her lip against the pain.

"I want answers," he told Alana. "How did this happen? Why did Caprice attack you? And which of you killed her? I know she is deadly with her blade."

Alana spoke the truth. "Krystal's blade proved deadlier."

Gregory spoke angrily. "If Caprice did this, she's lucky to be dead before I found her."

Krystal heard the door open and was grateful to see Gerta. The pain of Gregory's prodding had almost proven too much.

"Princess Alana, help me undress her. King Gregory, you should leave. I have to get to her injuries."

Gregory denied her. "I'm not going anywhere."

The healer snapped back. "Then at least turn around, for good-ness sake!"

This he did, though he growled, "You will not use that tone with me in the future."

Krystal could not help as she felt her clothes being removed. The air in the room cooled her bare skin. Someone, probably Alana, protected her modesty but left the wound exposed.

"Princess, you will help me clean it," Gerta said. "It will need stitching." Krystal heard water again and then a clicking noise.

The healer spoke again. "Sire, you must make her drink this."

Krystal felt a hand slide behind her head. She was almost beyond herself with pain. Her thoughts danced in and out of fog. It hurt to think.

"Come, my love," said a tender male voice. "You must drink this for me." He lifted the cup to her lips.

She drank and the pain began to ease. Krystal could still feel the prodding at her belly as Alana washed the cut. A hand touched and started to caress her forehead.

Krystal reached for it. "Jareth?"

Chapter 29

ANDREW CAUGHT UP WITH JARETH just outside the village. "Why did we fall back?"

"My uncle was better prepared than I thought," Jareth said. "His mercenaries nearly cut our army in half. If I'd ordered an advance, we'd all be either dead or prisoners right now."

"And we're still being followed," Calum said. "I suggest we get out of here—now."

Jareth nodded. "Once we make it to the trees, we'll split into smaller groups," he said. "Those men following us don't know the forest. It'll be easier for smaller groups to evade them."

Andrew tried to turn his horse. "I'm not leaving here without my sister."

Jareth grabbed Andrew's reins. Andrew's horse shrieked at the sudden yank. Damen barked loudly and sidestepped the horse's hooves.

"I have no intention of having to explain to Krystal someday that I let you get yourself killed!" the prince said. "Here is where your obedience will keep you alive. I'm putting you in charge of a group of men. Get them back to the camp or die trying."

"Are you sure that's wise?" Calum frowned. "He doesn't know the forest that well."

"He knows it better than the mercenaries." Jareth looked at Andrew. "Maybe being responsible for more than just his life will keep him in line."

Andrew knew the logic behind Jareth's order, but he hated leaving without Krystal. "I know a thing or two about responsibility. I'll get your men back safely. But what about my sister?"

Jareth looked back at the castle. "I only know one other way in now. And when you get back, I'm going to need your help."

Chapter 30

KRYSTAL SLEPT FITFULLY. She heard a good deal of shouting, and at one point, she saw Gregory and Alana's furious faces. When she awoke, she found Gerta leaning over her.

"You're awake," the healer said as she checked her bandages. "How do you feel?"

Krystal opened her mouth to speak and let out a croak. Gerta pressed a cup to Krystal's lips and let water trickle into her mouth. She noticed a strange sweetness in the water and looked up at the healer.

Gerta answered her question before she could ask. "The herbs will help with your pain."

"Thank you," said Krystal. "Will I be all right?"

Gerta sighed. "Physically, you will heal. Though I can't promise you'll thank me for it."

"Why not?"

King Gregory entered her view. "That's enough. You may go."

Memories rushed back to her as Gerta backed away. Krystal looked at him with wide eyes.

"Surprised?" he asked as he searched her face. He crossed the room and shut the door Gerta had left open. He returned to the bed and sat to face her. "I imagine you would be."

Krystal didn't want to ask the question that threatened to burst past her lips, so she chose another. "What happened?"

Gregory's hands reached out for her, but he forced them down. "Alexander revealed his true loyalties when my rebellious nephew and his band of rebels attacked the castle. We fought them off. I can only assume Jareth must have forgotten I've attacked this castle in my day. I know it better than anyone." He looked at Krystal. "I was better prepared than even *you* knew, I think."

She read it in his eyes. He knew she'd lied to him. "And Jareth?"

"I wanted to be able to tell you he'd been killed but I, at least, don't like to lie."

Krystal had no energy to pretend. "Since when? You lie very well."

"Not as well as you," he said. "You almost had me convinced you wanted to be my wife."

"What gave me away?" she asked.

"Looking back, I'd say the little shudders when we touched, the hesitation when I kissed you. You could not make a liar out of your body."

"It is not in my nature to deceive, no matter what you may think." Krystal looked around and recognized the room. "Where is Alana?"

"My traitorous niece? I have placed her in the tower to contemplate her sins."

"Helping her brother isn't a sin." Fear crept into Krystal's dazed mind. "You haven't harmed her?"

"Not even while she hurled insults at me for all to hear," he said. "I had to give myself time to contemplate what to do with her."

"What happens now?"

King Gregory looked into her eyes. "Maids will be in to assist you. They will feed you and dress you and prepare you for the ceremony."

Dread settled around her heart. "Ceremony? What are you talking about?"

"I'm not going to give you another chance to escape me," he said. "You and I will be married this morning. All the arrangements have been made."

Krystal's jaw dropped. "You must be joking. I will never consent to be your wife."

He spoke flatly. "I will kill Alana if you refuse."

"You would never kill your niece."

Gregory sighed. "Thanks to your corruption, I have no niece. She is wholly and utterly her brother's sister. She has committed treason and deserves execution."

Krystal paled. "Why would you do this? I know there are other women you could choose, more willing candidates. Why do you want to marry a woman who clearly doesn't want you?"

"You have ruined me for any other woman, I'm afraid. Once you are my wife and my queen, you will come to accept your new place by my side."

"Never," she vowed in a shaky voice.

Gregory's eyes grew dark. "I will see you at our wedding or Alana's execution. The choice is yours." He left the room.

Just as Gregory had said, Julienne and another maid entered shortly afterward with a breakfast tray. Krystal's eyes moved to the sullen, dark-eyed stranger as she hovered behind Julienne's shoulder. She returned Krystal's gaze with hostility.

"Don't mind Meaghyn," Julienne said as she set the tray on the bed next to Krystal. "She's one of the few of us who thinks we should serve the lord and master without questions."

Krystal sighed and leaned into her pillows. She had no hope. "Have you seen Alana?"

"No, but I prepared her tray and sent it up with a guard."

"One of ours?"

Julienne shook her head. "Please eat what you can. I've been instructed to dress you."

"For the wedding. Why is he going through with this?"

"I'm so sorry. But it's my head if you're not dressed and ready when he comes for you."

"I don't blame you, Julienne."

The maid gave her a hopeful smile and turned to cross the room. Krystal noticed the wedding gown hanging on the door of the wardrobe. Gregory had made thorough preparations. She turned her attention to the tray. She took a bite of biscuit and drank some of the water, but even under the watchful eye of Meaghyn she couldn't eat another bite.

Later, as she stood before the mirror in the lavish gown and veil, Krystal felt the reality of her fate descend upon her. She heard a knock at the door. Meaghyn opened it to reveal Gyles Bettencourt, the Grand Minister. "I have been directed to escort you to the palace chapel."

Krystal crossed the room and took his offered arm. From the

corner of her eye, she noticed that Julienne and Meaghyn followed them at a short distance. Behind the maids walked two of Gregory's guards. Krystal found a small smile. At least King Gregory had learned from his mistakes. He no longer dared trust her.

The chapel had been hastily decorated. Few people sat in attendance, and all of them had drawn expressions.

King Gregory stood at the front of the room. He looked somber but resplendent in black and green. Behind him she could see a colleague of the Elder Patriarch, one of the lesser patriarchs, in blue and white robes. Leodegrance Severin's absence seemed conspicuous.

The Grand Minister left her to walk down the aisle alone. He stepped into a seat near the back of the room. She looked askance at Gregory, and he nodded. Krystal could feel the maids behind her. Slowly she made her feet move forward.

Gregory took her hand as soon as he could reach her. She tried to pull away, but he wouldn't allow it. Krystal faced the Patriarch and tried to ignore the sinking feeling in her heart. She tried to block Jareth from her thoughts completely, but this proved an impossible task.

Krystal would never be able to remember the words spoken over her as the marriage proceeded. King Gregory had to squeeze her hand so she could give her consent. She momentarily returned to the present. Krystal had quite forgotten that in marrying Gregory she became queen of Demarde. A maid removed the veil from her brow, and Gregory placed the ceremonial crown on her head. The Patriarch placed a similar crown on the king's head.

Polite applause rose from the crowd when they turned and were presented as King Gregory and Queen Krystal Gildresleve of Demarde. She closed her eyes when he kissed her. Gregory led her to the dining hall where refreshments had been organized.

He positioned them near the door, and they greeted the guests as they arrived. Alana came into the room, escorted by a menacing guard. The young princess wore a black gown and her fair hair had been braided down her back. The two friends had no time to speak, as the guard moved Alana away too quickly. When Krystal looked around a few moments later, her friend had gone.

They moved to the table to eat the lunch that had been prepared. Again, Krystal could not eat much and only sipped at her water as she observed rather than took part in what unfolded. She felt her husband's eyes on her periodically but did not look at him.

When the meal was finished an hour later, the king and queen stood to leave. Krystal heard a collective gasp that spread across the table. All eyes were on her. Krystal followed their gaze and noticed a stain of blood across the front of her gown. She looked at Gregory.

He'd gone white to the lips. Without a word, he swept her into his arms and carried her from the room. A guard at the door received his order to call the healer to the king's chamber and took off down the hall at a run. Gregory carried her to his chamber and kicked the door shut with a booted foot. He set her on her feet at the foot of the bed.

"Hold still," he said in her ear. He removed his dagger and deftly slit the ties that held the gown closed at the back. With surprising care given his speed, he slit the sides of the gown and Krystal felt the fabric give around her. Gregory replaced his dagger, and with his hands, slid the dress off her shoulders. The ruined and bloodied gown pooled at her feet.

"Let me look at you," he said as he moved in front of her. The chemise and bandages still covered her, so for a moment she wondered what he hoped to see.

Gregory did not leave her long in doubt. Using the dagger once again, he slit the sides of her undergarment and pulled it away from her skin. She grasped at the lower half of the garment as he cut, or it would have slid down to her thighs.

She felt his warm hands on her flesh and flinched as he unwrapped her bandages

Gregory stopped and looked at her. "Did I hurt you?"

"Maybe a little," she said, not meeting his eyes.

"I'll be gentle."

The knock at the door felt like saving grace to Krystal. Gregory took his hands off her to answer the door. She looked down at her destroyed wedding gown. A woman had died for that gown, and it hadn't even lasted the morning.

Gerta bowed to Gregory as she swept into the room. "Let me see it," she said.

Krystal's eyes darted to him as she let Gerta help her back onto the pillows.

The healer understood. "Sire, I would appreciate privacy for my examination."

The king folded his arms. "I will not be ordered out of my own chambers. I can assist, I trust, as she is now my wife."

Gerta didn't argue. She asked him for water and cloths and he stepped away from the bed.

"It appears the morning's activities have aggravated her injury," she said. "I'll rewrap the bandages, but she needs absolute rest. She shouldn't leave this bed for at least a week."

Gregory returned to her side. Krystal shivered at the raw possession in his eyes as he looked down at her. "I hadn't planned on anything else."

Gerta continued in a more forceful tone. "What I meant, sire, is that she needs to remain undisturbed. She must refrain from any and all physical activity if she is to heal. If she is tousled about or anything of that nature she could bleed to death before I could help her."

A look of astonishment replaced his look of hunger as King Gregory gaped at her. "Are you saying I cannot bed my bride without killing her?"

"For a week, at least," the healer said. "I will continue to treat her with pain and healing herbs, but in order for them to be effective, Krystal must have complete rest."

"*Queen* Krystal!" he barked. "She is the queen, not some commoner!"

"Of course, sire. Forgive me."

The king growled his acknowledgement of her words and left the room. The healer continued to administer to Krystal.

"Thank you," Krystal said when they were alone.

"I've bought you some time," Gerta said. "I hoped the fear of your death would be enough to keep him from bothering you."

"I don't know that I should thank you for giving me time to dread it." Krystal sighed. "Though I confess I'm relieved to know I'm not as bad off as you made it sound."

Gerta chuckled. "You will be sore, but my healing potions are unsurpassed. If he hadn't insisted on dragging you from your bed today, you would have been nearly mended by supper."

Krystal grimaced. "But I am still his wife."

"A lot can happen in a week. I'm certain once Prince Jareth hears of your marriage, he'll stop at nothing to take care of his uncle once and for all."

As the healer mentioned his name, Jareth's face came into Krystal's mind. "How can we hope a second attack will succeed?"

"Because hope is all we have."

"I wish I could go to sleep and wake up to find this has all been an awful dream."

Gerta patted her sympathetically. "Poor child. I wish I could do more for you than wrap your wounds and mix up herbs."

"I've never had such excellent care."

"I doubt you ever needed this kind of care before coming to Fayterra. Now, let's get you into a fresh sleeping gown, and I'll mix up another pain potion. Then perhaps you can get some rest."

"How long do you think Gregory will be gone?"

"There's no telling. He's in quite a mood."

Thanks in part to the herbs, Krystal slept most of the day away. She did not dream.

Julienne had brought in a tray of food, but Krystal felt no hunger so she only touched the soup. The maid also tried to tidy up the room. When she picked up the remnants of the wedding gown, however, Krystal stopped her.

"What are you doing with that?"

"We have some skilled maids in the castle," Julienne said. "I'll take it to be repaired."

"It's sliced up and covered in blood," said Krystal. "I don't think it can be fixed."

"It's such luxurious material, though. I'd hate to see it wasted. Perhaps something else could be made from it. Some women make their children's clothes out of their wedding gowns."

Something deep within Krystal rebelled. She looked at the gown again. It seemed to represent all that had gone wrong. She never wanted to see it again.

"Throw it into the fire," Krystal said.

The maid raised her eyebrows at the order. "I'm sure something can be done with it."

"Don't argue. Just burn it."

Julienne inclined her head. "Yes, Your Majesty."

"Please don't say that."

"But you are the queen."

Krystal sighed. "It's like Gregory's brand, to be called queen. I don't mean to be harsh."

"I understand. So much has changed in such a short time."

Krystal agreed.

Julienne turned and walked to the fireplace and tossed the gown into the flames. She lifted a poker from the stand and stood over the fire until the gown was a smoldered ruin. Then she replaced the poker and turned back to the bed.

"Thank you."

King Gregory had ordered dinner for both of them in their chambers. He arrived just as they placed the food on the table. He dismissed the servants and closed the door. A knot had formed in Krystal's stomach when he walked into the room, and it grew when she watched the bolt slide home. She could not take her eyes off him as he put away his crown and sword.

Gregory walked toward her. "Good evening. How are you feeling?"

"I'm a bit tired, but the pain is tolerable."

"Would you like me to send for the healer?"

"Gerta said she'd return to check on me before I went to sleep."

"Good then." He turned to the table. "Are you hungry?"

"I'm not sure I can eat anything."

He looked at her. "I won't accept that." He moved to the table. "I will make you a plate."

Gregory filled both their plates and carried them to the bed. He handed her one then spread a cloth napkin over the bedspread and put his plate down. He poured his wife a goblet of fresh water and himself a glass of wine and carried them to her.

"Thank you," she said.

"You're welcome."

Krystal found herself able to eat more than she had thought. Still her plate remained half full when she set it aside. Gregory looked mildly reproachful but said nothing.

The king put his own plate down. "We need to talk. It's time we discuss our future."

Chapter 31

MUST WE DO THIS NOW?" Krystal asked, sighing heavily. "We haven't even been married one day!"

"I am weary of this uncertainty between us," he said. "What better time to ensure a positive start? You are my wife—my queen. I want to put the past behind us and look forward to our reign, our future, and our family."

"You forced me into marriage," she said as evenly as she could. "Nothing has changed."

"Everything has changed!" Gregory said. He calmed himself and continued. "I've repelled Jareth's attack, and I will do it again, provided he proves foolish enough to attempt it. Why won't you accept it? I am your future."

"I can't imagine what cooperation you can expect from me after a forced marriage. The future you describe is nothing to me except bondage. I will surrender nothing. It surprises me that you would deliberately choose such a life."

Gregory came to his feet and threw his hands in the air. "You are a queen!" he roared. "You have power and riches! How can you call that bondage?"

She sat up with difficulty. "I did not choose this! I did not want this!"

"You were willing enough to be Jareth's bride!"

"Choice makes all the difference!" Krystal said. "I have been forcibly engaged to a merchant and a king. I chose Jareth for myself.

You robbed me of that choice, and now you expect me to sit here and plan my future with you. If I had *chosen* you, Gregory, it would be different."

"You *did* choose me."

She shook her head. "I chose Alana's life. I chose the lesser of two evils."

"Regardless of how we came to be, we are now husband and wife. You are an intelligent woman, Krystal. You need to come to terms with your life and accept your path."

"Why? What benefit is there in that for me?"

Gregory looked at her for a long moment before he replied. "What do you want?"

Krystal did not expect that. She kept her gaze on him as she considered. "I know you want children," she said. "But I don't love you. I can't allow you to touch me."

"Unacceptable," he said. "We have a duty to provide heirs. That requires your participation." Gregory took a step toward her. "Someday you will long for children."

"Then I ask for time," she said. "Let me come to terms with my fate."

He frowned. "Many a woman goes to her wedding bed without knowing her husband. I don't know that you deserve any more consideration in that than anyone else. People expect that the marriage has already been consummated. Only we and Gerta know it has not."

"Who cares what people think?"

"You should. As their queen, you are an example to the people and have obligations to them. I will let you think about it."

Krystal knew that she could get no more from him on the matter.

"What else do you want?" Gregory demanded.

She'd never anticipated debating the terms of her marriage like some sort of contract. "Alana. Free your niece, Gregory. She cannot harm you."

"Granted," he said. "Though, I will be looking hard into getting her married."

"Why?"

"I can hardly look at her. That betrayal cut deep. More so, in some ways, than yours."

Krystal sighed. "I did not enjoy trying to deceive you. It was hard for me."

She thought she saw his eyes warm a little. "Any other requests?"

Krystal steeled herself. "Jareth. What will you do about him?"

"My feelings for him have not changed. I want him dead—more so now than ever." Gregory sat down next to her on the bed. "I don't feel we can move forward together as husband and wife with Jareth still roaming free." He reached up and stroked her cheek. "I want the opportunity to win your heart. I won't have that if you remain loyal to Jareth."

Krystal saw that Gregory's desire filled his eyes. She had the power to win Jareth's safety, she thought, but at a great price.

With a deep sigh, she took his hand. "You want a willing wife. You want someone willing to bear your children and rule by your side. I have one last proposition for you."

Gregory leaned forward. "And that is?"

"Give up on Jareth. Let him live. Give him his freedom. Do this, and I will be your willing wife." She took a breath. "I will give myself to you the moment I am physically able. I will bear your children and be your partner. I will give you my loyalty and learn to love you."

His eyes darkened. "You must love him a great deal to sacrifice so much of yourself."

She could not fool him. "I love him enough to value his life over my longing. But think of the benefit to you. Everything you want would be yours."

He turned from her to stare at the wall. Krystal remained silent and let him think. She didn't want to think of what she'd offered him.

Gregory looked at her. "How will you convince my hotheaded young nephew to accept your choice? I don't want to spend my life looking over my shoulder."

"Would you be willing to retreat to Demarde and let him have his kingdom?" she asked.

"And give him the means and the army to come after me? I think not."

"Then give him his sister. I will give her a message to deliver. You said already that it pains you to look at her. Reunite them as a gesture of good will."

"I must approve this message," he said. "No more deceptions, Krystal."

She nodded. "We will have no more secrets between us."

"And you will open your heart to me? You will let yourself love me?"

"I will."

"Promise me," he said.

Krystal knew what he wanted. He knew, as she did, that her vow would bind her. "I cannot," she said. "I've offered you all I can. Please don't ask for more."

He sighed and shook his head. "I am a fool, but I accept your proposal. I will be waiting for your promise, though. Jareth and I will never have an easy peace until I have it."

"And Alana?"

"I will send for her tomorrow morning. You will give her your message, and then she will be given the chance to pack her things and join her brother."

Krystal let out the breath she didn't know she'd been holding. "Agreed."

"I think we should seal our bargain with a kiss," her husband said. He cupped her head in his hands and pulled her close. "Don't worry, I will be gentle."

Unlike his previous kisses, this one was tender. Tears burned her eyes as she realized she would never kiss Jareth again.

They broke apart at a knock at the door. The healer had arrived. Gregory let her in.

Gerta looked uncomfortable. "Is this a bad time, Queen Krystal? I could come back."

"No, Gerta. I'm anxious to sleep."

"Then I will mix your herbs."

After she'd gone, Gregory shut and bolted the door. Then he removed his tunic to get ready for bed. He paused in removing his pants when Krystal gasped.

It had been involuntary, and when he looked at her, Krystal felt a blush creep up her face. His mood changed from annoyance to amusement.

She shook her head. "I hadn't considered this."

Gregory sighed impatiently. "I am your husband now."

"Yes, but can't we maintain our privacy?"

He shook his head. "You need to accustom yourself to my habits."

"Which are?"

"I prefer to sleep nude. I find it more comfortable."

"Could you at least, for now, wear something to bed? Please, Gregory?"

He sighed at her. "It seems I cannot resist a request from your lips, no matter the circumstance. I have some pants in a drawer I can wear."

He had a wicked sense of humor, though, and dropped his pants before walking to the dresser. Krystal shut her eyes once she realized his intention and kept them closed until she felt him climb into bed. He laughed softly and kissed her cheek.

"It's safe now. You can open your eyes."

She did. "That was cruel of you."

He smiled. "But entertaining."

The cocoon of pillows Gerta had created to keep Krystal comfortable meant Gregory had to essentially climb over them to reach her. But Gregory seemed content to be near her and settled into one of the pillows by her side to sleep.

Krystal lay awake a long time and reviewed their bargain. She longed only for Jareth's safety and his freedom. She'd meant what she said to Gregory. If she had to trade her future for Jareth's life, she would gladly do so.

≈

"Good morning, my queen."

Krystal's eyes fluttered open. "Hello, Gregory." She pulled her hand out of his and slowly came to an upright position.

He frowned at her grimace. "Are you in pain?"

"Perhaps a little. I've never had a dagger wound before."

"I had hoped you would be feeling better by now."

Krystal did not reply but turned her attention to smoothing the covers.

He sighed and climbed from the bed to dress. Krystal averted her eyes until after he'd settled the crown on his head and buckled his sword. Breakfast arrived, and after they'd eaten, Gregory sent for his niece. While she waited, Krystal brushed out her hair. Her hands shook.

Alana arrived minutes later. She looked pale, and her hair hung in her face. She kept her eyes on Krystal. She did not look at her uncle when she spoke to him. "You sent for me?"

"My queen has a message for you to deliver."

The young princess raised her eyes. "Message? For whom?"

Krystal looked up at Gregory. "Could you give us privacy?"

He shook his head. "Remember our terms."

"Then please step back a little."

This he consented to do. Gregory took a chair across the room and watched them.

Alana sat on the bed. "You're in bed. I thought you'd be healed by now."

"The wedding took a bit too much out of me," said Krystal.

"Are you all right?"

"I intended to ask you that," Krystal said. "How are you?"

"Don't worry about me," said Alana. "What is going on?"

Krystal took a deep breath. "I've bargained for your freedom."

"Bargained? What do you mean?"

"That's not important. You can go to Jareth. You just need to tell him something."

"What?"

Krystal caught Alana's eyes with her own. "Tell Jareth he needs to leave Fayterra. His uncle will not pursue him. But he must give up his claim to the throne."

"What about you?"

She shot a glance at her husband. "Tell your brother that I have chosen Gregory."

Tears sprang to Alana's eyes. "This will break his heart."

"Please tell Jareth I wish him the best of luck, but I cannot be part of his future."

Alana wiped her eyes with her hands. "I know there is more to this. You aren't fooling me." She nodded to her friend. "But I will deliver your message."

Gregory stood. "You have one hour to collect your belongings. The guard outside will escort you to your room and then out to your horse. You can find your brother on your own."

He opened the door, and Princess Alana swept out with dignity that impressed Krystal. An hour later, the guard reported Princess Alana rode away from the castle and didn't look back.

☙

Krystal felt utterly disconnected to the scene as she stood in the throne room next to Gregory, where he waited to accept the crown of Fayterra. The somber expressions on each face she looked at did little to ease her worry. She knew how they felt. She felt empty inside. Her fate would be sealed the moment they placed the crown on Gregory's head.

As she waited, she turned her gaze to the colored tapestry that hung behind the thrones. It had been beautifully made. Krystal found herself tracing the threads with her eyes. She gazed at the tassels that hung down the left side when suddenly she saw them flutter. Krystal thought nothing of it. A breeze from anywhere could have caused the movement. Still it caught her attention. She did not listen as the Grand Minister droned on. The tapestry moved again. A glint of steel flashed. Someone in the crowd gasped audibly.

Jareth stepped from behind the tapestry. Calum, Voltimande, Count Alexander, Alana, and her brother Andrew followed him. All of them save Alana had drawn swords. Damen followed them out from behind the tapestry and flanked Alana. He took a protective stance between her and King Gregory's guards. The princess sought out Krystal with her eyes before backing away. Damen followed Alana into a corner and stood protectively between her and everyone else.

Krystal could not take her eyes off Jareth. The young prince had locked eyes with his uncle the moment he stepped into the room. Krystal had never before seen such fury as what lit Jareth's face. It hypnotized her.

King Gregory wore no weapon other than a ceremonial sword. He signaled to a guard near him and took his sword. Then he faced his nephew.

"You've gotten our message, I see," he said to Jareth. Gregory indicated Alana.

"If you're referring to the nonsense Alana tried to feed me, you can save your breath," said Jareth. "I will never believe Krystal chose you."

"She decided to send Alana to you." Gregory's calm voice sounded almost surprised. He took Krystal's hand and pulled her to him. "Why can't you accept she preferred a life with me?"

Jareth glanced at Krystal. "I'm sure she thought of a way to keep Alana safe from you. I doubt she intends to be shackled to you for the rest of her life."

King Gregory kissed his wife. Surprised, Krystal did not struggle against him. "I wonder how you'd feel, Jareth, even if you get what you want. Krystal has been my wife for a week now. How could you live a life with her knowing I had her first? What say you to that?"

The prince's eyes narrowed to mere slits when he replied. "I say Krystal will make the most beautiful widow this kingdom has ever seen."

Krystal's heart warmed. Gregory had spun a convincing story, but Jareth truly knew her heart. He had seen through her ruse to get Alana out of the castle. Hope flooded her.

She pulled herself from Gregory's grasp. He looked at her, astonished. Krystal shook her head at him and backed away. Her husband's countenance lost its calm, and rage overcame him.

"I see," Gregory spat at her. "More lies. I should have forced you to give me your word."

"I didn't lie to you," she said. "I would have lived my life with you. But I realize I can't deny my heart's desire. I can't stay with you. I'm sorry."

"You may not love me yet, but you will." Gregory raised the sword with a yell. Krystal thought for a moment he'd aimed for her, but he lunged at Jareth instead.

The clang of steel reverberated throughout the silent hall. Guards surged forward to attack Jareth's followers. Krystal found she could not focus on one single fight. Gregory matched Jareth but Calum, Alexander, Andrew, and Voltimande engaged the guards in a half circle between the crowd and the dueling royals. She couldn't help but be impressed by her brother's skill.

Alana stood across the room. Krystal went to her. As she passed him, she stroked Damen's head. He licked her hand.

They clutched hands but did not speak. Krystal felt Alana's grip tighten each time Jareth or Gregory came close to injuring each other. Krystal's mind raced from one impossible scenario to another. Either Jareth or Gregory would die this day, and she was powerless to stop it.

"I've never seen Jareth so furious."

"I don't know that anyone has." Alana broke off as Jareth forced Gregory to stumble. Her grip on her friend's hand became painful, but Krystal didn't notice.

She saw the concentration on Gregory's face and knew he'd underestimated Jareth's skill. No longer did man fight boy. The prince had become a man, and Gregory was caught unprepared.

Her husband turned to look at her. He began to fight his way to her. He let Jareth back him up so that the only thing between him and his wife remained her great black dog.

"You can have your crown, Jareth!" he said. "I'll take my wife and be on my way!"

Jareth brought his sword. "You'll die first!"

He advanced. Gregory blocked him. Damen's hackles raised, and he began to growl. The king paid the dog no heed, so he didn't hear the warning growl emanating from the beast's throat.

Krystal's cry of warning came too late.

In a flash, Damen leapt onto the king. Jareth's eyes widened as he watched man and dog tumble to the ground. The king's sword flew wide.

Gregory's yell of pain echoed through the hall, but then he lay still. Damen stepped away. Krystal released Alana's hand and ran. She hesitated a second then and threw herself at Jareth.

With his free hand he embraced her. She turned to look at the fallen king. He stopped her. "Don't," he said. "It's horrible." Jareth kissed her then looked around. "The king is dead. Put down your weapons." No one moved. "I command it!"

Slowly Gregory's guards lowered their swords. They backed away from Jareth's men and sheathed their weapons. The prince sheathed his own sword and moved to stand before the Grand Minister. Krystal followed him. Bettencourt looked up into his face.

"Continue," said Jareth. "I am rightful ruler. I choose to accept my father's crown."

Andrew, Alana, Voltimande, Alexander, and Calum moved to stand between Jareth and the crowd. Andrew had been wounded, and blood seeped from his shoulder. Krystal looked at him, but he indicated she shouldn't worry.

A murmur from the crowd showed their approval. Trembling, the Grand Minister bade the prince to kneel. Jareth complied. The Minister raised the crown high above his head and spoke the ceremonial words aloud.

"I, Grand Minister of the kingdom of Fayterra, do hereby crown thee, Jareth Lochnikar, son of Emrik and Falina, King of this land. May your reign be long and prosperous."

He placed the crown on the former prince's head. "Arise, King Jareth!"

Applause thundered throughout the room. Krystal's eyes went to where Gregory's body lay. She did not want to look at it, but it seemed so out of place in a room full of celebration.

The newly crowned king seemed to agree. He walked to his uncle's body. Removing his own cloak, he draped it over Gregory and motioned two men forward.

"Take the body away." He then went to Krystal. "We have much to do. We must secure the castle and let my men inside. I want you to let Alana take you to your chamber."

Krystal put a trembling hand on his cheek. "I'm so glad you came."

He kissed her fingertips. "As am I. Go, my love. I'll come to you as soon as I can."

Calum tapped Jareth's shoulder. "I believe you need this." He held the amulet that had been around Gregory's neck. Krystal noted Calum had wiped the blood off first.

Jareth accepted it and placed it around his neck. It glowed with energy when he touched it. "Thank you, my friend."

Krystal returned to her chamber. She couldn't wait to hold Jareth in her arms again.

Chapter 32

ANDREW FOUND KRYSTAL in her chamber the next morning. Damen lay on her floor. The dog did not seem inclined to leave her presence. She invited her brother in and closed the door.

Alone with his sister at last, Andrew found himself struggling to find the right words. The awkwardness in the room caused Damen to lift his head and give Krystal a questioning look. She motioned him back with a wave of her hand, and he lay back down, watching them.

"Are you all right?" she asked her brother.

"Yes. You?"

"I am."

Andrew took a step toward her, and Damen growled. Her brother stepped back, the memory of the king's demise the night before fresh in his mind. "Does he have to be in here?"

"*You* try getting him to leave," said Krystal. "He will obey me to that point."

Andrew gave up. "So much has changed. I'm not sure where to start. I tried so hard to find you, and now that I have, the reasons I came looking for you seem so insignificant. I had to know what became of you. I tried to come to your rescue."

"Thank you," she said. "Are you going to ask me to go back with you?"

"At some point, I suspect I lost my right to dictate your future, *Queen* Krystal," he said.

She blushed. "I hadn't considered that."

"Regardless of what else has happened, you have wed a king, have been crowned a queen, and have been made a widow. It seems to me you have much more say about your future than I do."

She smiled. "What will this mean to you? What will you tell everyone when you return?"

"The truth will suffice, I think. The man who abducted you married you before I could get to you. You are a queen now." Andrew sighed. "If Curtis Belvey gives me any trouble about breaking the marriage contract, I'll be surprised. Once you wed Gregory, any hold I had over you was broken."

"But you'll tell them I'm all right? The family, I mean."

"Of course." He looked at her. "You've changed Krystal. You've been through a lot, and I think you deserve a little happiness."

She threw her arms around him. "Thank you, Andrew. I know I'll be happy with Jareth."

"You had better be. You fought hard to get to this point." He released her. "I think I'll head home tomorrow. I'm sure they will be glad to see me."

She grasped his hand. "Stay a few days longer. Be here for my wedding."

Her brother smiled. "I think I can do that."

☙

They buried Gregory the next day in a secluded corner deep in Falina's gardens. Jareth told Krystal he'd wanted to avoid desecration of the grave by any one of the people his uncle had wronged. She agreed. They stood outside alone for a while before the cold chased them inside.

Gyles Bettencourt met them near Krystal's chamber. "Sire, I require a moment of your time. Queen Krystal, this concerns you as well."

Jareth addressed him. "What is so urgent, Minister?"

"I have been told you intend to wed Queen Krystal in two days," the man said. "I must urge you to consider putting the date off a few months."

Jareth shook his head. "Impossible."

"Please, sire, consider this. If you wed her now, and if there is a child born within a year, there will be talk—speculation—that the child is not yours. You must understand it would be a logical conclusion for a woman who has had two husbands in as many weeks."

Krystal tried to speak, but Jareth put up a hand. He addressed the Grand Minister sternly. "I'm not going to let anything else delay my marriage to the woman I've loved all my life. We will be married in two days."

The shorter man bowed. "As you say, sire. All will be ready."

After he had gone, Krystal looked up at Jareth. "What if we *do* have a child right away? Aren't you concerned your people will suspect the child as being your uncle's?"

He knelt beside her and took her hand. "I don't care. I know that sounds unreasonable, but it doesn't matter to me. You have slipped through my fingers too often and are too important to me. Marry me in two days. Say you will."

She let it go. "Of course I will."

Jareth kissed her. "Thank you for understanding."

"I will try, my love, to give in to your requests whenever possible," she said.

The young king grinned. "I think I'm going to like marriage."

Krystal kissed him. "My darling, I promise you will."

Photo by Holly Nielsen

About the Author

CHERI CHESLEY BELIEVES IN magic and miracles. When not writing she can be found reading the dictionary for fun or improving her photography. She lives with her husband and numerous children in Tooele, Utah.

Look for updates on her latest works at www.cherichesley.com or check out her blog at http://cherichesley.blogspot.com.